MURDER IN THE HELLFIRE CLUB

ALSO BY DONALD ZOCHERT

Laura: The Life of Laura Ingalls Wilder
Walking in America
Books and Readers in Old Milwaukee

MURDER

in the

HELLFIRE
CLUB

by

Donald Zochert

HOLT, RINEHART AND WINSTON · NEW YORK

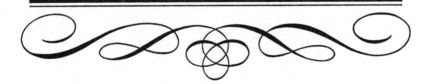

Library of Congress Cataloging in Publication Data
Zochert, Donald.
Murder in the Hellfire Club.
1. Franklin, Benjamin, 1706-1790—Fiction.
I. Title.
PZ4.Z854Mu   [PS3576.023]   813'.5'4   78-4702
ISBN: 0-03-022441-1

First Edition
10 9 8 7 6 5 4 3 2 1

Designer: Amy Hill
Printed in the United States of America

For Nancy

Author's Note

I t gives me pleasure to acknowledge at the beginning of this narrative, rather than at the end, the welcome assistance in technical matters of A. D. Moore, professor emeritus of engineering at the University of Michigan, Ann Arbor. I am also under obligation to the interest, assistance, and gracious encouragement of many other individuals, both in this country and abroad. For one reason or another, all have requested silent partnerships in this enterprise. Whether they are timorous or merely modest I cannot say. But I grant their anonymity.

The narrative itself is based upon lengthy researches in both England and America. Franklin's copy of Priestley was consulted shortly before the end of the War in a small museum to the northwest of London, to which place it had been removed for safekeeping. I am purposely circumspect. A fortnight after I consulted this rare volume, which bore Franklin's signature on the flyleaf and contained marginalia in his own distinctive hand, I felt obliged to return to the museum to confirm one or two of the more startling points in my notes. At that time I was informed by the keeper of the library that the book could not be found. I had the presence of mind to search the library's rather indifferent collection of religious works, thinking that perhaps some clerk in her wisdom had shelved it there because of Priestley's name. In this search I was disappointed, and conclude that like many books this very valuable one is now lost to posterity through the commonality of incompetence.

My notes (on Franklin's notes!) were fortunately preserved. They launched me on a quarter-century quest for what are today so charmingly referred to as the "true facts" regarding Dr. Franklin's many activities in the obscure arena of criminal detection—including his extraordinary Paris adventures with Duval, the French balloonist. Of this, perhaps, more at another time. The case at hand concerns more simple things than aerostatics. Sex and dissipation of the senses. It is, so far as I have determined, the first of Franklin's adventures in which he was obliged to unriddle such earthly pleasures, and certainly one of the more timely. But then Franklin's time was very near indeed to our own.

One more word. I confess to a certain reticence in bringing forth in such detail an account of this neglected element in the career of a great American patriot, especially as my own training and experience lie outside the literary arts. The recent success of various fictions, however, leads me to some sanguine hope for the prospects of an account based entirely upon careful fact. I fall back upon Dr. Franklin's own observation that "truth is my only cunning." In addition, I find that age loosens one's reserve even as it diminishes one's powers. I now feel closer to Franklin than ever before and am certain that his reputation can withstand whatever shocks the truth may deliver.

To the present narrative I have added only such "literary" touches as would seem most agreeable to the reader and least objectionable to the critic. On the whole I regret the advices of my publisher, to whom I reluctantly yield in such matters as this, that I forego the sort of elaborate annotation I know would please my more scholarly friends.

MURDER IN THE HELLFIRE CLUB

Prologue

The fog had lately lifted from the gray waters of Falmouth harbor. Like the parting of the first curtain of drama, it disclosed with sudden clarity a scene that seemed only faintly real but which grew familiar: the quay with its busy moorings and draymen, the red brick buildings of the town, the dark fields and hills that lay beyond. The air was cold, the wind rising. The morning light was tinged with ocher, such as aborigines use to coat the eyelids of the dead.

Packets rocked at anchor in the harbor. Between them and the waiting docks small skiffs shuttled back and forth with passengers. They left a white dissolving tracery on the water.

One of these vessels, presumptuous enough to bear the legend *Georgius Rex* on its peeling bow, carried seven men in unaccustomed proximity.

Two of the men were black, clad in yellow coats. They sat in the stern next to the steersman. Two others, like the steersman, were rough sorts. They pulled unevenly at the oars. The final two men were of more immediate interest. They faced one another but looked, as it were, through each other. One searched the steely Atlantic which lay beyond Pendennis Point and the open arms of Falmouth Bay. The other had his attention fixed upon the rapidly closing quay.

The first of these was in the flush of manhood, no more than twenty-six or twenty-seven years of age. A very pretty young gentleman, everyone said. His face was lit with excitement, earning his adjectives. Looking out upon the gray sea he was leaving so gladly behind him, his eyes danced with the prospect of long-contemplated pleasures.

The other man was older, and less pretty. He was in fact the boy's father, and in his face could be read nothing.

It was not the practice of Dr. Benjamin Franklin to betray his thoughts in the twist of a lip or the arching of a brow. This is not to say his face was inexpressive. On the contrary, it was fresh and sly and ever-changing. Behind it lay the struggle of many geniuses for release—printer, postmaster, diplomat, scientist, inventor, wit, raconteur, editor, spy, philosopher. These he held imperfectly suspended. They animated his face. But of his deepest thoughts he was decidedly the master.

At the moment he was gratified that his long journey across the Atlantic had come to a safe conclusion. This emotion was natural enough, considering the tediousness of the crossing and his own unnatural forbearance. Only once had he gotten drunk and spoken in plain language to the captain. Like his son, he too felt a quickening of the spirit as the skiff drew near to the quay. Unlike the younger man, he could name its source precisely. Behind him lay the arid colonies of

America, drowsing in the thin light of some future sun. Before him lay England, filled with old friends, comforts, and traditions, and darkened by an unmistakable air of dissipation.

There was nothing secretive, however, about Dr. Franklin's mission to England. He was charged—to use a potent verb—with bringing the light of reason to the brothers Penn in their management of the Pennsylvania proprietorship. This task was well-advertised, for the province already had two agents resident in London. They had failed miserably with the haughty Penns, and, naturally enough, babbled Franklin's anticipated arrival around town as though he were a rescuing cavalry. Furthermore, he had many friends and more acquaintances in the old city. They hummed with expectation about the visit of the man whose discoveries in electricity, if nothing else, had elevated him to the front rank of public figures on either side of the Atlantic. The shadow cast by his electrical kite preceded him. The town of London anticipated him.

With his arrival at Falmouth on the morning of 17 July 1757, Franklin's movements become a matter of common record.

His purse was starved down to two pounds, two shillings. Yet he hired a coach on the strength of his papers and set off across the desolate moors for London with his son, Billy, and their two black menservants, Peter and King. At Wilton the company stopped to refresh itself in Lord Pembroke's garden, then smoldering with summer color. In the neighborhood of Salisbury they paused to survey the fosse and earthworks of Old Sarum, and farther north lingered an hour on Salisbury Plain, where the great monuments of Stonehenge stood before them like doorways to some half-suggested mystery. They soon pushed on for London, covering seventy miles in a single day and reaching that contradictory metropolis well after dark. Franklin soon replenished his purse and fell in with his old and dear friend, the printer William Strahan, who had long expected him.

Having spent a good part of his voyage composing yet another treatise on the virtues of prudence and economy, Franklin gave over his attention to his wig and his shoes. He bought one of the former and several pairs of the latter, as well as a pair of gold spectacles, a watch, a handsome looking-glass set in walnut well rubbed, a sword, a silver-handled dagger, a blue hat for Peter (to prove his generous nature), and an assortment of shining buckles for his own person. He sat for a miniature. From the Bear Inn, at which he had taken his first lodgings, he moved his party to the house of the Widow Stevenson in Craven Street, off Charing Cross and close by the Thames. First he sampled the widow's cooking and her daughter's smile, and found both to his liking. Thereafter he busied himself with official duties.

Such necessary drudgery he disturbed with welcome visits to Vauxhall and Windsor, to the old printing house where he had first worked as a youth, and even to Drury Lane, where Garrick himself acted in a farce. Billy meanwhile was entered in the Middle Temple to study law. As he was a bastard, his way in life seemed clear enough.

These diversions took their toll on the elder Franklin.

They ended in a complaint of giddiness, humming noises, and twinkling lights such as come to even the stoutest men when age first makes its claim upon them. The Doctor was confined to his rooms in Craven Street. There he was subjected to a regimen of contrayerva, hartshorn drops, bark infusions (drunk in wine), and cupping, administered by another of his cronies, the physician John Fothergill. Like all medicines and extreme measures, these were eventually effective. Franklin was cured, gladly enough, after only eight weeks.

So far the record is certain.

But the skirts of night drew longer about London. The first fall storms began to brood over the spires of the city. There arose an adventure so unexpected and chilling in intent that even he hesitated to write home about it, and of which he left only the most elusive clues in his cramped account books, in scattered memoranda, and in the margins of his personal copy of Joseph Priestley's *History and Present State of Electricity.*

It was an adventure of envy, lust, blasphemy, and murder, to only one of which he was then a stranger.

One

Dashwood, excited by wine, reeled across the crowded room as though he were dancing the volte—with grèves and passaggios. His face was flushed a merry red, his voice a gull's cry above the tumult of the room:

"The Stone-eater! The Stone-eater!"

The Stone-eater had taken his place at the center of the room, standing upon a low bench so that everyone could see him plain. He was an old man with an ancient face that was seamed and split like an outcropping of granite. His clothing was coarse and loose, his manner enwrapped in an air of resignation.

He had already started to eat stones.

The room fell slowly silent. Playing cards were spread face-down on the green baize, their backs illustrating the varieties of venereal pleasures. Dice boxes stood empty as a gin-miller's heart. A hundred candles hissed and flickered in their sockets.

The crowd, all powdered and red, closed in noiselessly around the Stone-eater.

The old man pushed three or four more pieces of sharp quartz into his mouth. His jaws carelessly worked them. The splitting and cracking of stones sounded painfully loud.

The Stone-eater swallowed.

His lips wobbled into a weak smile, but his eyes remained cold and hard. They were like two polished stones set deep into the weathered flesh.

"God damn!"

"God damn!"

The Stone-eater did not acknowledge these accolades. He reached down to the scattering of stones that still lay spread out upon the table, taking up a piece of chert. Limestone followed, and flint, and several pieces of pink marble. When only a handful of pebbles remained he palmed them into his mouth as though they were so many dried peas. He swirled them around with a draft of gin, even gargled with them. And swallowed.

The crowd gasped.

Being done, the old man stepped down from the bench, leaning forward to grasp the table as he did so. He nearly disappeared beneath the craning shoulders of the crowd. He seemed to rattle. But still a loose, uncertain smile worked its way outward across his hard face, as if an idiot's grin were sufficient to forestall what he knew would come next.

The crowd pushed forward.

Dashwood himself suddenly appeared next to the little gnomelike man. He took care to smooth the scalloped cuffs on the sleeves of his frock and lifted them slightly, the better to discover his delicate well-formed hands. These clenched themselves into deceptive fists, and he struck the Stone-eater squarely in the stomach.

It seemed as though he had struck a sackful of stones.

"God damn!"

Another gentleman stepped forward. He was less spindly than Francis Dashwood. He waved a meaty, more malleable fist in the air and brought it sharply down against the midsection of the Stone-eater. Just as quickly he raised it again. His fingers writhed like snakes. He howled and spun off across the room in mock pain. A ghastly comedian.

The Stone-eater said nothing. But a wicked gust of laughter, a snarl, an animal growl, broke from the crowd as each gentleman pushed forward in turn. They were of a passionate temper. There was a flurry of fists and sly elbows, and the same hollow rattle. The Stone-eater's face turned gray. His smile faded into bewilderment. His chest heaved, and a red ribbon of blood and sputum began to run down his pitted chin. Clearly he had not expected such severe sport.

At last one of the ladies of the room—rouged and provocative—stood before him.

"Sir. May I feel your stones?"

The crowd roared its assent in one solid voice. The Stone-eater did not answer. But the question was only a matter of form.

The woman reached down somewhat below the poor man's midsection, got hold of him, and squeezed. The old man's mouth opened in a scream that no one heard, for the crowd itself exploded in a storm of cries and laughter.

Dashwood's voice rose through it like a knife, a frenzied soprano:

"Holy Ghost Pye! Give this man a slice of Holy Ghost Pye!"

The gentlemen in the crowd picked up the cry:

"Holy Ghost Pye!"

"Holy Ghost Pye!"

"Holy Ghost Pye!"

The Stone-eater's mouth was fixed—cavernous and empty. Above him a vulture twisted mutely on its wires, a great scraggly beast with a blood-red neck. Its glass eyes were cold and hard, like two polished stones.

But the attention of the crowd had fled from both him and it. The rattle in the room was that of dice.

Two

~~~

Something in the scene worked upon Franklin—the coziness of the log fire, the closeness of good company, the contrasts between the drowsy eating room, so neat and commodious, and the passionate cries that came from behind the gaming room door.

He had watched that door all evening. It opened and closed as gentlemen and their ladies made for the stairs and the rooms above, or returned to their more public recreation. In those moments the cries grew louder, washing across the semidarkness of the eating room. Franklin was able to catch a glimpse now and then of the bright interior and the fevered man who would be host, flitting about in his scarlet coat and crying for Holy Ghost Pye.

The obvious indecencies of the mob in the next room, being in right proportion to the more civilized wine and Welsh rabbit of the dining room, bespoke a certain precarious balance—one might say in the souls of men as well as the life of London.

But they unbalanced Franklin's tongue.

He sat off to the side of the crowded eating room near to the fire and not alone. His companions at table were William Strahan and John Fothergill. Not by any accident did Dr. Franklin's return to the London of his youth find him thrown together with these particular gentlemen.

They were ancient friends, having known each other's company since those amber days of a quarter-century previous when the world itself seemed younger—when Franklin leaped naked into the Thames and swam spouting to Blackfriars, performing all the strokes of Thevenot. Since then the tides of life had driven them in different directions. Franklin, who spurned the advice of his friends that he establish himself as a swimming instructor to the wealthy, had made his way back to America. Strahan had become a printer and publisher, one of the most prosperous in all of London. Fothergill had taken up the mysteries of medicine.

But the chain that bound them together had not been rusted by the distance that kept them apart. In the Vulture Tavern the distance of years dissolved in wine.

William Strahan: Like Franklin he leaned toward corpulence, and would have appreciated the pun. Red-faced and ambitious, he had that catholic and compelling curiosity so characteristic of those in the printing trades, and, like them, the inability to put it to better use. Of course he drank. He thought of himself first as a printer, which was an honorable thing, and dreamed of himself as a Lord, which was not. Nevertheless he threw himself into tavern politics at his every opportunity. If there was news, he had it at his fingertips. If there was no news, he could invent it. He was one of those men who are often befuddled but rarely at a loss. His geniality was as constant as the tax on tea.

Fothergill by contrast was thin and dry, a consequence of his long studies at Edinburgh. His rather large reputation as a pathologist was based upon his rather small pamphlet entitled *Account of the Sore Throat Attended with Ulcers.* This had brought him a measure of esteem, which he disclaimed. For despite his obvious eminence in medicine, John Fothergill made room in his life for other interests, among them quietude, conchology, and exotic botany. These were necessarily solitary. He maintained, in other words, a division between his public and his private life with a strictness that was a signature of each.

In this Franklin saw something of his own predicament, and a decent guide to conduct. But his predicament at present was somewhat less profound.

Three times during the long evening—now a fourth—he had been approached at table by an earnest, full-bosomed young woman of the house. Her frank country face was reddened with rouge and showed to be slightly pocked, despite the thickness of the powder. Her lips twisted into a sharp smile. Her purpose was plain. She hoped to hook both his heart and his pocketbook. "Come along with me, sir, come along, and I'll show you how it is to treat a gentleman such as yourself." She curtsied. Her voice was a soft whisper.

Each time Franklin scowled and shook his head ponderously from side to side, as though he were being bothered by a fly. Not until the woman stepped off disappointed for the fourth time did he turn to his companions to explain the obvious:

"I'm being highly flattered."

"She's a bit frosty, Doctor."

"You don't look at the mantelpiece when you're poking the fire."

Strahan was in a fine mood, Fothergill less so. Franklin himself was inspired.

For the first time in weeks he was loose from illness and felt a taste for something that would aid his circulation. He found the Vulture satisfactory for that. From his comfortable vantage with his back to the fire he had watched John Wilkes rush in from the street shortly after seven o'clock, look nine ways at once, and disappear into the gaming room across the way. A cheer burst from behind the slowly closing door. After no more than two or three minutes, however, Wilkes emerged in the company of a painted lady and vanished up the stairs, from which neither had descended during the long hours that followed. Meanwhile, Strahan pointed out George Selwyn, a grave-faced gentleman said to be the greatest wit in all of London. But as he slept over his beer at a small table in a corner of the room all evening, the claim went untested. He seemed the very model of dullness.

This scene momentarily disappointed William Strahan. A week earlier he had caused to be advertised in two newspapers a small notice announcing that Dr. Franklin would dine on this particular night at the Vulture. By this very modern stratagem he hoped to induce a flood of characters—perhaps even a Lord or two—through the greasy door of the Vulture Tavern, and thus provide some amusement for his friend.

He was wrong to worry. The three cronies needed no more amusement than their own cordiality (although Franklin kept an eye cocked on the gaming room door and the steady parade of couples up the stairs and down). Strahan's spirits were restored. The conversation turned from turkeys to murder to vellum paper, and thence to Baskerville type, only to wander off to the prediction of weather, and to snakes, and the natural productions of the New World.

They each saw the bottom of their cups, and filled them.

Strahan tried bravely to discuss Hume, whose publisher he was, but Franklin would have nothing of it. Fothergill contributed a dour soliloquy on the decay of morals, manners, and intellect. It was his hobbyhorse. Learning was in decline, literature had grown increasingly rotten (not to say indecent), fashion ruled the mob. Franklin listened with an air of bemusement before leaning forward:

"It's the common practice of men to complain of the badness of their own times, sir."

The hours flew by uncounted. The motley population of the dining room gradually diminished, and still the cronies did not stir from the deepening comfort of their cups. To keep the draft off their feet, more logs were thrown on the fire. More wine came to table. The conversation continued. Not even the arrival of the late supper—a meat pudding served by the Vulture's hawk-faced porter—disturbed its erratic course. From the Gulf Stream and flying fishes the talk leaped unaccountably to Fothergill's coreligionists, and from there to the manufacture of wrought iron, to the nature and properties of dust, to the establishment of foundling hospitals, to farting, to mistresses. It came to a happy conclusion at last on the mysteries of satisfying the fair sex, a subject that fairly matched Franklin's pent-up mood. "Touch them in one place," he observed, "and you touch them all over."

Strahan snorted.

"Yet a manservant is no substitute for a handmaiden," he declared, taking note of Deborah Franklin's absence from the Doctor's mission to England, and reaching once again for the Madeira.

"She will go round the world gladly enough, but will not cross the ocean," Franklin sighed. His face bore a trace of unhappiness.

"No man should be so long without the services of his wife, else his virtues will rust," Fothergill chided, as much in the spirit of the thing as he was able. He was not much able.

"Else not."

Strahan poured his own glass full again, and Franklin's as well.

"I shall get her to cross the ocean easily enough and lay you a guinea in the bargain," Strahan said suddenly to Franklin. "By the next post I'll tell her how you stand open to temptation, how the light of your reputation has come before you and warmed the hearts of London's women. Hah! How on every side you are endangered by their attentions—even by strumpets!"

Strahan's eyes shot triumphantly over toward the pockmarked serving girl who found the portly Dr. Franklin an objet d'art (not realizing that an objet d'art is a very small item indeed). The wench stood idly by the stairs, curling her dark hair with a provocative finger. Next to her stood the surly porter, and both fixed Franklin's table with a look of undisguised interest. It seemed as though the porter were urging the girl upon him once again.

Franklin sighed, hoping not.

"Enough," he said at last, waving the fancy away. "I'll send her some silver and some cambric and perhaps a miniature of myself, and she'll be happy enough."

His eyes once again took on an unhappy cast. Silence filled the empty bowls of Strahan and Fothergill. But Franklin's was still half filled.

The hour had grown very late and the eating room itself was now nearly empty.

"Gentlemen," Franklin said finally, lifting another forkful of spotted dick to his mouth. "Who is the master of these indiscreet ceremonies in the next room?" He shook his head roughly toward the gaming room, from which—despite the closed door—another roar of laughter could suddenly be heard. Above it floated Dashwood's voice, as shrill and specific as though he were a taunter at Tyburn.

For a moment neither of Franklin's companions said a word. They looked at each other. At last Strahan sputtered: "Dashwood. Francis Dashwood. I believe." But that explained nothing to a man from so far away as America.

Fothergill felt the call of duty.

He roused himself from the half-sleep into which he had helplessly fallen (knowing nothing about mistresses), and leaned forward. His eyes appeared as yellow as a cat's.

"The most dissolute rake in all of England, sir. The very Devil himself."

Franklin's face rounded into a look of sudden amusement. But there was no mistaking the disapprobation in Fothergill's cracking voice, which he held to a hoarse whisper.

"He's a gambler, an idler, as corrupt and wicked a man as ever walked the Strand. A fit subject, I might say, for his friend Hogarth. Indeed! There's talk that—"

"Although more handsome than the rakes of Hogarth, from my small look at him," Franklin observed.

"Not yet disfigured by his vices," Fothergill hissed.

Strahan reached over and patted Franklin's knee. "If you seek gossip of the most vile sort, satisfy yourself that you shall have it!" He folded his hands carelessly across his ample stomach in a gesture of passive resistance and turned his face, beaming and appreciative, toward Fothergill.

The Quaker physician disregarded him.

He leaned back in his chair and pulled his words with him, so that Franklin was forced to bend forward to catch their import. In doing so he reached out at the same time for the Madeira, finding it convenient.

Like all men addicted to the cause of righteousness and moral reform, John Fothergill was well stocked in scandal of all sorts, even vile. Strahan was right. From his hogshead of whispers Fothergill proceeded to draw a portrait of Francis Dashwood highly colored by contempt.

Of Dashwood's indecencies and indelicacies there seemed to be no natural bound. They fitted the times, Fothergill said. In sum he was the heir to one of the great fortunes of the age and by it supported a life unparalleled in excess, venery, and masquerade. As a youth Dashwood had fallen in with the Bucks, who, like the Bloods and Mohawks and other gangs of that day, tortured the upright and innocent with obscenities, and thereby claimed the virtues of wit and courage. The simple countrymen of his native Buckinghamshire returned him time and again to Parliament, no doubt in ignorance of his true character. It was true he had grown into some small reputation as a patron of the arts. He had encouraged the preservation of some obscure pagan monuments and memorials. True he was a clubman. But in an age that counted Ugly Clubs and Farters' Clubs, what virtue was that?

"His whole life is a rebuke to reason," Fothergill declared. "It's common talk. He took his Grand Tour as a lad and used it for unrestrained license. In Russia he dressed himself as Charles of Sweden and undressed the Empress Anne, trying her virtue. So it's said. She had no virtue to begin with, so this was no great achievement. But it shows the man! In Turkey he passed as an Oriental and embraced an entire harem of women—"

Fothergill warmed to his subject. His temples pulsed.

"A jolly dog!" Strahan interrupted with a mighty laugh. "Don't hold the sins of his youth against him. He's no longer so young as to try a harem. . . ."

Fothergill brushed Strahan aside. His voice quavered with indignation. "While in Rome 'tis said he dressed himself as the very Devil—turning nuns back on their heels—scourging worshippers in the Sistine Chapel. I've no sympathy for the Church of Rome, sir, but if we credit all that's said of him— why!—he stands against both man and God! Age is no excuse! It hasn't cooled his fire! He still acts the Buck and Nicker!

He thinks to call himself a priest of learning. Faugh! He surrounds himself with women who pray with their knees upwards!"

Fothergill spit the words out.

"A knave in grain!" Strahan exclaimed happily. He clapped his hands smartly together.

"The town talks of him! I'll not be drawn into any loose gossip!" Fothergill said earnestly, ignoring Strahan and directing his attention toward the placid Dr. Franklin. He was now quite overcome by his own revelations and somewhat more vocal than he had intended. "He's a blasphemer! He profanes what good men hold dear! He's re-created a secret order of disorder!" For a moment he stopped, pleased with his phrase. *"He has resurrected the most infamous of all societies, sir—"*

Strahan waved a mediating paw in the air. "He kneels before Miss Brown, is all," he explained to Franklin with a sly wink. "Folly refers to the infamous Dilettanti Society, or the Divan Club, is all."

"God damn!" Fothergill exploded, to his own surprise and that of his companions. He drew himself erect in his hard chair.

"Of all his masquerades, this comes closest to the truth," he declared with vehemence. "I was going to say—Indeed!—I was going to say, it's said that Dashwood has lately presided at the resurrection of the forbidden Hellfire Club! Devoted to worship of the Devil! Such utter nonsense! Spending himself in the collection of maidenheads, more likely! Strahan! Leave off calling me Fotty! Have you not heard the same—"

But Fothergill abruptly stopped.

For some time the door to the gaming room had stood open. The candles inside still blazed and gleamed, but the occupants had departed. All but one.

A tall, dark figure filled the doorway and strode forcefully into the eating room. As he neared the fire his face turned even deeper crimson.

"Dr. Fatsides!" the gentleman squealed in an excited voice, sweeping aside the skirts of his scarlet coat and dropping into a low bow directly before Franklin. His eyes were fixed on the table, not Franklin. "In the absence of a proper introduction—believe me, I cannot win one—I am Francis Dashwood."

Fothergill's yellow eyes closed. He slumped back in his slatted chair.

But Franklin looked benignly up at the stranger.

Dashwood's face was well formed but flushed with wine. He seemed to have been christened in pump water. His eyes were bright blue, clear and piercing. They were articulated with thin brows of surprise. Except for his radiance there was little enough especially devilish about him. Life did not measure up to art.

He rocked back and forth on his heels.

He was silent, as though he had not thought his way beyond his blustery introduction. His eyes darted toward Strahan, then came to rest momentarily on Franklin.

When he spoke again it was in deadly earnest.

He stammered uncomfortably, "If you would be so good, sir, as to visit me in Pall Mall—my lodgings—or if you would permit me—at your convenience—I say, there's a small matter of some little importance, perhaps of interest . . . it's no matter! Of some importance to me, I say, and perhaps to others . . . danger—sooner is better than later . . . if not tomorrow, I say, then perhaps . . ."

His voice trailed off uncomfortably. An appeal that began with hope disappeared in despair.

Dashwood bowed deeply again, and Franklin could not help but see the dark cloud of concern that crossed his face. But as Dashwood straightened up, the cloud vanished.

"—at your own convenience," Dashwood said softly.

"Should there be any way that I can be of service to you—it's only fair—use me—call on me, sir, and I shall . . ."

"There may be one trifling request," Franklin interrupted, speaking to Dashwood for the first time. His eyes twinkled.

"Ah! Permit me!"

"Might I have a small slice of your Holy Ghost Pye?"

For a moment Dashwood did not move.

But his sudden burst of laughter, when it came, startled everyone in the eating room—even the snoozing Selwyn.

Three

Pall Mall was nearly empty. Here and there on either side of the wide street a carriage was left unattended, shuddering before the wind. Sheets of old newsprint rattled past the doors of houses and shops. It was already late afternoon. The weather was changing.

The blue carriage of B. Franklin turned the corner at the west end out of St. James's Street and clattered onto the cobbled Mall. The wind caught the driver's blue cap and sailed it into the air. But the carriage did not stop. It flashed out of the sunshine and into the shadow, sweeping past the stately mansions which lined the south side of the street. Here the Schomberg House, where lived the notorious Lord Sandwich, once First Lord of the Admiralty but now quite out of favor (although not yet quite out of bed). There the residence of the Walpoles, such queer chattering sticks. Next the more modest house where once had lived the immodest Nell Gwyn, the King's whore. Franklin turned his head. Down at the end of the street Bubb Dodington's mansion stood with sooty shoulders against the gray sky, looking for all the world like a coke furnace. Beyond it could be seen the ineffectual spire of St. Martin's Church, casting its mild rebuke upon those various seats of dissipation and luxury.

The high facade of houses hid the low sun. It drew a wedge of premature darkness down into the street as the carriage began to slow.

Dr. Franklin had much to think about. He had lain abed until nearly ten o'clock, so slight was the penance exacted for his exertions of the night before—which by the by had continued long after his return to his rooms in Craven Street. When he finally awoke it was with a start. His mind was still busy with the diversions of the evening past. All night he had dreamed about the Vulture Tavern—doors opening and closing, women laughing, muffled voices and an unseen scream, smoke, and red velvet. It made him dizzy and uneasy.

These dreams had fled. But morning brought with it the nagging thought that they signified more than the sum of their separate parts.

Even half awake he stood at the edge of a dream he could not quite touch with words. Why had that pock-faced serving girl singled him out for her suggestive pleasantries when there were younger men about who seemed more answerable to her purposes? Did he look so fat with prosperity? He thought not. Why had Francis Dashwood approached him at the end of the evening? Dr. Fatsides! Where had he learned that intolerable nickname? What a strange sort he was— brusque and vulnerable at the same time. Eccentric. What dark thought troubled him that could not be spoken in such a place as the Vulture?

These questions floated upon the light of day. Franklin felt suspiciously like a fat pike eyeing them. He was wary of the hook, yet his mind was hungry. The thought drove him down into the pillows for another hour's slumber, so deep that he did not dream at all.

Breakfast had been biscuits and balm tea, sweetened with honey and seasoned with Mrs. Stevenson's complaints. She scolded him for his late hours. He thought of home. Polly, the widow's daughter, did not come to table. She peeked at him from around the landing of the stairs. With her light brown hair swept up and her white shoulders bare she looked as fresh and smooth as she had some hours since, when he returned to the sleeping house from the Vulture. Franklin sighed, and thought of his late hours. Take your medicine where you find it. His face was a tolerable approximation of innocence.

He had sent Peter away to Pall Mall as soon as he appeared downstairs. The servant was back to Craven Street before the morning table had been cleared of its crumbs, announcing that Dashwood would be pleased to entertain a visit from Dr. Franklin that very afternoon (after his headache had passed off). Mrs. Stevenson read aloud from *The Times*. Franklin did not want to hear it. He closed his ears. The forenoon he spent impatiently in sitting before the parlor window, watching the London sky turn slowly toward darkness.

Strange images drifted through his mind—doors opening and closing, women laughing, a pock-faced girl, muffled voices, a tall man in red velvet sweeping into a low bow with a cloud of fear upon his face, a single word let slip: *danger*—until at last the carriage stopped.

Peter leaped down from the driver's bench, opened the carriage door, and Franklin stepped unsteadily out—tapping his walking stick on the cobbles. His leg had gone gouty.

"Where's your hat?"

"I've lost it, sir."

"Find it. It's a measure of my esteem for you."

A wave of his hand sent the carriage clattering away. Save for three men arguing with some animation outside the house of Mrs. Missenden several doors back, the street once again was silent.

Franklin turned his eyes to the house before which he had been deposited, hoping to read the character of its occupant. It was one of the peculiarities of his nature to search everywhere for details, and to draw from them conclusions to light the path of his conduct. When called to an audience with the Devil himself, what should one seek?

He pondered. The house, like the others on the long block, was set back only a few feet from the street itself. Built of rusticated marble in the Italian manner, it was neither imposing nor especially modest; it was ordinary, and perhaps a bit small. Yet if appearance must be measured it was rather more imposing than modest, or it would not have been situated in Pall Mall. It stood only two stories in height and was very narrow. In the architecture of the block, it was an afterthought. But its tall leaded windows, its bas-relief stonework, its magnificent hooded doorway—architrave carved with scrolls of some anonymous, exotic leaf—gave it a heavy, ornate air. Its upkeep was no doubt considerable.

The Doctor's practiced eye, however, noticed that the house stood next to the little alley called Pall Mall Court, in which lodged (he could see) John Winkles, Jellyman to the Prince of Wales, and a number of other small shopkeepers serving the Court and wealth of London. Being situated so closely to a seat of commerce, no matter how distinguished, Franklin thought, its value must be correspondingly diminished. It was a town house, no more.

While thus engaged in speculations of property, and all the while standing incautiously outside the pedestrian posts, he was called to sudden attention by the noise of a carriage behind him. It was Peter roaring by, waving his blue hat.

At the same time the door to Dashwood's house was flung open as if on signal and a ragamuffin boy of eleven or twelve years burst from the darkened interior. The door immediately slammed shut, and the boy—scullery rags flying— dashed past Franklin, crossed over the street, and ran off so fast that not even the wind could catch him.

This flurry of noise and activity urged Franklin forward. He stepped up under the portico.

For a moment he stood there without moving—a short, substantial figure in his plain blue coat. Then with the end of his dark malacca walking stick he neatly flipped the brass knocker on the door. He smiled faintly. The knocker was cast in the shape of a devil's head, horned and leering, its lips drawn back in what he supposed was a snarl of contempt.

There was no answer.

He banged the knocker down with more force.

Silence.

He looked about. Down the street the three men who had been arguing had amicably vanished, perhaps into one of the silent coffeehouses across the way. Franklin puffed his cheeks.

Had he not just seen a ragamuffin boy burst from this very door? He sighed, and the door swung open. An elderly servant, crooked with age and obviously out of breath, peered around it, showing only his face and one shoulder.

"Franklin," the man declared.

His voice sounded like a punctured concertina. It carried more than a touch of impatience, an undesirable emotion in a servant. The man's eyes darted this way and that like a snake's tongue, never quite coming to rest. Franklin no sooner stepped

into the house—entering directly into a long hall or room—
than the door clicked shut behind him. The servant had already slipped away, hissing to himself.

The great high-ceilinged hall in which Franklin found himself was unlighted and unnaturally dark. It was empty of
furniture save for a bare sideboard about halfway down and
what appeared to be a writing table and two or three chairs at
the far end, in front of the French windows.

There too, outlined by the soft light between the draperies,
Franklin saw the figures of two men—one standing, the
other seated. Neither spoke or gave any indication that
Franklin had entered, although the fact could hardly have
escaped them.

Franklin stood for a moment, allowing his eyes to grow
accustomed to the semidarkness of the room. From either side,
high on the walls, dusky family portraits peered down at him.
Silence ran in the family; they did not speak either.

"Mr. Dashwood," Franklin finally said, announcing himself. The click of his walking stick sounded sharply on the
polished floor as he made his way toward the other end of
the long room.

"Mr. Dashwood, sir."

The room was silent. Dashwood stood like stone before
the window and did not turn away from his reflections even
when Franklin came up directly behind him. It was as though
one of them were not there. But which?

Franklin glanced over at Dashwood's companion. At least
this gentleman's head moved. He had followed Franklin's
progress down the hall and now looked squarely at him—a
thin, delicate face locked tightly. He did not speak. Franklin
dropped his glance to the great oak table. Its surface gleamed
in the white light of the windows and was as barren as his
welcome. He looked past Dashwood's shoulder out across the

bare mounts and the King's garden. The trees bowed slightly in the wind. Dead leaves spilled through the air. There seemed to be a snuff of snow curling about the brown hedges, but perhaps that was an illusion. Illusion! Was not Dashwood supposed to be a master of illusion and masquerade?

Franklin cleared his throat.

"Dr. Fatsides has arrived," he said reluctantly.

Dashwood came suddenly to life. He turned abruptly on his heel away from the windows and exploded in his high astounding voice.

"Doctor! Forgive me! I am—I fear I am distracted. Dr. Fatsides! Indeed! I *am* distracted. John Raleigh is dead!"

"John Raleigh," Dashwood's young companion said matter-of-factly.

Dashwood ignored him. He seemed to moan. The words tumbled out more quickly than he could control them. "Hah! Your reputation, sir! And I dare to say 'Fatsides'! Forgive me! Philosopher! Scientist! And now a member of the Royal Society! Is it not so? Everyone talks of Dr. Franklin from America! Bah!"

Francis Dashwood seemed insensible and excited, as though someone had dazed him with a blow to the head. Or heart. He threw up his hands in a gesture of helplessness. Franklin blinked. Dashwood began to pace back and forth before the window, hands flying.

"But that's not it!" he cried. "I've read your almanacs, sir! Indeed! Poor Richard! Indeed!" He laughed cruelly despite himself. "You're crafty! You're a fox, sir, among the hens of this poor bedeviled world! Indeed! Bring your goddamn arse to anchor!"

Dashwood had forgotten himself again, but Franklin took no notice of it.

He seated himself obligingly in a straight-backed chair

next to the table and stretched out his gouty leg. Dashwood really did appear to be distracted. His pointed brows were arched even more dramatically than on the evening before. His face was still flushed red, less from wine than from some new agitation. In his hands he twisted and untwisted and twisted a heavy sheet of writing paper, which he now tossed carelessly upon the empty table (where it slowly untwisted itself).

"Is this your son?"

"My son!" Dashwood exclaimed. "Forgive me! Eugene Toplady! He's a student, a brilliant student. Isn't that so? He's part of my household. Forgive me!"

Eugene Toplady unfolded himself from the chair in which he was seated. He bowed stiffly to Franklin. Then he refolded himself. The lad had manners.

Dashwood marched back and forth before the windows again, banging a palm against his forehead.

"I had not intended for you to come here under such circumstances!" he said suddenly. "This is darker than I considered! I thought—God damn!—John Raleigh!" He threw back his head and laughed. A single word shot up his windpipe and lodged in his throat. "Murdered!"

"John Raleigh," Eugene Toplady repeated. He looked knowingly at Franklin.

"I know neither the name nor the man," Franklin said. "I know little enough about murder. I know nothing of why you have called me here. I supposed you had some intelligence on the proprietorship, or some message from the Penns, or perhaps were to offer me a piece of your Holy Ghost Pye. But I have no connection with murder."

"You misunderstand!" Dashwood cried. "Forgive me! But I must explain."

"I hoped you would, sir."

Dashwood ceased his wild pacing. He stared directly at the seated Franklin. He was frozen still, and his voice suddenly turned cold.

"Do you often think on death?"

"Not often, sir," Franklin answered. "There is too much to life—"

"Too much to life!" Dashwood cried. Suddenly he was off again. "Too much to life! My reputation! And what do I care for it? Reputations are like coats—put them on, take them off as the season turns. My own, sir, forgive me, is that of a . . ." He sawed the air with his delicate hands.

"Patron of the arts," Toplady offered. "Bon vivant."

"Hell-raiser," Franklin said benignly.

"Hell-raiser! So it is, sir! Christ on the Cross! God damn, sir!"

A wild, helpless look fixed itself upon his face. His fist came down sharply on the table and he sank meekly into a chair across from Franklin. The truth was, he could not bring himself to begin, and seemed to realize it. He edged the crumpled parchment across the tabletop toward his guest with trembling fingers, as though he did not wish to touch it.

"A pretty puzzle," Toplady said to himself.

Dashwood moaned. Franklin looked at him through half-closed eyes. In the face of snakes, wild bears, and players he was usually contemptuous. He called loudly for the servant who appeared momentarily in a doorway off to the right.

"Something to clarify our minds, sir," Franklin ordered, without turning his head.

The old man soon returned with a black tray on which were balanced three crystal glasses and a large decanter of canary. The wine was poured. The servant backed away, to take his place behind the door. Franklin reached out and picked up the twisted paper that Dashwood had pushed toward him.

He held in his hand a quarto sheet containing a verse of some kind. The paper itself had once been neatly folded and sealed. The crease still showed. But the seal had long since been broken open, and what little wax still clung to the paper was without a mark. The sheet was discolored by Dashwood's constant attention.

Saint Francis—[it began, by way of salutation]

What foul description's fair enough for thee,
Sunk beneath all decency?
Betrayed by hellish appetite, you shrink
From virtue. Drown, you reprobate, and sink!
You art all over Devil's child!
Your band of miscreants beguiled!
Beware, foul-minded reprobate,
Abandoned to your revels late—
Arrived from Hell, you'll soon be back
To try thy wit on flame and rack!
But first the pathway must be paved
With thirteen hearts of souls unsaved!

Beware!
Revenge!

It was Franklin's turn to laugh aloud. He looked sharply at Dashwood.

"My good friend Fothergill could have done as well as this—given time enough to cool the heat of his mind. Is this what sends you off into such ecstasies, sir? *Saint* Francis? Surely a man of your estate—you do not expect the world to bow politely? But—or did you wish me to print it up? I am but a poor printer, sir."

Dashwood did not laugh.

"Here's the noose to hang me by," he said flatly. The enthusiasms of a moment before seemed to have been crushed out of him. "To hang all of us. Here's our Newgate and Tyburn all in one."

"Yes," Toplady said.

Franklin drew himself up silently in his chair. He reached for his walking stick, but Dashwood interrupted him.

"Please. Please, sir. When I called myself to your attention last night, I had only a puzzle on my tongue. A pretty puzzle, Eugene says. So it is. Today John Raleigh is dead." Dashwood's hands fluttered in the air. The color was drained from his face. "Please, sir. Please!"

Franklin sank back into his chair. "Very well," he sighed.

Dashwood began quickly, eager of his opportunity:

"I have some small acquaintance with art, sir. This devilish verse has no such pretensions—am I right, Eugene? The rhymes are bad. It does not scan. No, what we have here is a prophecy—to ignore, as I've ignored it, at peril."

Dashwood was very intense. He had at last caught onto the control that had eluded him.

"It was brought to this house from the street at an unknown hour and by an unknown hand. But I recall the day very well—because I do not recall it at all. I was drunk. I am not often drunk, sir, for all that you may hear in this town. I'm a man of moderation, and I hope a few sensibilities. . . . Leave that aside. As it is, I was drunk.

"Our summer revels came to their conclusion on the twenty-second of July. I returned to the city on the following morning and fell in with—with bad company. Clergymen. Now, I know two clergymen tolerably well, sir. These were not with me. Had they been, I should have stayed drunk for sure. As for those who were—well! I can hardly say I know them. I showed *them* the civilities of White's, they showed *me* the whores of St. James's. And no doubt thought the bargain was mine. Between the two amusements I extended myself somewhat more than usual—"

"You were exhausted from the revels," Eugene Toplady said.

"Yes," Dashwood answered. "I'm no Buck. Forgive my manners, Franklin! Death has distracted me. We did not learn until—we are—confession doesn't suit me."

"Indeed. You rousted in the park," Franklin said quickly, to forestall another eruption of temperament. Dashwood closed his eyes for a moment, and then opened them.

"My servant called the—the message—to my attention on the twenty-fourth. I was still abed. A wonderful antidote, sir, for license."

"To lie abed?"

"Hardly, sir! The antidote is death! Mr. Brackett told me he found the letter on the day previous, slipped beneath the door. I have no reason to disbelieve him. He's an old man, sir, and frightened. Look on the back of that sheet—there—you see a devil's head. A crude sketch. As incompetent as the verse itself. But does it not carry its own warning? He was frightened, sir. Not all my scoffing could cure him of it. I love the man, sir, and know his—"

"Please," Franklin said. "There is no need to smother me with such niceties. I'm not used to it, and daresay nor are you. Leave off the 'sir.' "

"Very well, sir. This arrived the day previous, which is to say on the day I myself returned from Med—"

"Which is to say in the very week I arrived from America," Franklin interrupted. "But before my coming on to London."

Dashwood's head snapped up. "I don't suggest you sent it, sir!" His smile was hard.

"Only in passing," Franklin explained, "the better to fix

the occasion. There is nothing so reliable as the word of a trustworthy servant. Nor so rare. Your Mr. Brackett waited until you were sober. Indeed. You opened the letter—or did he?"

"I did. The seal was unbroken. It's curious how these things act upon one's mind. My reaction—well!—it was the same as yours. A harmless prank. Some jealous friend trying his poor wit. How often we did such things at the University, and thought they qualified us for Heaven! But—more canary?— it's curious. For a time I couldn't sleep. By day I laughed at such nonsense. By night—my sleep was disturbed by visions, sir. Not of women, would that they had been! No. By visions of danger. Of knives flashing in the darkness. Of blood running from my heart. A death beetle gnawed at my brain, sir, and—"

Franklin leaned forward. "I don't read dreams. Who would wish you harm? Perhaps by placing your attention there you will find some natural cause to—"

"Ask a man to judge himself!" Dashwood sputtered. "Were I to introduce you to all of London, it would fall short of an answer. Who would wish me harm? Many men nurse the wounds of wit long after they've been inflicted. For myself— I do not. But these are times of private bravery, sir, and by that I mean great mischief. Who would wish me harm? Might as well ask that of yourself! It's a part of the age! More than once I've fought at close quarters. Always on the side of honor. I am no coward. But these things usually end—how shall I say?—not amicably, but honorably. Surely you have fought in duels—"

"Not once. I am a coward."

"They don't have duels in America," Toplady offered.

Dashwood rushed on: "I've hurt or injured no one. Believe me! I'm a fair judge of emotion, sir, and the means by which it's concealed. I've searched the faces of my friends.

I've observed their actions. They're innocent. Perhaps not to your taste, or to the taste of the population, but innocent enough of this foul thing! They yield me their affection! Better to look in the dark world—"

"Is Mr. Toplady in your society?" Franklin asked.

Dashwood drew a deep breath. "My society?"

"The Hellfire Club."

"The Hellfire Club," Toplady repeated flatly.

Dashwood's hand made hesitant circles in the air. "He is—yes—he is a member of the Society of St. Francis. It is not—"

"Did he attend the summer revels you spoke of?"

"Yes. He did."

"Did he accompany you back to the city, or did you return in your own company? I'm not clear—"

"I returned alone, as I said, and fell in with two clergy-men—"

"And you, Mr. Toplady, returned to the city alone, or with others who can attest to your company?" Franklin asked, turning to the slack young man.

"No. Alone," Toplady answered quickly.

"I see," Franklin said. "Then you were here on the twenty-third of July, the day following the revels and the day on which Mr. Dashwood supposes that this message was anonymously delivered."

Toplady's face turned crimson, from the bottom up.

"He was not, sir!" Dashwood said sharply, turning first to Toplady and then to Franklin. "You are not so much a fox to elude me! Eugene is a student—a student of languages. He's a member of my household, but his studies carry him to libraries—public and private. He attends to phlogo—philigol—"

"Philological," Toplady said quickly.

"—matters. He's had an audience with Dr. Johnson. He has friends outside my acquaintance. He's not required to—"

Franklin smiled and shrugged. He turned his palms upward, cupping the air.

"I merely raise the point as a hypothetical," he said. "Mr. Toplady was not here, he was somewhere else. That explains everything, sir. I commend his industry." Franklin smiled again, but it was a poor disguise.

"Leave it off!" Dashwood said, somewhat testily. "My friends yield me their affection and their allegiance without duress. There is no need to abuse their—"

Franklin reached for his walking stick.

"Another possibility suggests itself," Dashwood interrupted again. "That some woman burned with a grievance against the Brotherhood—felt herself badly used—but I dismiss it! The ladies who attend the Brotherhood burn with something other than grievance."

But Franklin had already tottered to his feet.

"You speak of this Brotherhood as though it were common knowledge," he sighed, "and yet to a stranger it might be supposed to be a collection of little friars."

Toplady laughed.

"Friars of pleasure, sir!" Dashwood said. "Don't bother yourself. To the public we are a Hellfire Club. I hear them chatter. Nothing of the sort! You know there is no such thing as a Hellfire Club. There are orders against it. We are—we devote ourselves to pleasure, to company, to a few harmless excesses." Dashwood laughed. "We amuse ourselves. None of our sins is deadly, sir. None such as this."

"Do you amuse yourself, sir?" Franklin tapped his stick rather forcefully on the floor. "I'm a patient man, but it is *you* who abuse *me*! You commend my reputation and then treat of it as though I could neither see nor hear. Forgive me! You puff yourself up with the emotions of a peacock! If you wish to go through life with a gallows hood, wear it! My blessings! Half the truth is a greater lie than none of the truth."

"Half the truth?" Dashwood was crestfallen. He had come around the table and grasped Franklin's arm.

"The truth, sir, is that I propose a legitimate hypothetical, and you oppose it with an absurdity. The truth is that the Franciscans are a Club of venery. You are too modest! You use half the whores of London in some abbey on the Thames! You celebrate the Black Mass! You unloose the tiger, sir, and cry aloud because he stalks the land! I did not come here with my eyes unopened. I'm not prevented from making inquiries. I'm not a fool, sir! I've met in a month more dissemblers than I'd wish on an enemy in a lifetime."

Despite his gout, Franklin fairly danced with emotion of his own. He broke loose from Dashwood's hand.

"The Penns condescend to treat me with contempt! The Parliament—of which you are a part—can be purchased! Would that I had the fortune, the world would be more at ease! Call a cat a canary, it will not sing! You stand at the head of a Hellfire Club, sir, orders or not! You are a rod on the roof of disaster and must expect the lightning!"

The look that fixed itself on Dashwood's face could have been taken for anger had not his hands, sawing the air, trembled out of control. He spun round on his heel with his back to Franklin, and stared out of the high windows. The gloom of the afternoon had given way to darkness in the King's garden. In the glass, Dashwood's own image quivered before him like a ghost. When he turned again to face Franklin he wore a mask of resignation.

"I am blind, sir, and see only with my heart," he said. "For a long time I disbelieved this business. I flew from fear to disbelief. Poor Richard! When you were pointed out to me last night—by Schiff or Pennant, I cannot recall—I thought to—"

"By Dieter Schiff," Toplady said.

"—I thought to invite you into this pretty puzzle. For what? Not a moment before you arrive, Henley sends his lad here with news that Raleigh is—dead! It distracted me! A vicious, wonderful man, sir! A man of great talent and terrible wit, trust me! No more suited for the duties of a porter in the Vulture Tavern—poking fires, sweeping up the leavings of the mob—no more fit for that, sir, than you for hauling slops."

Franklin's brown eyes were instantly round with interest. His lips pursed themselves, and his eyes rose beyond Dashwood to the windows.

"You say the porter at the Vulture is found dead," he said to himself. "The porter at the Vulture."

"More than that," Dashwood answered. "A Franciscan. One of the thirteen."

Four

N ow that darkness had fallen, the streets of London were crowded—not only with the fur-capped fops and dandies who were always to be seen, but with wandering children, with clots of peddlers, and with the poor. The last seemed to hide from daylight and grow bold by night. They were driven from their hovels into the crooked lanes and thoroughfares by the burden of cheap gin and the hunger of unhappiness. A cold wind brought the high, angry whine of their voices to the windows of Dashwood's great carriage.

Here and there Franklin noticed bonfires in the streets and ghostly crowds gathered around them like witches hunched over the lip of a cauldron.

Franklin's audience with Francis Dashwood had been more impassioned than expected, but ended in a way that could not have been anticipated. His curiosity had overwhelmed his discomfort.

It was not the fact that Dashwood had been threatened with bad verse; the world is always threatened with bad verse. Nor was it the fact that a certain John Raleigh had been found dead in the Vulture Tavern, or at least not that alone; of him Franklin knew next to nothing. He was not compelled by sympathy for Francis Dashwood, for sympathy was not one of Franklin's defects. Indeed, he found Dashwood rather disaffecting.

None of these things drew Franklin into the web of mystery over which Francis Dashwood presided like a helpless spider. Something else caught his attention—something Dashwood mentioned early in the interview. A lesser man would have disregarded it. Franklin did not. When coupled with a certain fact, it gave rise to an interesting line of speculation. Franklin had not missed it. He was fond of fact, but even more fond of speculation.

Dashwood had given him more than enough food for this. Before leaving the comfort of the house, Dashwood called for more wine and some cheese. Toplady sat aside with a plea of weak stomach. But Franklin and Dashwood were less finical. The subject of their discussion was the Hellfire Club.

Secrets are ill kept in large numbers, and Dashwood conceded that he had indeed founded the order some four years previous, in contravention of the Orders in Council. He acted from the most catholic of motives: boredom. It amused him to give some regulation to the use of willing women and to dare the insensible populace with his parodies of religion.

The Brotherhood was divided unequally into two orders— inferior and superior. Into the inferior order crowded all of London who dared to claim affiliation but hesitated to exercise it. The superior circle was limited to twelve members, not to count Francis Dashwood himself, who stood at their head. Thus "the thirteen."

Franklin and Dashwood turned each name over, looking for the maggot of discontent.

The members of the superior order had been chosen for a certain convergency of interest, but like quicksilver these interests shifted elusively beneath the thumb. The majority claimed a devotion to the literary arts, chiefly satiric and pornographic. Two were clergymen, and one of these was an expert boxer. Another was a bookseller. Eugene Toplady was a student, and indulgent of that easy life. Yet another was a quick-witted pamphleteer with an idiot wife who thought she was a cow. Three of the members were also members of Parliament. Some of them followed Dashwood's suit and held interests in antiquities, art, natural history, or electricity. All were gamblers by temperament and practice. All felt the buck of manhood in their blood, even doddering old George Bubb Dodington, and sought to satisfy it with the most pliant and successful women.

They were, in other words, Englishmen—the glory of the race and the very foundation of Empire. Each had the potential for either mischief or magnificence.

"Here's the thing that nags me," Dashwood said. "They are damaged angels—I love them!—we all are. We are men of our time, sir. What use is there for genius, lest it play to its own tune? I can't distrust them. Not a one!" He glanced off into the distance. "Although it's true I've shared this— this verse—with none of them save Eugene."

Toplady smiled weakly at Franklin.

"He's examined it from every side, I assure you," Dashwood continued. "He's an expert at words. He's a student of language, sir. I've seen him take a word apart and put it back together differently or make a word that reads both ways at once. He's found no wit in this, no clue of any sort to tell who sent it."

Dashwood called for more canary. Franklin stretched his gouty leg and folded it and stretched it again, considering Dashwood's plea that he give the circumstance his attention. He mused. He hedged. He swallowed his canary. He doubted very much whether his faculties were suited to such an undertaking. Finally, with the third glass empty, he connected the curiosities that had bothered his mind. Idleness had made his gout more painful than before, but he assented.

Thus the great coach shuddered eastward into the City. Dashwood slumped pathetically in one corner of the coach seat. Franklin bounced uncomfortably in the other. Eugene Toplady, his stomach worse than ever, sat across from Dashwood; he was wrapped against the cold in a long golden coat, and it nearly swallowed him.

They rode in silence until passing under Temple Bar, where the skulls of traitors grinned down in the torchlight. They were reminded most forcibly of death.

Franklin spoke up. "In all these confessions, you conveniently leave off John Raleigh. Think carefully of his character and allegiance. His wit, if he had any. Is it possible that your warning comes in his hand?"

"I know his hand as well as my own," Dashwood said softly. "I know his mind and heart. He was my Brother—"

"Your brother?"

"Not of flesh, sir."

This man, as Dashwood explained him, had once been a youth of distinction and promise. He exhibited poetic gifts. But as often happens, fair weather was forecast and rain came. John Raleigh was given over to the pleasant vice of violating other men's wives—an enterprise in which he employed not force, which after all is rarely necessary, but iambs and dactyls. In the Barbados he would have been a bucca-neer. In ancient Greece, a bucentaur. In London he was merely a rake, but a dangerous one at that. A title or some equal estate would have preserved him from the consequences of his vices. But he had inherited only a facile wit and a modest competence. One of these he wasted, and found it hard to survive upon the other. He was driven to a furtive, anony-mous existence by the fear of harm, which was not only real but warranted, and which was wished upon him generally by the affronted gentlemen of the town. That is, those simple trades-men whose wives fell into bed too easily with a man who said he was a poet.

For a time he contributed to the journals of the City, scrib-bling satires over the cognomens *Succubus* and *Cock*. But this was not enough to keep a rat alive. The praise of his peers did not pay hunger's bill. Besides, his choice of subjects raised up enemies even where he could claim no vice but virtue.

Some cuckolds took their wives more seriously than others. Raleigh was hounded, startled by threats, chased more than once by bravos—hired thugs. He drifted from bagnio to bagnio along the Strand—fists empty, forever looking back over his shoulder, and gratifying his passions on flower girls (who, on the whole, he found less accomplished than the ladies who had yielded to his sonnets). Necessity drove him to the composition of pornographic verse, that and a certain easy competence. One might weep for the abuse of talent, but there was an enormous market in pornography. London lofts were filled with etchers leering at their zinc and draw-ing fine copulating lines. Raleigh was one of those who supplied the thousand words to accompany each picture. The profit went to booksellers, however, and even this low muse turned bitter.

Raleigh began to use the actual names of his former conquests in his verse, holding their husbands up to the cucking stool of public ridicule. Their husbands could not fail to notice. In their loneliness, they were the chief devourers of pornography. Life was a vicious circle. His need for masquerade became double.

To his various indulgences must be added one other. His calendar of debts, had he kept one, would have looked like this:

To Mr. Carey, Who shall break wind loudest: One crown.
To Mr. Morgan, Roll of three dice: Three pounds.
To M. Fleur, Direction of wind at 6 o'clock A.M.: Three crowns.
To Mr. Smithson, Depth of water in Hungerford gutter: Five guineas.
To Mr. Beddoes, Fighting of cocks: Two pounds.
To Mr. Carey, On whether Mr. Henerson will stand or fall: One pence. (No bet.)
To Mr. ———, The color of the next horse to turn into King street: One guinea.

&c.

He was, in other words, a deep player; not so much by the sums he gambled, as by his constancy. No uncertainty was beneath the laying of a wager. Of his skill in such diversions no more need be said than that his opponents found his behavior obliging in the extreme, and found their purses growing fat on his recurrent hopes.

By finding work as an anonymous porter he was able to

43

feed his stomach on scraps and make his wagers on what was left over. He stayed out of harm's way. Dashwood by chance discovered him at the Vulture and embraced him for all his dangerous principles. Poverty has a way of exciting the rich. John Raleigh soon found himself accepted by the Brotherhood that had gathered around Francis Dashwood, for hunger and danger had given his wit a fine, hard edge. And, of course, he was once more free to satisfy—during revels and less stately occasions—his original indulgence: to work upon other men's wives.

During the nearly three years he had kept Raleigh in his company, Dashwood explained, not once had the man seemed near to either harm or discovery. He stayed to his place at the Vulture during the visits of the Brotherhood, and lived upon an annuity of affection from Dashwood himself.

"Ha!" Franklin said. "Here are a million reasons to find a man dead! Jealousy. Failure to pay his debts. Revenge. Payment for pain inflicted."

"I count four," Toplady said.

"And you say 'murdered,' " Franklin continued, "knowing nothing of the matter save what a scullery boy has told you. He was starved to death! Undernourished! Natural sickness. . . ."

Franklin received no answer from Dashwood. He pulled the collar of his coat around his throat and settled into a grim silence.

The coach trembled on noisily over the cobbled streets. It shook loose a flock of curiosities in Franklin's mind, like blackbirds rising from a stubbled field in the backcountry of Pennsylvania. He watched them wheel in silence, but did not sort them. He peered from the carriage window at the faces that slipped by beyond the spokes, and at the lamps and open fires that flickered in the dark wind. His face settled into a mask of indifference.

The carriage, having passed around near to Paternoster Row and St. Paul's, turned the corner into King Street. A small crowd was gathered in front of the Vulture Tavern.

Mr. Henley, the keeper of the place, elbowed his way out from the middle of the mob as soon as he saw the carriage. When he recognized the sign of its owner, he nearly sprang at the door. At his elbow was a boy in rags. Behind them Franklin made out the expectant figure of his friend William Strahan, who had come to the Vulture for supper and a hand of hearts and who had stayed on account of the excitement over the strange event that had occurred there, and of which he felt himself a part.

Henley looked every solid inch a tavernkeeper. His skin was sallow as a butcher's dreams, full of gristle and sinew. His body was squat, a condition made more noticeable by the filthy apron he wore over his enormous belly. His face bore the same brutish aspect.

His huge hands clutched at the air, and he talked in several directions at once—even before Franklin eased himself down from the carriage.

"As I'm sayin', sir—ye look to be a pretty one!—it was near to midnight when I missed John Raleigh and could na' find 'im, the danglin' bastard. Ye was still here yourself, sir, and your friends, and Mr. Dashwood. Why! Mr. Dashwood! How ye be? And me, b'God, with all the cookin' and haulin' port from down the stairs and lookin' out for the ladies, such as they are. To have the pother of John Raleigh, who's supposed to be at my right hand! Now! I'm telling ye! The bastard's gone, and na' for the first time, I'm sayin'. We emptied out and I sent a girl to look after 'im, but she comes back empty as a sack of coal in summertime, sir! *Empty*'s the word! Empty-handed, empty-headed! Tho' if it's a good time ye be wantin', why sir, she's the very one! I give it up, considerin' the hour."

Henley slapped his hands against his belly in disgust. His mouth gaped for words. Franklin tottered on his walking stick in the face of the innkeeper's assault. He had tried to interrupt twice, without effect. Strahan pushed forward to hear better, and an even larger crowd began to gather on the stone walk in front of the Vulture.

Henley surged ahead. "As I'm sayin', I give it up and went to home. I returned here at ten on the clock this mornin'. My usual hour, as in the rhyme. I'm regular as a clock wound tight, believe me, sir! I'm hopin' to find John Raleigh slunk back, the cowardly cur, and plan to box 'is ugly ears in the bargain, do I!" Henley shrugged his massive shoulders. "He's nowhere about, and a bit harder to find than that, I'll say. I start to work. I'm used to it, sir! It seems to me in recollection that I passed those stairs a dozen times afore it strikes me that the door to Annie's room is shut up tight as the notch of an untried maid—"

Franklin managed to interrupt by waving his walking stick in the air with some menace.

"Annie, you say?"

"Aye," Henley answered. "I've given her a room, sir—na' a large one, but all the same—and hardly ever used and who's this? Mr. Loptaddy, I'll say!—hardly ever used except for—for—"

"Yes?"

"Why! Except for Annie, sir!" Henley exploded in surprise, as though he had just added one and one and got two. "She's the very one I'm tellin' ye about! That sometimes entertains a gentleman, as ye know! The other rooms is all upstairs, save for this—direct across the kitchen and with the door bein' under the stairs. If it's private ye be lookin' for, it's up the stairs with you! Mr. Dashwood, isn't it so? But if ye be wantin' some of Annie—there's such as appreciates it, tho' na' such gentlemen as yourselves, I'll swear. She's light-headed, it's true, but she's light on her heels as well, and I'll back it!"

Henley suddenly became aware of the crowd pushing around him on the walk. Franklin's stick once again was rising in the air. Henley turned about and waved Dashwood's party after him into the Vulture. In the eating room, forks stopped in midair as the piper passed through.

"Now! As I'm sayin', the door's closed tight as a duke! Locked! As ye know. I called for Annie, thinkin' her inside. Not a peep. I calls for John, the bloody bastard! I'm hopin' to beat the devil from 'im and send 'im on 'is way faster than a cat what has its tail trod on. As I'm sayin', the door's locked plain enough—bolted from the inside—so I takes a sledge from out in back—takes a sledge, sir!—and breaks down the bloody door at the latch!" Henley slapped his hands together for effect.

"And what do ye suppose I see? I ask ye that! The bastard's dead! Dead as the pharaoh's heart, I'll say. And lyin' there all the night. Dead!"

Henley's tale ended just as it should have, for like most tavernkeepers he had a fine sense of timing. The party had reached the worn stairway in the little hallway back from the eating room and alongside the kitchen, from which came an overwhelming odor of cabbage.

A large wooden keg blocked the door about which Henley had spoken. He wrestled it out of the way and gently pushed open the door, which shivered on its hinges. The inside bolt, still thrown shut and secure in its latch, wobbled latch and all from a few splinters of wood.

"Aye!" Henley announced grandly. "Dead as the pharaoh's very heart! But you'll need a lamp!"

The room was indeed dark. Henley pushed his way back

between Dashwood and Strahan, waving away the crowd of curious that had followed them halfway down the hall. He grabbed down a hissing lamp from its bracket and rushed back into the room, which Franklin had already entered.

"Nothing has been touched?"

"No, sir, it has na'. I just blocked it off, as ye can plainly see unless you're blind as well as fat. It mystifies me, I'll say! But then it come to mind to call on Mr. Dashwood here, because I know he's acquainted—"

Franklin blinked. "When was the body removed?"

"About noon, sir! To the care of Westminster!"

Franklin nodded.

The apartment was small and sparely furnished. Inside the room, a single low bed was pushed up against the wall to the left of the door as one entered. Next to it stood an old oak washstand. A small rug lay crumpled up on the floor. Directly across the room from the bed was a spindly gate-legged table, leaf thrown and sadly secondhand, pushed against the wall beside a small stone fireplace. The walls themselves were merely whitewashed, and were without ornament except for two sconces, one on either side of the bed, and a small print of a dog hung carelessly above the fireplace, where it had become darkened by smoke. The floor was earthen and swept clean. Opposite the door was a small casement window without covering except for dirt. Beneath it was a scuffed chest, the only other piece of furniture in the room. There was not even a chair on which to sit—a disadvantage not only to the occupant, but to a man with the gout.

"Right there, I say!" Henley began to babble. "Beside the bed is where he lay! He was—"

Franklin stared him to silence. He walked round to the side indicated by the innkeeper and bent carefully over the empty washstand. He examined it closely, running his fingers thoughtfully across the amber top.

"This piece of amber is—"

"It's not new, sir!" Henley interrupted. "The stand's not new, I'm sayin', and John Raleigh thought to improve it some with that block of amber—and I daresay he—"

"This Annie you speak of," Franklin said softly, almost as though he were alone in the room. "She has a pockmarked face? A bit frosty?"

"Why! That's her! You have her!"

"She was entertaining John Raleigh in this room?"

Henley considered.

"Why, no sir!" he sputtered. "That's foolish on its face! The bolt was thrown from the inside, and there was no one here save Raleigh."

Franklin eased himself with some effort to one knee beside the bed, where but a few hours previous John Raleigh lay dead. The carded, crumpled-up rug was damp to his touch, although not with blood or urine. He placed his fingers against his lips. Then he lifted the cream-colored bedcloth and peered beneath the bed.

"She makes this room her residence? She lives here?"

"I should say na', sir! She only works here, and na' too well at that!"

"Can you call her in here? I would like to speak to her. And if you gentlemen would—"

"But as I'm sayin', sir! We have na' seen her. She is na' here! The wench has gone and—"

"So much for that," Franklin sighed. He rose from his knee with a grim smile. Once erect, he tapped the floor next to the bed with his walking stick.

"The murdered man lay directly here," he said aloud, "and the—"

"But 'murdered,' sir?" Henley exclaimed. "Mark my word! I saw 'im! He was na' murdered! How do you say 'murdered'?"

49

"Worse than that," Franklin said. "Something has gone terribly wrong for the murderer." His eyes darkened, and half closed. "Of course!" he said at last, although not in response to Henley's incredulous question. Rather to a question he had asked himself.

"And the washbasin," he said, "the washbasin is . . ." He turned slowly about, walking stick extended at arm's length. "It is—*there*!" he said emphatically.

The stick pointed steadily toward the gate-legged table. Indeed, beneath the table, where the light from Henley's lamp did not immediately reach, a large copper washbasin lay tilted against the molding of the wall. Franklin leaned down and kicked it out with his stick. For a moment his attention seemed to be caught by the baseboard. But he picked up the basin, gave it a cursory glance, and placed it carefully atop the table.

There anyone might examine it: a plain copper basin, with a hole for hanging punched into its lip. There were no marks upon it.

Franklin hobbled over to the casement window. "These have not been opened, and the door itself was bolted shut," he murmured. "From the inside."

"I should say na'," Henley said with a rush, coming across the room and wiping his greasy hand across the dark glass. A lace of cobweb came off in his hand. "And if they were na' opened, then who opened the door? As I'm sayin', I'm no dunce, but if murdered—surely you mean—"

"Not a dunce," Franklin said. "Not a dunce?"

He tapped his stick impatiently on the scuffed wooden chest. Henley stepped quickly to open it. But the lifted lid discovered only a few petticoats, a shawl, several shifts of a plain nature, some yellowing linen.

"This is very unusual, is it not?" Franklin said, turning

back toward Strahan and Dashwood, who stood side by side in the doorway. Toplady's wan face floated behind them.

"I suppose—the man bore no evidence of violence, you say?" Franklin asked with a sharp glance toward Henley. "He was not hanged by the neck. He was not run through. There was no ball, no gunshot. He was neither beaten nor—"

"No, sir! And na' a one. The lads from the hospital remarked the very same, for all their—"

"It is now near to twelve hours since a man was found dead in this room," Franklin announced. There was an uncharacteristic trace of excitement in his voice. "For perhaps eight or nine or ten hours previous—we do not have the number—he lay here equally dead. Consider what we have set before us. There is no sign of struggle. There is no blood. The door is locked—we can assume through the agency of John Raleigh himself. Murder enters without his invitation or assistance. We see him there by the bed. He dies and falls—let me think aloud! Let us say he dies and falls, striking the basin and knocking it to the floor. Is that sufficient? Just so! But the room—the room is not his. His business here is—what? Mr. Henley?"

"He was the porter, sir, and often enough—"

"The porter. So! There is nothing out of the ordinary in him being here. We must expect him to be here. But then— then we should expect—Faugh!"

Franklin strode abruptly toward the doorway, and stopped.

"Gentlemen, we should have a cause, having the effect before us," he said. "Shall we say that Porter John died of a broken heart?"

They all spoke at once.

"Broken heart?"

"Broken heart?"

"But *murdered?*"

"By a *broken heart*?"

"Thank you!" Franklin said with a laugh that surprised the others. "Can you think of something else? Something we have overlooked, perhaps?"

"*Else?*" Strahan's eyes swept from Franklin to the still-thrown door bolt, hanging from its thread of wood with the latch still attached.

"There!" Franklin said with a flourish. "We've a very pretty puzzle, do we not? But what can we do at this hour? We are concluded here. Mr. Henley, should you find this woman Annie, I should like to know of it immediately. Send your lad. I will leave the address. Save her here and send for me immediately."

"Very well, sir. As ye say!"

"I am very slightly *rotund*. That is different than fat, sir." He turned to Dashwood. "I don't know the secret of your prescience. This interests me. I fear I owe you a small apology. More than that. You've set my poor mind to working. Come aside here."

He beckoned Dashwood off to the side. "Whatever danger you imagined," Franklin whispered, "it is here. In this room. In this town. Beware of it."

With that, he pushed his way past his startled companions. He hobbled down the hall, sniffing at the mingled scent of ale and cabbage. But he did not stop for supper in such a cursed place. He moved directly to the door, entered the street, and pulled himself up into Dashwood's carriage.

The others followed—even Strahan, who gave up his hand of hearts and squeezed himself between Toplady and Francis Dashwood, the better to face his friend.

"I fail to see—if the room was locked, the bolt thrown— I see no way . . . You mean to tell us that the man was murdered, yet you do not—or do you really mean to suggest that he—No! On the face of it I must say—I mean to say!—If he was murdered, one would certainly expect—"

Strahan babbled on.

Not until the carriage reached Craven Street, turning off the Strand at the corner past the shop of Deard the toy-maker, did Franklin rouse himself from his thoughts.

"You overlook the obvious, Strahan," he said.

"The obvious!" Strahan sputtered, glad at last to have someone speak besides himself. "Why, sir! But if you say 'murdered'—"

A faint smile crossed Franklin's face as the coach came to a stop.

"There is a wonderful amount of credulity in the world," he said softly. "Did you not see the mousehole?"

Five

The body of Annie Martin, scullery maid and some-
time whore, was found floating in the brown Thames
two days later. Her throat had been slit rather dramatically from ear to ear. The drayman who made this discovery at first mistook the peeling flesh of the poor woman's
face for a cabbage, as she was found off the stairs at
Hungerford Market and only her head could be seen bobbing
along in the slow current.

The drayman's error was soon discovered, however, when
one of the market women noticed the open cavity of the victim's mouth and the dark pools of her eyes, an unnatural
thing in a "cabbage," and fainted dead away into a stall of
real cabbage.

This intelligence was carried by William Strahan to Dr.
Franklin. Franklin received it in the parlor of his house in

Craven Street without comment, and indeed almost as though he had expected it.

The Doctor's gout had grown worse. He had not stirred from the house since his last visit to the Vulture Tavern. Now he sat spread-legged on the carpet in a patch of sunlight that fell through the window—his pantaloons pulled up, his white stockings pulled down, and his pale legs exposed to the solar principle. He was surrounded on the floor by a dozen small musical boxes and other mechanical contrivances, part of an experiment in which he was then engaged and which played all at once as Strahan puffed up the stairs and burst into the room.

That ruddy-faced printer, his pockets bulging with oranges from Hungerford Market (which lay only two streets away), sat patiently on the settee after having delivered himself of his brief news. Franklin looked vacantly at him, as though his mind were elsewhere. The visitor relaxed himself, waiting for the miniature orchestra to wind down to an intermission and for Franklin to free himself of its unmelodious jingle.

Strahan himself had not been idle.

After depositing Franklin in Craven Street two nights previous he had sought out Fothergill and arranged (on Franklin's request) for the dour pathologist to examine the body of John Raleigh, deceased. This, unfortunately, Fothergill was unable to do; the body had already been dissected and disposed of in the noble cause of a new generation of anatomists. But Fothergill had inquired the next morning after the master anatomist at Westminster, a certain Dr. Chowder, and obtained a report from him.

Raleigh, so it turned out, had in life been a healthy man with venereal disease, of moderate stature, and about forty-one years of age. Rest his soul. His brain was larger than the normal and bore some slight calcification on the left anterior lobe, although nothing so serious as to have impaired any of his functions. His liver, however, gave evidence of deterioration—a sort of decohesion of the tissue (not always a sign of alcoholic abuse)—as did the lining of his stomach organ. His vessels were open. His heart was distended, and had burst; this, Fothergill concurred, was the proximate cause of death. The small toe on his left foot was missing, probably the result of a childhood accident, and there was an old scar of undetermined origin on his left knee. On the inside of his left thumb the dissectionist discovered an unhealed wound of about an inch and a quarter in length, with the flesh burnt—as though he had grabbed hold of the wrong end of a poker. An occupational hazard of alehouse porters with more than one thing on their mind. Except for the slightly putrid appearance of his privates there were no other marks on the body worthy of commentary, and certainly none to indicate that he met death in any manner other than the one Dr. Chowder surmised—a burst heart.

Fothergill wrote this report out from memory for William Strahan, adding at the bottom a notation of his own for Dr. Franklin: "Bursting of heart not uncommon among dissolute rakes."

Having passed these observations along, Strahan was placed by Franklin in the charge of an investigation or two of his own, a task he relished.

The first was to locate the missing Annie Martin and bring her to Franklin's door. In this he succeeded in a perverse way, although only partially, merely by happenchance. He obtained the woman's address and made his way to her lodgings above Holburn Court, but could find no one who had seen her. Indeed, he found only one person who had even heard of her, a bent and crippled old woman who appeared to be the landlady and who complained noisily of Annie's irregularities—"a bloody whore with ballocks for a brain and not a pence to pay her rent," the hag called out—even after Strahan had backed into the sanctuary of the hansom cab and pulled shut the door. It was not until he wandered past Hungerford Market that success blessed him.

Another task was to return to the Vulture Tavern and find there, as Franklin put it to him, the "other mousehole." As Strahan had failed entirely to notice the first mousehole, he was not entirely sure what game he was after. But he went forth lightly.

The tavern was closed to the public when Strahan sought to pursue this curious charge. From the street window, however, he could see a group of people milling about in the hallway—a knot that tightened and unraveled with excitement. His rapping on the pane aroused the attention of Mr. Henley, who was showing a small collection of friends through the room in which John Raleigh had been found so mysteriously dead. Strahan was granted admission.

He prowled about for the better part of an hour, and often on hands and knees—a posture common enough to him in his younger days but endured now only because of the importance which Franklin appeared to place upon his search. He counted six large yellow cats, all mousers; there should have been no mouseholes. In the eating room he found two buttons made of brass, a broken shank bone with the marrow sucked out, and a garter of blue silk; in the gaming room, nothing. In the kitchen he found only a sleeping dog. He let it lie. With Henley's leave he explored the upper story, the Elysium of those carried off by passion, and found there three rooms furnished in much the same mode as that in which the dead man had been discovered: beds in various stages of undress, washstands, tables, round white chamberpots. But no mouseholes.

When at last he made his way downstairs again and stepped

into the "death room," as he had come to think of it, he found the mousehole plain enough beneath the gate-legged table next to the fireplace.

"How easy it is to find something if only you know where to look!" he exclaimed happily. And then remembered he was to find the "other" mousehole.

He looked about. The fireplace and the flue were recessed into an interior wall, although there were no other rooms on that side of the Vulture. He nodded briskly. Stepping quietly through the eating room and back out into the street, he saw at once that the last six buildings at this end of King Street were built as one, or at least had become amalgamated with age. They shared a common roof of tin, and no doubt had walls in common as well.

"Harrumph!" he snorted.

The sign of a draper hung from the doorway of the small shop next to the Vulture. A closer inspection, however, showed that the shop itself was deserted. The windows were clear of obstruction, although the door was bolted shut. Boarded shut, in fact, for Strahan could see the end of the timbers on the inside from his vantage at the window.

Through the dim and vacant interior he also spied a crack of light at the rear door of the shop.

Strahan made his way noiselessly around the far side of the Vulture, which was the last building in the row. He slipped between the end of the building and a set of nasty brambles most carefully, and discovered himself in a narrow alley. This led up the length of the block. He tiptoed past the rear door of the tavern, catching snatches of Henley inside crowing gladly to a new group of his friends: "That's it, sir!—b'God!—murdered, as I say!—The bastard was dead as—"

When he came to the rear door of the draper's shop he found it was neither bolted nor boarded shut. It stood half open.

Strahan pushed the door inward gingerly with his foot, his large eyes eager for the sight of a mouse.

He stepped into a large and empty room, one of two into which the shop was divided front and rear. A doorway in the dividing wall showed him the windows at the front. Dust and cobwebs were hung everywhere. Soot traced patterns of accusatory fingers on the low ceiling. The walls were stripped bare. All the fixtures of the place had long since been removed, either by the owner or by vandals, save for a massive oak worktable—perhaps too heavy to move, or in too poor a condition. It was pushed up against the wall to the left of the door. Alongside the fireplace. Next to the mousehole.

He saw it at once.

Fortunately his sense of excitement did not outrun his keen powers of observation. In addition to the mousehole he also noticed that the tiny creature had left chips and scrapings of fresh wood alongside it, and at that had done rather a neat job on the hole itself. With another hasty glance around the desolate room for a mouse, Strahan departed the premises in a mood approximating joy.

He rushed to relate all of this to Dr. Franklin, with somewhat more drama than a straightforward telling has room for. Franklin, for his part, slapped his hands together twice, but whether to catch a gnat or confirm a hypothesis, Strahan could not say. Having received the news of the mousehole and registered his emotion, Franklin lapsed back into the nap from which Strahan had awakened him. Strahan was left as confused as ever.

So it was that on the following day, grazing with curiosity, he wandered down toward Craven Street, stopped by at the Hungerford Market to fill his pockets with oranges, and was by happy circumstance present when the squeamish market woman fainted dead away into the bin of real cabbages. It was fortunate that Strahan's nagging interest in the matter had carried him into the neighborhood. He provided the identification of the drowned and silent woman in the Thames by noticing the initials *A.M.* on the inside of her watery boots.

The sight of the scullery maid being hooked so unceremoniously from the water, fluids streaming from her gray body even after she was safely ashore, made Strahan himself feel rather silent. But he fortified himself in the knowledge of the pleasure Franklin would take in the receipt of such intelligence.

In this, as has been noticed, he was mistaken. Franklin received the news of Annie Martin's death in a rather passive manner, almost with indifference. But he was not immune to his friend's obvious consternation in the affair.

Strahan pulled an orange from his pocket, peeled it, and replaced the peelings in an empty pocket.

"For Dr. Johnson," he explained. "He saves them."

"You shall have to arrange an introduction," Franklin said.

The musical boxes had fallen still.

"If the room was locked, sir—"

"My dear Strahan. Don't trouble yourself. Do you know all of Fothergill's stories?"

"Of Dashwood?"

"Indeed."

Strahan laughed. "I've heard them all, not alone from him. 'St. Francis,' he calls himself, and his Club—call it that—the Franciscans, the Friars of St. Francis, the Monks of Medmenham, the Hellfire Club. It's an age of clubs. Like interests demand a means of expressing them. There's a club for every—"

"What do you make of him?"

"Of Dashwood?"

"Indeed."

Strahan thought a moment, and shrugged. It was a subject he had not previously considered, being practiced in taking the world as it is.

"These are loose times," he finally answered. "No worse than you or I, if we had money instead of brains." A self-satisfied smile spread across Strahan's face.

"Harmless then? A fool?"

Strahan thought another moment, and shrugged again. He was uncomfortable. He was not used to playing the philosopher.

"Every man has the seed of danger in him." He shrugged once more, thinking it appropriate. "Under the proper conditions—Why, you're a botanist, and know this."

"Precisely. While you've answered your charge, I've attended to mine," Franklin said. "Does he set a good table? I'm to have supper with him. Tonight. And his Club."

Franklin rolled over like a beached seal, to face Strahan more fully.

"Don't trouble yourself," Franklin said, resuming a lost thread. "If you cannot declare a murder was done, can you deny it? Two murders, although one is more obvious to you than the other. And here, sir, is my proof of both."

Franklin held out his hand into the sunlight.

Strahan's brows arched with curiosity. He bent forward to look into Franklin's outstretched palm. It was empty.

Franklin sighed, and sank back onto one elbow.

"Murder's a most simple thing to do, in its great majority. I leave off the thought that nine men in ten are suicides. Consider it, Strahan—the mode and means are always at hand, depending only upon ingenuity and the strength of passion. Should I wish to murder you, sir, would it not be the heart of simplicity to withdraw a pistol from my pantaloons and shoot yourself as you sit there with your orange? Indeed. So close do you sit to eternity. Or might I not just as easily run you through with a sword, or plunge a dagger into your great and good heart, or draw it across your helpless throat? Simplicity itself! Against my sudden intentions you are without recourse."

Franklin actually smiled.

Strahan did not.

"But is it prudent?" Franklin went on. "I think not. One cannot easily hide the brutality of the knife. A ball in the heart is soon found, as being both out of place and out of character. Nor could I easily move so proportionate a man as yourself, should death prevent your cooperation. And I must think of Mrs. Stevenson, who at this moment I believe is at work in the kitchen below. The woman is as sagacious as a cat, and has ears of the same order. She would hear you squeal! And thus discover me! Ahhh—but perhaps I should poison your orange. . . ."

Franklin began to enjoy himself.

Strahan did not.

"This is more elaborate, I grant, but it places me at one remove from your death—the thought of which, dear Strahan, already makes me shudder. Count my disadvantage. For a consideration of safety to myself, a hedge against discovery, I have foregone certainty and sacrificed swiftness. But is my safety more than an illusion? No. I think not! I must obtain the poison from some public place, an apothecary, and risk the memory of a clerk. I must secrete the poison in your orange, in some manner unknown by yourself. I must feed—"

"But you are only thinking aloud, I should hope!"

"Indeed," Franklin nodded congenially. "If I am truly serious about remaining undiscovered, the poison must be fed to you over a period of weeks, and in the proper proportion. You must consume it without knowing of it, or tasting of it.

Of course! But I can see by the way you eat, this after all would not be so great a problem. Strahan, if you would chew your food forty times to the side, your digestion would be greatly improved."

Franklin leaned forward and rubbed his bare legs.

"And what am I to do, sir, if you suddenly develop a taste for apples, or walnuts, or decide to live entire upon lavender water?" he suddenly burst out. "What if you should take up nutmeg? I'm undone! Let's leave you confirmed in your orangeness. It's far easier. I call out your consideration. Whether swiftly or slowly, it appears I deceive myself to think I cannot be discovered in murder. Or that I must necessarily save my own skin by taking yours in strips rather than whole. You see the point, Strahan. Yet is this not the most glorious age of invention? The times yield innovation on every hand. We must expect novelty, my friend, or surrender to its surprises. Even in murder. Especially in murder. We must prepare ourselves to expect murder that is both brilliant and astounding, that has the poetry of material progress in it, and not allow ourselves to be blinded by it. Even murder may be raised to a fine art. Yes, of course I am thinking aloud." Franklin sighed.

"But no matter how brilliantly executed," he said thoughtfully, "murder alone is of little consequence. Although I say it is pretty enough. And I daresay that here it holds more than the common interest, being that it's the very first use of—No! We are obliged to put the saddle on the right horse. It's the murderer himself who must engage our attention. We must enter and read the motives of his heart—for that is the only way he can be discovered out. And *there,* sir, is the true realm of darkness. *There* we must grope for his motive force with no candle but our wit."

Strahan seemed to be chewing his orange an uncommonly long time.

"But there, sir, is where you have me blind and lost and halfway turned around in the bargain!" Strahan interrupted at last, with a citric sputter. "The slut's easy enough, in death as well as life. It's not natural to swim with your throat cut through! But for the life of me and two shillings, sir, I don't easily see how you count the porter murdered, unless you mean to suggest by sudden poison. Or do you say by slow poison? By what—"

Strahan leaned forward emphatically in exasperation, turning the pockets of his mind inside out, empty.

"By what means do you call that poor man murdered? The room in which he was found—the murder room was locked, was it not? And at that, from the inside. Fothergill himself assured you that failure of heart was not to be unexpected in such a scoundrel. The man bore no marks of notice. It was not *his* throat cut through! Why, sir, everything argues against it—except, of course, your own confounded assertion!"

Franklin's face softened.

"My dear Strahan," he said patiently. "Regulate your mind. You've heard my old argument on behalf of the crossbow as the most perfect weapon in warfare. No rain can wet its powder, for it has no powder. It's silent and does not discover the vantage of the man who wields it. It's certain death, so strong is its force. It is death, we might say, administered from a safe distance. Now. Let me ask you. May it not also be the perfect weapon in murder as well as more general warfare? Is it not possible, Strahan, to fire a crossbow through a window—let us say—from which a single pane of glass has been removed, the room all the while remaining locked? From the inside, as you say?"

Strahan looked stunned.

"But the panes were intact!" he finally answered. "The window was not disturbed!"

Franklin sighed. "The glass was intact," he repeated. "The window was not disturbed. I credit your recollection. But my dear Strahan, can you not remove a pane of glass from the outside of a window without notice and then replace it?"

Strahan looked confused. Finally he sputtered:

"I . . . I did not notice, I confess. I mean to say, why—I don't know! Of course not! It's *impossible*!"

"Sir. It is *very* possible. There is no other way to do it."

Strahan looked dumbfounded.

"But, of course, a crossbow was not used," Franklin said softly.

Strahan looked relieved.

"Particularities, sir," Franklin went on. "I've given you one. That the room was locked is of no consequence, except as it gives us the order of things. A happenstance, a side dish, sir, although I should think calculated by the murderer to sow confusion in such simple . . . in credulous minds." He grimaced. "Sharpen your wits! Here's another. Fothergill. Did he say that bursting of the heart was not unexpected? So much for that! Another of his drolleries! He said only that failure of the heart was not uncommon. Of course not! What could be more common than death? The murderer, my friend, is uncommon. That his victim—I speak of Raleigh—that his victim should die in such a manner, so swiftly and without a discernible mark upon his body, is mightily to be expected!"

At this inopportune moment Mrs. Stevenson entered the room from the stairs, clad in a plain housedress and her customary smile. She brought tea and a gentle reminder of the hour.

When she glided away, Strahan spoke. "You remarked, while we were yet at the Vulture, that something had gone terribly wrong for the murderer. Raleigh is dead, is he not? And you say murdered. What, then, has gone wrong?"

With some effort Franklin lifted himself to a sitting position.

"My dear Strahan," he said. "Everything has gone wrong. You must pay more attention to particularities. It's the particularity that gives us the direction toward the generality. One point standing alone is only a single point, nothing more. But two points comprise a line. A line, sir, possesses direction. By the careful observation of particularities, and by their accumulation, we might hope to understand the general laws that govern not only the natural world, but the minds of men as well. Even the minds of murderers."

Strahan was silent. It was contagious.

"You are right," Franklin said after a long time had passed. "I *am* only thinking aloud. A fruitless exercise. Of the two murders before us, the second is the less interesting. Its motives are the more obvious."

"Obvious?"

"Two may keep a secret if one of them is dead."

Franklin tilted back his head, the better to fix Strahan in his gaze. "If the woman was an accomplice at the murder of John Raleigh, as we must assume—"

"An accomplice?"

"Yet a coin has two sides," Franklin continued, "even a coin counterfeited on the anvil of passion. Perhaps she was uninvited. Her throat was opened to close her mouth. That much is clear. But why was the man in the room at all? *There* is our question! You see? There! The room itself is essential—of course—and if essential, it could not be used without the knowledge of the girl."

Franklin's head began to nod unceremoniously.

"Essential," he said.

Suddenly he sat bolt upright.

"Have you yet written to my wife?"

Six

S trahan's departure left only an air of bewilderment in the room, and the faint scent of oranges.

For a moment Franklin sat alone.

Absently he turned the keys on two or three of the musical boxes and set them to playing at once. He added another one. The effect, in concert, was disconcerting. But before they had time to run down, he lunged unsteadily to his feet and hurried himself slowly up the stairs. The odd, disharmonious sound of the musical instruments drifted after him, until it too was lost in the silence of the third floor.

Not until he reached the sanctuary of his own room did Franklin hear the soft voice of Mrs. Stevenson calling plaintively to him from down the stairs. "A gentleman to see you, sir, if you're not yet indisposed."

The widow called from the second-floor landing, where she stood wiping her hands on the small French apron which now covered the front of her plain dress. She wrung something genteel from the word *gentleman.*

Franklin grunted. "I'm forever disposed."

He slowly made his way down the staircase again and entered the parlor. He could hear Mrs. Stevenson below, commending his hospitality. A moment later she ushered into the room an old gentleman who leaned stiffly upon a stick of bright yellow wood. He presented a very respectable appearance, mitigated only by the wheezing which the stairs had extracted from him. A crown of silky white hair floated carelessly about his head. He was attired in pale lemon pantaloons, a gold cravat fashioned boldly about his neck, a worn blue frock, black shoes so highly polished that they caught the last glint of the red sun from the westernmost window. But his face suggested something quite the opposite of the gaiety of his dress.

"Take care of the boxes," Franklin said inhospitably, pointing to his miniature orchestra.

The old man stood still. His nose, pink and mobile as a rabbit's, wrestled about above his mouth.

"Oranges," he announced at last.

"Indeed."

"You are Dr. Franklin. From America."

"I am that. Have a seat. And take care of the boxes."

The old man lowered himself by a series of jerks into the settee, as though he were guided by a system of unseen winches and pulleys. His hand, decorated with liver spots, rested lightly on the head of the walking stick, which remained erect before him.

"Do you represent a charity? I'm very busy, but not ungenerous. State your business. The hour is—"

"I am Hector LaNeve. The name means nothing to you. But perhaps in France, in the neighborhood of Châlons-sur-Marne, it might yet have some small meaning. Several nights since, a man was found dead in the Vulture Tavern."

Franklin's eyes went around. His easy smile vanished. He seated himself carefully across from the visitor.

"Indeed."

"A scoundrel. A piece of scummery."

"That may be, sir."

"He was murdered?"

"Indeed."

The old man lost his stick. It clattered to the floor, and he jerked down to retrieve it. "Forgive me," he said. "I am told you have a certain interest in this matter."

Franklin retrieved his smile. He shrugged as though he were indifferent.

"Where have you heard that?"

"From talk. This is a town of loose tongues. They talk of nothing but scummery." M. LaNeve squared his jaw. "I too have an interest in this affair."

"Which is . . ."

"Not easily put. Although painfully clear. The dead man was a member of a Club known by many names, a despicable Club, call it what you will, proof of the course of the world, a Hellfire Club. My son . . . his name . . . here lies the point of my interest . . . but I see—I am obliged—"

The old man was moved by old manners. He abruptly swept his hand about the room to indicate the musical boxes scattered on the floor, the loose sheaf of newspapers which Franklin had left on a side table that morning, the look of impatience that suddenly crossed Franklin's face—as though recognizing the measure of his interruption.

"I ask your indulgence, sir."

"I'm generous. Not indulgent," Franklin said sourly.

The old man bowed his head. "I meant to come to you when

I first heard of this affair—of your interest in it, I mean to say, for news of this low creature's death swept the town like news of a cure for the pox. I have some knowledge of your reputation, but not—I confess—not of your interest in a man such as this."

Franklin lifted himself half out of his chair.

"If you mean to complain of the world, do so elsewhere," he said. "This room is in a state of undress. My mind even more so. I have an appointment, sir, that cannot be put off. This is not Trinidad or Tobago. Tonight I'm obliged to seek my supper elsewhere than at this house, so that if you could arrive at your point within the minute—"

"A minute! You *are* an American! Thirty years in a single minute!"

The old man rattled a deep sigh, but then he squeezed himself stiff.

"I believe my son to have killed this man," he said.

LaNeve's cheeks flushed red, adding yet another color to his ensemble. Franklin sank gently back into his cushions.

"I see that causes you no surprise. Just as I thought! He is—"

"By what means?" Franklin asked sharply. "To what purpose?"

"He's an excellent swordsman. He's a dragoon, injured out. He is—what?—temperous."

"The dead man was not killed by a sword, I assure you."

"No. Of course he wasn't. Something more devilish. Some have said the Devil himself. Some suppose witchcraft. I've heard that poison was used. It's very much a mystery—I know nothing of it. But I know that behind it is my son—it's his affair—and he's well able to carry out the threats I've heard from his lips these last two months. He's a dragoon, sir, and would have captained a company were it not—"

70

LaNeve laughed dryly at the cruelty of the world. "I must take you back five years since," he said suddenly.

"I will not miss my supper."

"There's no help for it. I'm an old man. Five years since!"

LaNeve's eyes closed, showing weary red lids. He waved a frail hand in the air.

"We were at that happy time still resident at Châlons-sur-Marne, as my family had been for generations before me," he said resolutely. "My family, LaNeve, have roots in the province of Champagne as deep as the fleur-de-lis. I remind you of that, sir. The estates numbered more *arpents* than an American could count. My son managed them. For *my* father, rest him, I had done the same. My wife is dead these many years. Here you have my history! I had only Hector—my son— and my estates. And, of course, my butterflies. They are perfect, as various as God's blessings.

"In other words, we possessed a certain position in the order of things as they have always been, and as I fear they will never again be. In small ways the order changed. You are not a young man, sir, but you require my years to see it. Hector quarreled with a peasant and left him dead. A small quarrel! Spanish blood! He inherited *that* passion from his mother— and his red hair from God knows where! I have no reservations that Hector was in the right, but this is an old case, sir, of no interest except as it illustrates something of his character and . . . But of course it was only the beginning. He defended his good name against a peasant, who like the other peasants took upon himself somewhat more liberties than were his due. Death was that poor man's reward, as well it should have been. As for Hector, he joined the army. Not as an act of cowardice—I read your expression, sir—although there was something politic in it, considering the low estate of the courts. I'm his father! I urged it. It was an act of

71

allegiance to the state, which was his obligation. I myself served with the Fourteenth Guard."

LaNeve's throat rattled with faint memories.

"With Hector gone to make a soldier, the responsibility of the estates was once more placed upon my shoulders," he went on. "In this God tested me with drought, insolence, and little brown bugs I never was able to identify. The crops failed. Several of the peasants were carried off by a strange sickness. The others worked less and less. The harmony that always existed between the LaNeve family and the society of those estates began to seem—it seemed only a dream, the tale of a grandfather. I see this in retrospect. At the time I was shut up in the manor house—heir to all the ills of those who find their strength eroded by age. I brooded among the cases of my butterflies—and how they seemed to me symbols of all we once enjoyed at Châlons-sur-Marne! Dead beautiful figures! Silken wings that could not fly!

"This is an age of fashionable infidelity, sir. Under such burdens as were given me to bear, I sought to have Hector returned to me from the army. Prefects and politicians who once had formed in lines to be of service to the LaNeves now laughed at me! I cringe to remember such humiliation. *Impossible, impossible,* they all said. I was awakened out of my sleep! You recall the peasants, how they gathered to take the rabbits and birds which were not theirs to take! It forced me to thoughts of our times. The King, forgive me—debauched and given over to the most gross infidelities. Pompadour, forgive me—ruling with that defamed white hand. The courts sunk in the grasp of the peasantry and cheap politicians; the Church given over to worldly passions; the class of which I proudly call myself a part shut up in close houses. Like butterflies!

"By God's good grace, Hector was sent out of the dragoons.

He had suffered a slight wound of the leg, inflicted by his saber. His heart and his mind were as strong as ever, but he was prevented from making those sudden movements so necessary to a soldier. He rides with pain. Afoot, he limps. But it is nothing. By God's grace, all that I could claim was mine again. When I resolved to sell off the estates—like you Americans, to liquidate the past and start out anew—Hector gave me his allegiance. I am blessed, sir, for all the terrible turnings of these times.

"We removed here, to London, with a fortune large enough to live upon but small enough to remind us of all that we had lost. We sought to find that ordered state of things, that rational society, in which a man can live an upright life in obedience to his conscience. I'll be open with you, sir. We have not found the success we hoped for. Not only are we pent up in this stink of a city, but this society shows itself as disordered as our own. There's no enlightenment here! Poverty I can endure, if it is somebody else's. It's less easy to bear this anarchy, the discontent of even the most righteous men, the indecent excesses of those whose position demands they exhibit—"

"If your head is made of wax, sir, don't walk in the sun," Franklin interrupted. "My stomach complains."

"You're a practical man," LaNeve said quickly. " 'My stomach complains.' And I was led to believe you had certain sympathies with philosophy, that you were a man of sound reason and scientific taste, a doctor of—"

"I have decided tastes, which are at this moment unsatisfied. I've heard your excellent history, and now if you'll be good enough to—"

"Very well. I'll be practical. I'm capable of it, old as I am. One year ago my son married, and moved from Great George Street. His woman was a fine girl, I grant it—Valetta

LaNeve. She bears my name. I myself was struck by her—her features, her carriage, the ease of her laughter, her strong emotion. It's apparent to everyone who sees her. She brought a certain brightness to George Street, and she restored to my son the manhood he'd lost sight of. So much for that. He's endured much. He was raised up without women, and the work of such a girl as Valetta was enough to make visible at last those qualities of contentment that have always marked the family LaNeve. They married with my blessing and moved from Great George Street to St. Martin's Lane, taking up apartments above a music shop. I saw them there often."

The old man paused as though considering some scene of domestic tranquillity. A shudder ran down his gaunt frame.

"This is an age of infidelity," he said with a hard edge to his voice. "Valetta was shortly guided by her passions into the most foolish practices. She claimed equality with her husband. She fell off in her cooking—they could afford no servants, sir. She fell in with low company, hell raisers and lechers—St. Martin's is crowded with them posing as artists and furniture makers. We were forced, my son and I, to confess on each other's shoulders how little we really knew of her true character.

"Even this he endured. Yet there soon came a point— Valetta was taken off by this group of rogues who call themselves a Hellfire Club. Of her own volition, I assure you. She's high-spirited! Not a woman open only to the exercise of force! So much for that! She accompanied those knaves— so we learned in time—to their infamous revelry, to be used and abused in turn. I dare not tell her usage. In truth, sir, she could scarce walk unaided. Three men—they fashion themselves monks and devotees of the darkest arts—three men had taken her aside into some dark cell and done their devilish work masked against her recognition. She came home—repentant. God's grace, I said. I'm of a liberal mind. She's been punished for her infidelities, and so far as my eyes saw was restored to faithfulness."

LaNeve sniffed at the air.

"My son, however, could not summon up that same sense of great forgiveness which is urged upon us by the example of our Lord. Can you blame him, sir? He gathered up such small goods as he had, brought them to Great George Street, and there gave me—his poor father!—a most lamentable farewell. As though—Do you have a son, sir? Then you would have known what it meant.

"To have seen him thus, both wounded and possessed—he reminded me of his mother, forgive me. He vowed revenge to every member of that godless Club, knowing neither the names nor the faces of those—those three men. He took his shirt, his brace, and his sword. With his sword he slapped me on the shoulder and uttered such a cry as I haven't heard since the Fourteenth Guard. And was gone!"

Once again the old man closed his eyes. His last words came out with a gasp. His face had grown very small, as though a seamstress had sewn it tight with painful thread.

"I have not seen him since. I fear I never will—on this earth," he said in a voice that was barely above a whisper. "Should you find him, I pray, bring him to me one last time."

Franklin was moved, but not very. He arranged himself differently in his chair, and looked long and hard at the withering Frenchman before him.

"I'm interested in your collection of butterflies," Franklin said. "What became of it?"

The old man looked startled.

"Butterflies?"

"Yes."

"I sold my butterflies."

"Necessity is the easiest economy. Did you sell them to your son?"

"To my son?" LaNeve answered incredulously. "No, not to my son, sir. I sold them to the Academy."

"Your son, then, was not interested in butterflies?"

"Hector? Interested in butterflies?"

"Your son had no interest in such things? For instance, did he geologize?"

"Oh! No—he had—"

"He had no interest in the study of natural history," Franklin went on, "or in the ocean's currents, or in the various effects of the atmosphere? Did he study the electrical fluid? It's quite the rage. Was his interest in physic? Had he informed himself in any way of medicine?"

"None of that, sir. He's of a more active turn of mind. One-quarter Spanish, I'm afraid. His mother—"

"So he did not care for your butterflies."

"He helped me catch them when he was a boy. It was a game, nothing more. He had no interest—"

"I see. Very well. Indeed," Franklin announced.

He carefully removed his spectacles and placed them on the broad arm of the chair.

"Mr. LaNeve," he said with a grave smile. "From the circumstances of the case it strikes me as improbable that your son had any agency in the death of John Raleigh. If you would be kind enough—your narrative is well-calculated to elicit sympathy. You have mine. We always tend to overestimate the powers of our blood, and the efficiency of our sons."

LaNeve thrust himself shakily out of his chair. His hand was palsied. But he reached inside his blue frock and withdrew a soiled sheet of paper, folded four times.

Franklin reached for his spectacles.

"Hector is alive," the old man said. "He is well. I do not

76

underestimate him. This came yesterday in the post. A day earlier, as I discover, that rogue was found dead in the Vulture Tavern. It set me to my inquiries. More than that, it set me to the hope that with the blessings of God he might be restored to me—I might—in some manner—"

But Franklin was reading:

Mon père—

For the glory of the family LaNeve, I long to be at your side. But first the pathway must be paved with thirteen hearts of souls unsaved. Let there be twelve!

In fidelis Deo,
Hector

Seven

Shortly after eight-thirty o'clock on the evening of the same day, the door to No. 7 Craven Street opened again. Franklin himself stood on the sill.

The old Frenchman had been discharged into the gathering dusk long before. He carried with him Franklin's promise that should the latter's researches into the affair of the Hellfire Club carry him across the path of young LaNeve, he would seek to reunite the lad with his father. It was a pledge made in silence, with a nod, as Franklin still held the son's note in his hand.

With the old man departed and the lamps in the house not yet turned on, Franklin had retired successfully up the stairs to his room. There he lay in darkness on the soft bed to clarify his mind and rest his body for the ordeal ahead.

His mind would not clarify.

The longer he lay there, the more hungry both it and his body became—the one for some insight into how Hector *fils* could have parroted the exact language of Francis Dashwood's dangerous correspondent, the other for less airy nourishment.

He felt the push and tug of events.

Even before Strahan had confirmed his worst suspicions about Annie Martin, Franklin had set in motion his own program of operation. He asked Dashwood to arrange a special revels of the Hellfire Club so that he might see at firsthand the company from which the dead man had come. No excuse was too small for a revels, and Dashwood quickly agreed— setting the date (on quick notice) a few days hence. No excuse was too small for anything. Prior to the special revels, Dashwood suggested, Franklin might attend dinner in Pall Mall and accompany the members of the Hellfire Club to the annual Squeezer of John Montagu, Lord Sandwich, which by common consent inaugurated the season of masques and ridottos in the town of London.

So it was that when the door opened again in the house on Craven Street, it was Franklin who stepped into the night.

He was an unlikely amalgam, wearing a plain hat, a Holland shirt ruffled at the wrists and bosom, and a pair of black broadcloth breeches that had recently acquired a new seat (the landlady's daughter supplied it). Luckily enough, his sagathy coat came down well below his hips and kept this a private matter. In his hand he carried a half-worn carpet-bag with gold clasp. It was already arranged that he spend the night for the lateness of the hour.

The street was dark. The sun that had warmed his gouty leg all afternoon had also raised up the temperature of London, and given the town an illusion of summer. It had brought out the mayflies of the mob for a turn along the

Strand—parading down from the City to Charing Cross and then back again. He heard their hubbub at the head of the street.

Franklin had a sudden taste for trout. He turned to his left and began to make his way on foot toward the hum of the crowd.

It was no democratic impulse that made him a pedestrian. The blue coach was not available, being in the shop of T. Bowman for the repair of a wheel from which the manservant Peter had dislodged the iron rim on a careless turn. Twice the wheel had been pronounced repaired, twice the carriage had been returned as fixed. Each time the rim had worked loose and come off again. Now the master craftsman had the coach back for a third attempt. Franklin tried not to become angry thinking about it.

Perhaps it was a blessing, for walking exercised his brain as well as his body. Repose had done little enough for either. But walking shook loose the strangest ideas. Even during his late illness, an observer in the Stevenson household would have seen the stout doctor make his circuit of all the rooms in the house, march slowly up and down the stairs, until he had accumulated by his own reckoning the distance of one mile each day.

The music of the hautboy players drifted down toward him from the Strand through the darkness. It was a strange, Eastern sort of music.

Whitefish would do as well as trout, three or four sides well buttered.

Franklin's appetite was whetted not only by natural hunger and the fashionable tardiness of supper, but by the anticipation of dining with a murderer. It moved the blood. The unlikely coincidence of Hector LaNeve's note merely drove him deeper into the gearwork of his own mind and the possibilities of the case. A doddering Frenchman, an unpredictable boy, a "fine" girl who had been taken into the Hellfire Club.

He attempted to reason, plunging into the crowd of dustmen and nightwalkers in the Strand. He was nearly sandwiched between two erratic post chaises. When he reached the other side of the street he stood for a moment and then more carefully crossed back, coming finally face to face with his own reflection in the darkened window of Deard the toymaker's.

The other Franklin looked wan and ghostly. Yet it alone stood still and solid against the moving pattern of strollers behind it.

The shop was closed. He wished it weren't. He often came down to this corner of Craven Street and the Strand, telling Mrs. Stevenson he was after a spot of air or bound for the baths at the Turk's Head—for William Deard kept a barrel of cold ale in his workroom "to temper the mind and steady the hand." He found Deard an ingenious man in his way, and wished he were about. The toymaker devised miniature dollhouses for which the rich paid dearly. He assembled intricate mechanical dancers out of walnut and fine cherry, and created assemblages of lead shot, curved wooden runways, and tiny tilting buckets by which an idle public added to its ennui. Having concocted clockwork, Deard knew all the ways in which one thing led to another. He was a dealer in consequences, but a master of innards. Franklin would have liked to try some of the alternatives of the case on the toymaker's deliberative mind.

Franklin himself had been credited with being a practical man, and indeed he was a practical man. But his spirit rode on the deeper sea of metaphysics—something the world, being blind, did not choose to see. To himself and his closest friends, however, he confessed too strong a penchant for hypothesis. It indulged his natural state of indolence.

This at any rate was the reason he stood so long before Deard's dark window, confronting in reverse the reflections of the world. Riding the swells of chance, of possibility, of character, of hypothesis. He calculated the names of the Hellfire Club members—those Dashwood described as belonging to the superior order. Some he knew little enough about. Others were common figures in the town, and thus had small hope for secrets.

Eugene Toplady he had at least met. A thin, runny youth given over to the privacy of learning, he seemed inadequate to such a public act as murder. His nearness to Dashwood raised possibilities, but for the moment Franklin dismissed him. Leave him to his participles and homonyms. John Wilkes he had seen from a distance, and so he had George Selwyn, who sat guard over his pale beer at the Vulture on the night John Raleigh died. The town made one man out to be dangerous, the other witty, but could not prove either. Bubb Dodington: Selwyn's patron and a power at the Court. For his size and his influence, he could not so easily be dismissed. Nor could Lord Sandwich himself, a squinting ugly man whose interests ran singularly toward young girls. He considered himself their benefactor, so the town delighted to say, breaking them into the ways of the world. There was John Raleigh, now dead. There was Francis Dashwood himself. . . .

Franklin nodded at his reflection in the glass. He had stood so long with his backside to the world that when the watch called the hour it was already nine by the clock. He was immediately late.

He gave off his considerations and crossed the Strand again. On the other side he turned west with the crowd. There were children underfoot. They jostled his carpetbag, loosened his plain hat, nearly trod on his toes. He hurried as best he could. Of the shops and houses he knew, he passed in order those of John Anderson, hosier; the Widow Wadsworth; Benjamin Cox, grocer; John Swann the bookseller (opposite Northumberland Street); Edward Orphen. He was forced out into the street in order to make his way past the Castle and the Coach and Horses, two adjoining taverns with clienteles that commingled. At the corner shop of Thomas Jeffery, printseller, Franklin turned north into St. Martin's Lane. Only part of the crowd turned with him—bound for the celebrated taverns at the upper end.

The lane was as dark as Craven Street and surely more dangerous. But by this route he avoided the Golden Cross tavern with its crush of coaches, horsemen, and trunks. And he saved a moment toward supper. He crossed St. Martin's Lane a little way up, entered Woodstock Court, and made his way through its dark corridors into the still darker Royal Mews. This was a wide expanse of open ground, an exercising yard more used by people than the intended horses. It was a place in which no less than Horace Walpole had once been robbed of more than fourteen hundred pounds sterling, and many a lady had been relieved of more than her rings and riches. Yet Franklin was neither Horace Walpole nor a lady anxious of being relieved. If any cutthroat watched him pass through the shadows, he held his cry for a more promising target.

Dr. Franklin hurried onward under the obligations of the hour, oblivious of any danger. Besides, he had suddenly acquired a taste for beef well roasted, with cranberries on the side. And almonds. And perhaps a pint or two. Or three.

He was not used to such hurried exercise.

He came out from the Mews, not at the regular entrance but at the mouth of Hedge Lane. This allowed him but a short distance to his left in order to come into Cockspur Street—which he cleared just ahead of the Portsmouth Flying

Machine, the daily coach coming down late toward the Golden Cross. He heard the click of the wheels behind him as the coach flew past. At the curb he took a moment to catch his breath, looking down through the thin dust toward the statue of Charles I, the mob that had poured into the center of Charing Cross to welcome the express, the men who swarmed like black flies about the door to the Black Horse Tavern. All of which made him thankful he had had the wits to seek a shortcut.

He pressed on, hurrying up the westerly side of Cockspur Street past the clutter of closed shops—past Rhymer the shoemaker's, past the Red Lion, past the shop of Christopher Moore the victualler, past the open mouth of Warwick Street, and finally past the notorious toyshop of Chevenix, who made up for the deficiencies of his trade by the exhibition of human freaks, lucrative enough in any age. This course brought him directly into Pall Mall, at the east end.

Again he paused to catch his breath, which left him at an alarming rate. He steadied his hat. He put the carpetbag down upon the stones. Secretly his hand reached around behind and felt the patch on his breeches, to discover it secure.

By day Pall Mall had been as quiet and deserted as the main wagon road west at Gnadenhutten on the Pennsylvania frontier. By night it was vivacious and alive. Franklin looked up the length of the street into the glitter of lamps.

London was many things, but here was *London*. The Mall was choked with coaches of various color, all agleam in the lamplight and parked at every which way along either side of the wide thoroughfare. That the rich, the witty, the gambler had no order in their lives, within or without, this certainly proved. Nor was this all. Both the sidewalks and the street were full of people—crossing, coming, going. It seemed as though a fair were in progress, so thickly did the crowd swarm about in all its ancillary motions. It could have been a saint's day in Spain. The hum of idle industry rose up from the street, punctuated now and then by sharp, piercing cries—but whether of contentment or pain it was not possible to say.

On the north side and but a short way off, three men wrestled together on the ground, turning over and over and over again in the dirt like a beast with six legs, four arms, and perhaps only three ears left intact. A chain of coaches—one blue, one deep red, one yellow—interrupted Franklin's view for a moment. He watched them edge through the mob, the monogrammed coach doors gleaming in the light: RStM, HLN, A. The middle coach was driven by a woman, standing erect on the board. The horses too caught the light on their shiny coats and then broke free, rattling their carriages around the corner near to Franklin and flying off free down Cockspur Street. Dust rose into the air. Through it Franklin could still see the three-backed beast rolling on the ground, and hear the encouraging grunts of the ruffians and gentlemen who stood about it.

He picked up his bag and began to walk.

It was far worse than the Strand. He felt out of place. The younger women, some with a gentleman on each arm and a third sniffing along behind, laughed gaily at him. Their companions scowled. Franklin considered the ruffles on his shirt. Perhaps they were too small. Mrs. Stevenson had picked it out for him. He considered his sagathy coat. Perhaps it was too worn. No—perhaps it was the fact that his shirt had pulled partway out of his breeches, making him seem stouter than he was. *Appearance. Seem.* He spit gently into the street, but these thoughts were not so easily dismissed. They occupied him until they were crowded out at last by the notion of thick chops with a white marble of fat along the edge, and a fruit glaze. He had worked his way through the sweet potatoes and the roasted almonds and the bowl of brown sugar and reached the tiny iced cakes set four to a plate when he finally came to. He was halfway up the block, deep in the crowd, and standing almost unconsciously at the arched doorway of Francis Dashwood.

Perhaps it was only the old carpetbag that made him conspicuous in this sea of dandies and young ladies. His ruffles were large enough. He wiped his mouth and turned in, finding himself face to face with the glinting brass of the devil's head.

A deep sigh escaped him.

Behind him was the tumult of the street. Before him was the tumult within—which he identified easily enough. It was the final bars of "Sally in Our Alley," lustily sung.

He blinked twice. Then he knocked.

Eight

The door swung open before Franklin had a chance to draw his hand back from the devil. Mr. Brackett reached out impatiently. He hissed some unwelcome word, took the heavy bag from Franklin's grasp, and snatched the hat from his head. Franklin stepped into a room as changed as all of Pall Mall had changed.

Where once had been darkness, now was light. Heavy lamps and their reflectors lined the walls and were ablaze with illumination. Where once had been a bare room was now a hall of exquisite decoration. The narrow sideboard had been removed. In its place was a walnut table of magnificent proportions, set to damask and glittering with glass and silver. In the corners were canisters of incense giving off a pleasant fragrance. Dashwood's family portraits had been retired in favor of a collection less domestic: satyrs, nymphs, surrendered women. Two of these paintings were anamorphoses, startling the eye from the perspective of the doorway with their graphic pleasure. Seen straight on, Franklin knew, they would dissolve into a pool of meaningless form and color. There could be no doubt that he had entered the realm of the Hellfire Club.

Dominating everything was the very work of art Franklin had heard whispered about—Hogarth's portrait of Francis Dashwood at his devotions. It showed the redoubtable host draped in his monkish habit, his adoration directed not toward the suffering Christ but toward a pink and naked Venus lying supine before him, her knees slightly bent and her thighs separated just enough to reward Dashwood's scholastic scrutiny.

This alone would have cast a proper tone over the assembly.

But added to it was a knot of gaily dressed men—some short, one or two tall, one very fat—gathered in the center of the room. They started in over again on "Sally in Our Alley"—as was their custom—despite the presence of the stranger in the sagathy coat.

Franklin was not unnoticed, however. Two men immediately broke from the chorus and rushed toward him, arms outstretched. They seemed opposite halves of a whole.

The first was short and squat, and could have been taken for a butcher. His brutish face was dark, his eyes were fixed intently upon Franklin from deep within their dark sockets, his bushy brows were twisted up in anticipation. There was something menacing about his rush forward across the room. There was nothing menacing about the second man: Eugene Toplady. He glided. His head seemed made of porcelain, the skin creamy white, the cheeks rosy. A smile was fixed upon his face as surely as if William Deard had painted it there.

"Dr. Franklin!" Eugene exclaimed happily, taking up Franklin's hand.

"Dieter Schiff," growled the other, taking Franklin's hand away and—unbelievably—kissing it.

The two men clasped Franklin affectionately on the back.

"The honor—"

"We are—"

"So we have you at last."

Franklin could only blink. Dieter Schiff and Eugene Toplady pawed at him, as though he were a lost dog come home.

"My hounds!" declared Francis Dashwood in his piping voice, breaking between them. His blue eyes betrayed no emotion save good humor.

He took Franklin rather too tightly by the arm and directed him toward the center of the room, leaning down in confidence. "Everyone has come," he whispered. "We lack only Sandwich—it surprises me—but we'll see him soon enough."

Franklin smiled warmly, as though Dashwood had asked his hat size.

"Your harmony is impressive," he said aloud, thinking to commend the company's rendition of "Sally in Our Alley."

"Harmony!" Dashwood cried, throwing back his head. His burst of laughter silenced the singers.

They stood an awkward moment confronting one another: Dashwood and Franklin on one side of an invisible boundary, the company on the other. Then Dashwood steered Franklin past them to a single chair on the outside of the long table—a Chippendale padded in red leather. He waved the members to their seats behind the table. They scurried like a covey of quail.

It was then that Franklin noticed one young gentleman wobble to his feet from a chair near to the window, where he had been hidden from view. The young man shuffled to the table like a sleepwalker. He was dressed entirely in orange, with a loose-hanging blue sash thrown carelessly over his left shoulder. The flicker of a smile played about his lips. He had been busy with something stronger than singing or carcavello.

Dashwood edged round the table to take his own place at the center, opposite Franklin and between Schiff and Top-lady—obviously his favorites. Above them was Hogarth's telling portrait. A very good likeness.

Franklin sat alone on his side of the table. He confronted a row of silent faces, all but one devoid of expression. The brief moment of awkwardness had settled into something more wary and substantial. The exception was the man in orange, at the end of the table to Franklin's left. He smiled knowingly at his silver plate, and was greeted by his own reflection.

"The place of honor," Dashwood said, gesturing through the heavy silence toward Franklin.

Franklin bowed slightly, not an easy thing to do while seated. "The better to see you," he said.

"The better to eat you!" exploded a high voice on his left. Franklin did not see who possessed it. But a wave of low laughter rolled down the length of the table.

Dashwood clinked his knife against an empty goblet.

"We are pleased to have you. I've already explained to the Brotherhood before your arrival—"

"Which was very late!" came a voice from the right.

Dashwood struck the goblet sharply again. He glared left and right.

"I've explained to the company—you can see, some of them have improved their time at the wine—we hope you'll accompany us down to the Squeezer. I trust you've decided to stay the night, for one cannot expect—"

"I brought my bag."

"I didn't see it. One can't attend a Squeezer with one eye to the clock. Consider yourself at home. Consider yourself among friends, as we are one to another—a brotherhood. Devote yourself to pleasure—forget philosophy! Tonight the pleasure of food and drink, and of good company, and of—"

There was a sudden crash.

The young man at the end of the table had dropped his face into his plate. From Franklin's vantage he looked like a mound of orange silk. John Wilkes, who sat second from the end with an underhung grin, put a sharp elbow into the young man's side. It brought his head up.

"They're all devils, sir!" Dashwood laughed. He talked three ways at once. "Hand me that wine! That's it! Be that as it may—God damn!—we'll have your company at our revels, sir, and you can—"

"Freeze your arse," someone said under his breath.

Dashwood sighed in defeat.

"I assure you," he said, "you couldn't do as well in all of London for fine times. These are the Monks of Medmenham, the Friars of St. Francis, the talk of London, the Hellfire Club, sir!" He waved his hands to either side.

A deep roar of appreciation greeted the announcement. Dieter Schiff jerked to his feet and reached awkwardly across the table, grappling for Franklin's hand. He wanted to kiss it again, but settled for the butter dish.

"We swim with affection," Dashwood cried loudly. "Let me introduce—"

"And roll from whore to whore!" bawled the man in orange silk. "Which in this case we have not got!" He was suddenly awake, although he talked only in spurts. His head rolled from shoulder to shoulder. "I need some wine to stiffen my neck!" he cried, banging on the table.

"That's not all that needs stiffening!" answered a voice

from the other end of the table. Franklin looked quickly down to see George Selwyn blinking blindly at a candle set before him. He seemed to be trying to blow it out with air from his nose.

Dashwood called his attention back.

The man who dressed in orange and wore a smile that would not go away, and which itself was rather orange, was William Reeve, a painter who labored modestly under the influence of Carracci and Giuseppe Borgnis. Dashwood used the names as if he knew them. Reeve was connected (besides being a charming fellow). His brother was governor of Bengal, and it was through him—Dashwood explained—that the Brotherhood had been supplied with those two blooms of Eastern culture, the *Kama Sutra* and bhang—something one smoked, not unlike tobacco.

Selwyn blew out the candle.

John Wilkes, who sat next to the smiling painter, needed no introduction. Close as Franklin was, Wilkes seemed less ugly than he had from a greater distance in the Vulture Tavern. Perhaps like Dashwood's obscene paintings, the meaning of Wilkes's terrible squint varied with the vantage of the viewer. From below was perhaps worst of all.

Next to Wilkes sat Thomas Potter. His broad nose, gaping mouth, and slightly bulging eyes gave him the aspect of a fish too long out of water. Brilliant and uncouth—a happy combination—this was the son of the Archbishop of Canterbury, proving once again that inheritance has its natural limits. He was now, Dashwood explained congenially, a hairsplitter, a rogue, a follower of Old Nick the Devil, and fine company.

"—and the father of Dean Warburton's baby!" someone cried from down near the other end of the table. Potter jumped to his feet and bowed in every direction all around, conceding that he still had some ecclesiastical interests. He was slammed back down into his seat rather abruptly by the hulking gentleman who sat beside him.

It was natural that these two should be placed side by side, although Charles Churchill towered over Thomas Potter.

Churchill was an atheist, a satirical poet of mean wit, an expert boxer, and a ruffian on general principles. He was also the son of a clergyman at Rainham, Essex, and was himself a priest in the Church of England, having received his orders the year previous and not known quite what use to make of them. It was not by mistake that he answered to the name *Bruiser*. His hair was cropped short, the bones of his brow were bumped and rubbed thick directly above his placid eyes, his neck and arms were swelled with obvious strength. Franklin had seen him caricatured in the press as a bear. Yet he was good-natured, even if Potter had reason to think otherwise. He drank beer instead of wine because he was a democrat, and spent himself on low women rather than ladies of fashion for the same noble reason.

Samuel Pennant sat next: black-bearded, moody, and churlish. His expression was nothing less than malevolent, although a pound note or two from Franklin's hand might have changed that. Pennant was a dealer in pornographic and occult books, and a printer of the same. His shop was in Bedford Street, over against King Street. It was Pennant, Dashwood explained to Franklin, who built his prosperity on the erotic scribblings of John Raleigh.

Mentioning Raleigh was a mistake—not of fact but of judgment. The observation chilled the temper of the table and restored the sullen air of distrust that had marked Franklin's reception. Everyone looked sharply at him, and then looked away.

Eugene Toplady's name, however, was greeted with an

outburst of jeers. The table came alive. His cheeks grew more rosy as Dashwood gave him a luxurious introduction warmed by real affection—the youngest member of the Brotherhood, an earnest scholar, every bit a match for Dictionary Johnson, a sweet and easy temperament, a pilgrim of truth, an experimenter in the electrical arts.

Toplady signified his discomfort by a glance across at Dieter Schiff, but Schiff at that moment was discreetly counting the tines of his fork (there were two). George Selwyn, who had reignited the candle before him, extinguished it with a whistle.

Like Toplady, Dieter Schiff held a favored position over his companions. But unlike Toplady, who was a dilettante, Schiff was the Garrick of electricians. Dashwood had only to mention his name in order to draw forth a thunder of hoots and catcalls that more than matched the one accorded to Eugene Toplady. Franklin blinked in surprise. Schiff was never surprised. He rose dramatically to his feet and delivered a tremendous sweeping bow to either side. He resumed his seat to hear the host commend the inventiveness of his mind, the variety of his interests, and his immense showmanship in the presentation of his well-attended demonstrations with the Leyden jar.

"We'll see one tonight at the Squeezer," Dashwood said directly to Franklin. "You're familiar with Dr. Schiff's wonderful works?"

"I confess, sir, I am newly arrived—"

"In the best of them," Dashwood interrupted, "he dresses thirty confederates as monks—they join hands, sir, in a show of brotherly affection—and are subjected to such a charge that their feet simultaneously leave the stage. I've seen it at Covent Garden! It works a wonderful abuse upon religion! He makes angels of them!"

Schiff held his palms up high, fingers outstretched. There was no applause. Only a few helpless giggles came from the far left, where a servant was pouring more wine into the bottomless glass of William Reeve.

Dashwood noticed it, and interrupted his introductions momentarily to call for dinner (which Franklin welcomed). The servants scurried forth with silver carts, served the table, and then stood back as Dashwood called upon the next man in line—Old Paul Whitehead—to deliver the devotion. The honor fell naturally to Whitehead. He once delivered a sermon to a congregation of cats, and he owned a chair that had once been owned by Shakespeare. These were proof of his eloquence.

"Prince of darkness, chief of all the powers combined against the light," he began, "champion of vice, sacred font of all that's lewd and cunning, lord of the lobcock. . . ."

Franklin permitted himself a faint smile, and eyed the entrée.

But Old Paul was more than a comedian, Dashwood explained between mouthfuls. Tall, thin, and gray-headed, he was best known as a poet and political satirist. He lived by his wits, quietly, and was not often hungry. He was High Steward and Treasurer of the Hellfire Club, collecting dues for lechery and drink; it showed his trustworthy nature. Some fine distinction of spirit kept him from the more public pleasures of the Brotherhood, although Dashwood himself vowed for his prowess in private. The source of his knowledge went unstated. Besides, Whitehead had a wife who thought she was a cow. He was devoted to her, an odd affection. But he was equally devoted to Francis Dashwood—that was plain enough by the pout of humility with which he greeted the latter's praise.

"How his silence drinks up all this applause!" Wilkes

noted, looking sharply down the table. But, of course, no one was applauding.

Least of all the mountain of fat and purple silk that sat to Whitehead's left. Born plain old George Bubb, he had added the name of Dodington to round it out, but himself needed no rounding. His broad face was colored in the manner of olives, showing that whatever he worshipped it was neither sun nor fresh air. His eyes looked out from beneath half-closed lids, even when he was most awake. The newspapers made him out an oaf, a pompous ass, an ineffectual womanizer, the butt of everyone's jokes—and were not far wrong.

"Fatherless and motherless, and born without a skin," Samuel Pennant intoned solemnly to his goblet, "he spoke when he came in the world and never spoke again."

"The old fart!" Churchill answered quickly, and everyone laughed at the riddle so old it didn't need to be rehearsed.

But the old fart did not stir. Bubb Dodington was sixty-six years old, the eldest of the Brotherhood and a founder of the order. He moved to the harmonies of ambition, which are not heard by every man. His house, located down near the end of the street, he once enlarged to make the largest in Pall Mall—knocking down four others to do so. His estimation of himself increased by the same proportion. Everyone despised him—his indolence, his ostentation, the slightly sour smell he seemed to exude, even as they calculated his influence at Court.

Last in the long row sat a smaller carbon copy: George Selwyn. Franklin recognized him easily.

Much younger than Bubb Dodington, Selwyn nevertheless shared all of the older man's allegiances and not a few of his vices. He loved death, suffering, and good times. He fell asleep easily and often, yet seemed to hear everything. His nose was as noble as his middle name, which was Augustus, and his eyes were green as a watery grave. Dashwood warmly called him "Bosky," acknowledging his affection for wine and ale. Selwyn had earned the name over and over with a career of dissipation, dangerous oaths, drunken quarrels, mock Communion, and such stinging bon mots that they surprised everyone into thinking him clever. He wrote them out beforehand, however, and practiced them with care.

It was an odd crew—as odd as could be assembled in a civilized town.

Supper was delicious enough. The Breasts of Venus—two small pullets set side by side under a rich glaze, and each topped by a glistening red cherry—were done to a ripe brown turn. The Devil's Loins were equal to it—a cold buttock of beef carved by hand into the shape of Venus's more private parts. The meal was punctuated with violent thrusts of forks (except for Dodington, who ate with his fingers), with parries of hard wit, with abusive elbows, with perfunctory belches.

Yet there was no joy in it. As supper wore on, the talk wore out. Every so often a ripple of laughter spread in a low wave down the table, nervous and uncertain, until it broke in silence on the empty places at the far end. One belonged to Lord Sandwich, who was obligated elsewhere. The other belonged to a dead man.

The absence of John Raleigh, deceased, did not need to be explained or remarked upon. It filled the increasing silences. When Old Paul Whitehead toppled his bottle of wine over with an awkward hand, no one leaped to his assistance. No one rebuked him, for that matter, or tried their wit upon his misfortune. Everyone sat speechless—knives and forks poised in the air (except for Dodington, whose fingers were erect)— and watched the red stain spread out across the linen. Then once again there was the scratching of silver against silver. Toplady ate nervously, in quick little gulps. Dieter Schiff smiled solicitously across the table. Churchill chewed on the silence.

Franklin bent to his plate. He ate slowly—looking up now and then at the faces across from him, noticing Dashwood's preoccupation, digesting the unsettled estate of the Hellfire Club as well as his supper.

When Dashwood cried for Holy Ghost Pye the huzzahs were startling, because they came from a silence that had grown oppressive. Baked with angelica root, the Pye was crusty and dry. Franklin broke it apart with his fingers and washed it down with port.

"Exceptional," he said with as much good cheer as he could muster. "A dinner worthy of condemned men. I should take the receipts home for my landlady."

He smiled, drew the linen cloth across his lips, and shifted his gouty leg.

There was silence.

"You're welcome to them," Bubb Dodington finally said, his jowls and chins barely moving. "Americans make me uneasy—"

"Condemned to Hell, I say!" Potter laughed with a mousy squeak of pleasure.

"Nevertheless—"

"Americans make *me* money!" George Selwyn said brightly. "My plantations—"

"Your nutmegs!"

"Nevertheless," Franklin continued, folding his napkin gently over his lap, "I acknowledge my pleasure. Such a meal—"

"When is the Squeezer to begin?"

"Such a meal puts me in mind of a small experiment I once proposed for the banks of the Schuylkill in America—"

"Spell it!" Toplady demanded.

"—America—it is a river, upon which is situated a city called Philadelphia." The tone of Franklin's voice had grown as hard as the edge of a knife. "The organizing principle was this: Spirits to be fired by a spark sent from side to side through the water. A turkey to be killed for dinner by electrical shock. The same to be roasted by an electrical jack, before a fire kindled by the electrical jar. The healths of all electricians to be drunk in electrical bumpers, under the discharge of guns from an electrical battery. The whole to illustrate—"

"Nonsense!" Dieter Schiff announced with a dark roar. The table buzzed.

"—the whole to illustrate what a marvelous age it is in which we live. That I could come all the way from America to dine here in Pall Mall on Breasts of Venus! Is that a marvel or not!" He sank back into his chair with an innocent smile.

"Nonsense!" Schiff repeated. His black eyes were fixed upon Franklin as if in a dare.

"Here I sit," Franklin shrugged, and wiped his lips again.

"The *great* Dr. Franklin should condescend to such a *stunt?*"

"So you should talk," cried Samuel Pennant, darting a glance down at Schiff. "With your *Electrical Kiss*! With your *Conspirators*! You are worse than a—"

"A fool," Toplady said earnestly. "A fool! Every company has a fool. Don't be put off by the airs of—" He turned directly to Schiff, leaning round Dashwood to do so. "Kiss my cooler, sir! This is Dr. *Franklin!*"

Schiff smiled a ghastly smile. His lips wrenched back to discover his straight teeth.

"You do not condescend to such a stunt as you describe," he said slowly to Franklin. "With your honors—with your—"

"Of course not!" Franklin laughed. "Mr. Schiff is correct.

I merely educate the world by my hypotheticals. Nor did I fly my kite! Nor did I—"

"So I thought!" Schiff turned triumphantly toward Eugene Toplady, who looked stunned (being a student, he believed more than he should have).

Franklin's hands were raised.

"I didn't kill a turkey, I confess" he said. "But I *did* nearly kill a goose!"

"A goose, he says!"

"Who is the condemned man? Did he say—" the painter William Reeve asked foggily from far down at the end of the table.

"While *trying* to kill a turkey for Christmas dinner," Franklin smiled. "Through carelessness I took the stroke myself, in my arms and body. A universal blow from head to foot. I neither saw the flash nor heard it, nor felt the stroke. But when I regained my senses I trembled for half an hour!" He lifted his hands again. "Dead flesh, gentlemen! For half an hour!"

A stir ran down the opposite side of the table. Franklin followed it with his calm, brown eyes.

"But the world goes forward, does it not? On my way here tonight I suffered a stroke fully as severe as that one."

Toplady wiped his hand across his pink brow.

"From the bottle, do you mean?"

"*You* are the *fool,* sir!" Schiff exploded, twisting his neck about and snarling at his young rival.

"No, no, no," Franklin continued, shaking his head. "More severe indeed. And so would you gentlemen, to see the young and beautiful Valetta LaNeve coming out of Pall Mall, atop such a handsome carriage, and all alone at that!"

When it came to calculating the course of a conversation, weighing its disparate elements, and encouraging its most profitable direction, Franklin knew the way.

Dashwood's jaw dropped. So did George Selwyn's fork. The Bruiser sucked in air.

Franklin looked directly at Francis Dashwood.

"Half the truth is often a great lie, sir," he said.

"Hector LaNeve? Here?" Toplady piped, the color draining from his face.

"He means to provoke us," Schiff said thickly. He pushed back his chair. "I hope that—"

"He that lives on hope dies farting," Franklin answered sharply. "The carriage was deep red. The trim was golden. The horses were bays, sir, and very fine at that. The woman was—"

"They know the woman," Dashwood said suddenly.

"A mole below the left breast," the Bruiser said, lying back in his chair—as calm as though he were about to fight. "High on her right thigh you will find a—"

Dieter Schiff bolted to his feet. His face was dark with blood.

"It's true that you *lie!*" he cried at Churchill.

The muscles tightened in the Bruiser's face and set themselves in a taut smile. He rolled forward in his chair and was on his feet.

"He *lies* with Valetta LaNeve!" Selwyn squeaked sarcastically. Bubb Dodington nodded drowsily in approval.

The table erupted in shouting. The veins in Dieter Schiff's temples pulsed in and out. Churchill sniffed at the air like a thoroughbred. Dashwood instantly leaped to his feet and waved the adversaries to silence.

"This was a private matter," he said impatiently to Franklin. "You have—it was—we're all familiar with the woman, but especially Mr. Churchill and Mr. Schiff—"

"It was *I!*" George Selwyn suddenly shrieked. "The man behind the mask was *myself!* And I can tell you, sir—it is not her *left* breast—you butcher!—but her *right!*"

He collapsed against the table in a fit of giggles, delighted with himself. Bubb Dodington reached over to pat him gently on the head.

But the Bruiser growled down at him: "You're dished up, jackanapes! Jack Pudding! You're a hobbledehoy, and wouldn't know what to do!—dished up!—and two stone underweight—"

He made a sudden move, as though he were about to strike.

"Perhaps it was *Hector* LaNeve," Toplady said, almost to himself. He looked absently over at Franklin.

"As for *you*, Dominie Do Little!" boomed the Bruiser. "You're both—why!—you're but a dilberry on the fundament of St. Francis, and if I'd my way—"

The dinner table was in disarray.

Shouts and curses filled the air. Two more wine bottles spilled down on the table, one soaking the lap of Samuel Pennant. Pennant also lost his plate to the floor when he realized he sat between Churchill and Toplady. Only the calming hand of John Wilkes—he reached over across the bewildered Thomas Potter—cured the Bruiser of thoughts of immediate violence.

Franklin's round eyes smiled.

"Gentlemen," he said cordially. "I was told that your passions were reserved for pleasure—but perhaps even there I was misled. . . ."

Dashwood was red in the face, stammering his unbrotherly Brotherhood to silence once again.

"Very well," he exclaimed, when order was restored. "However you happened by the name of this woman—I credit you—you see her effect. We thought at first she was but a flapper, an apprentice in the arts of whoredom—isn't that right?—because, sir, she was light-heeled, I'll say. She went for the balum rancum—the dance without clothes—and was savagely acrobatic. I'll wager she's Irish! But could we know?—could we know she was married to a captain in the guards or some such thing?—I'm not sure—a Frenchman—"

Dashwood looked for help up and down the row of sullen faces.

"She came to our last revels, it's true—by whose invitation?"

"Toplady's," snapped Samuel Pennant, the dark-eyed pornographer.

"Yes—it's true—she'd attended a party or two in town—the Vulture—this very room," Dashwood went on. "We don't dragoon women, sir. Through an unfortunate instance she was—roughly treated. God damn! We had to have Dr. Underwood down from Meddy. We made arrangements—she was cared for—she was returned to the city, b'God! But of course she seemed to be—abused—slapped about a bit, I'll say—"

"By that monkey butcher who calls himself the Bruiser!" snarled Dieter Schiff.

"Hold yourself, jackanapes—"

"By a man who was masked—as we all were, it's true," Dashwood said quickly. "By one of us—I suppose—who hasn't the courage of cock alley."

"I saw him," Churchill claimed. "A thin man."

"You were drunk on diddle!" answered Schiff, peering round Dashwood.

"Ha! Then how could it have been me?"

"It was *me*, I tell you!" George Selwyn said meekly.

Dashwood struggled to keep the lid on.

"The fact is," he said, "Mr. LaNeve has made some claims about town—we've all heard them—he's offered to—he threatens—not that we're afraid—"

"He'll have their plug tails in his pocket," announced Selwyn. Bubb Dodington cleared his throat appreciatively.

"The fact is—" Dashwood tried again.

"And if it's *you* who done it," the Bruiser answered, "he'll have empty pockets—"

"The fact is," Dashwood explained, "Mr. Churchill and Mr. Schiff here most certainly attended this woman—"

"As did Raleigh," Toplady said.

"*May* have used her, sir—so he claimed—but not to the point of complaint." Dashwood shrugged his shoulders. "The fact is, it's made them both blue as a razor—you can plainly see—the whole affair's squeezed all the good nature out of them, and I'll be—"

"I'll be!" Bubb Dodington said loudly. "We have a *Squeezer*! Academy's adjourned!"

He slapped the table with his powerful fat hand, cast a disdainful look at Franklin, and tottered to his feet—a gay balloon rising slowly over the ruins. There was a chorus of eager agreement from the remainder of the Brotherhood. They scratched back their chairs on the floor and milled past the seated visitor. Only Eugene Toplady remained at his place, running his finger idly around the rim of a goblet still half filled with carcavello.

Dashwood came round and stood next to Franklin, leaning quietly over to his ear.

"It's a circus, you can see," he whispered. "I credit you—I put no importance on the woman, yet she excites them more than she should. I'm not blind. Compose yourself. Eugene will stay to show you the room. Come down, if it suits you—I'm not sure—to come down to Lord Sandwich—then come. Eugene will bring you. Perhaps you can learn—I fear—you are more important than ever."

Franklin's eyes were unsmiling. "I merely stir the soup," he said softly.

Nine

"**I**s there a bigger fool than Francis Dashwood?" Franklin asked brightly. "He takes me for a goose."

Eugene Toplady regarded him with a pinched and anxious expression. The other members of the Hellfire Club had long since fled the house, leaving the two men to the silence of their carcavello. Two maidservants and Mr. Brackett, the manservant, had come in to strip the table. They, too, had disappeared.

"I'm not sure but what we're all fools," Toplady said. "I can't see that he treats you more lightly than the rest of us. Not everyone, sir, is granted admission into this room—or into this company."

"Except for fools and murderers," Franklin responded.

The lad looked disconsolate.

"You'll not likely find a murderer in this company."

"I've already found him," Franklin said.

"And *I* am the Prince of Rajhib," Toplady said wearily. "Let me show you the house and your room—we'll be off. Are you going? You'll find the Squeezer more diverting than my poor company. This is all a masquerade, is it not? Men are the best marionettes."

He rose from his seat like one of William Deard's mechanical dolls, a creature made of painted wood, with fragile china features. Franklin followed him about like a dog following a bone held above its head, taking care to seize his advantage when it came.

"So you're a philosopher," Franklin said in the morning room.

Toplady did not answer.

"These are impressive gentlemen," Franklin said in the drawing room.

Toplady did not answer.

"S-c-h-u-y-l-k-i-l-l," Franklin said softly as they stood near the rear door of the house, spelling each letter out.

"So!" Toplady turned around with a look of joy upon his face. "And pronounced as though it were *school-kill*! Just as I thought!"

"An orphan, adopted into English," Franklin smiled. "Is it any wonder that our young people cannot spell? But perhaps Dr. Johnson in his wisdom can mend it."

"Johnson!" Toplady exclaimed happily. "Wilkes has fixed him in the *Advertiser*!"

"How so?"

"Ha! In the grammar to his dictionary, the old Bow-Wow declares with his usual certainty—he's bullheaded, sir!—he says the letter *h* never begins any but the first syllable of a word. The letter *h*!" Toplady laughed aloud. "Wilkes answered in the *Advertiser*—calling him a man of quick appre-*hen*sion—compre*hen*sive genius. Flattered him!—all the same, saying his be*hav*ior was un*hand*some to the priest*hood* and the widow*hood,* sir, and charging him with in*hu*manity to man*hood*!"

Toplady laughed quickly, a china doll come to life. Franklin laughed along.

"I would not have guessed that Wilkes had—"

"Oh! He has a dangerous mind, sir!"

As simply as that, Franklin had touched the nerve of Toplady's passion—the curious nature of language and his hopes for the reform of spelling. Franklin himself had some small interests along these lines. He listened pleasantly as Toplady spoke animatedly of diphthongs, silent letters, secret codes, root words, words that are spelled one way and sounded another. The more tedious the subject, the livelier are a scholar's enthusiasms.

"I confess, sir, it wraps me up!" Toplady declared cheerfully. "There's nothing so amusing to me as language."

"Nor so dangerous," Franklin added.

Toplady looked surprised.

"It's the means by which we communicate, one to the other," Franklin explained, "and thus mislead each other."

"Oh! It's deceptive, sir. And imperfect."

"It's perfect for deception."

Toplady fell silent. But in a moment he brightened.

"Well!" he said. "You don't wish to hear any more of this —a subject fit for poor scholars sitting over their books. There's a Squeezer on." He led the way back into the morning room at the front of the house and onto the stairs that led up to the second story. "You'll find your room comfortable enough—the beds are well made and the pots are large enough to hit in the dark!"

Franklin followed after him.

"Perhaps not, perhaps so," he said. "It's always difficult to know what I wish to hear, or to say what I wish to know. You see? I'm becoming a philosopher! At my age there are few things that pass me by without raising the edge of curiosity in my mind."

"Or mine."

"Then you're a philosopher too, as I said. Question begets question! I'm intrigued to know why Dashwood plays me for a goose—that's plain enough!—telling me not a word about the beautiful Valetta LaNeve. Can you keep a secret? I'm on to him—like a dog after a rag—and won't let go! And I would like to know this woman, too, who exercises such a—"

Toplady stopped halfway up the stairs and turned round to face Franklin.

"There's no secret to it, sir. Everyone in London has heard of LaNeve and his vows. Someone is always threatening the Brotherhood—if not him, someone else—and we've grown to live with—"

"Then everyone has heard, certainly, of the threatening verse Mr. Dashwood received, and its poor rhymes."

"No, sir. We've kept *that* a secret, as it were."

"Among whom?"

"Mr. Brackett, Mr. Dashwood, and myself. Dashwood wished it that way, until the author of it could be discovered out."

"And *you* can keep a secret?"

"Surely."

"And have told no one of it—your friends—or—"

Toplady shook his head.

"More than that, sir. I've told no one in the Brotherhood of your purpose here, nor has Dashwood mentioned it. *There's* a secret! If they knew, it would amuse them."

He turned about up the stairs.

"There! You see!" Franklin said after him. "Question

begets question! It's the way of philosophy! I'm intrigued to learn your path into such a company—you're still a young man and more sensible than—what age are you, sir?"

"Twenty-six," Toplady answered without looking back. He had reached the top of the stairs.

"Twenty-six!" Franklin exclaimed. "At twenty-six I lived upon crusts and water, and a few crumbs of hope that I could make some small way in the world as a printer. *I admire the young their insolence! These are long stairs!* And in this very town, yet I should never have hoped—you're a prodigy, Toplady! Allowed a life of reflection. Pursuing your studies. Surrounded by congenial circumstance." Franklin puffed a bit as he also reached the top of the stairs. "I envy your opportunities."

"To be honest—yes, to be honest, I had always hoped to live a different life than this. To live more—"

"Dangerously," Franklin finished for him.

Toplady's pink cheeks flushed red. For the first time Franklin noticed that the lad had a small white scar beside one eye.

"The dream of every scholar," Franklin said.

"Yes! To live dangerously!" Toplady made a face, like a child who's been told the right answer to a riddle. "Instead I'm fitted up for study—for dusty books, for closed-up rooms, for long hours over questions that amuse me but interest no one else. The mysteries of language! You spoke of dead flesh. . . ."

He turned away and led Franklin down the long hallway which divided the rooms on the second floor. On his right he indicated Francis Dashwood's private chambers and, at the far end of the hall, his own. The door to each was closed. But at the end of the hall on the left, opposite the lad's room, was an open door.

The room was neat enough. A large four-post bed with heavy curtains dominated the square space. A lamp burned on the dressing table. In the corner, beneath a dark window, was a small chest made of walnut. Two quilts were folded neatly on the chair next to the bed, and at the foot of the bed sat Franklin's carpetbag.

"Excellent," Franklin said, sitting on the quilts and looking about the room. He peered past Toplady into the dimly lighted hall. He could see the closed door to Toplady's room.

"I'll have the window opened for the air, and—"

"I'll open it later," Toplady said. "And turn down the clothes."

"Mr. Brackett has already been here."

"Yes. The pisser is under the bed. When St. Francis has a lady, here is where she stays. But the walls are very thick, sir."

Toplady turned and walked out of the room.

"I'm flattered," Franklin said, following after.

Midway on the left side of the hallway and directly next to Franklin's room was another room, closed up. Toplady opened the door lightly and extended a lamp into the darkness, disclosing a few bulky shapes covered with sheeting and and a low feather bed with its covering wrinkled as though someone had sat on it or napped there. This room, Toplady explained, was unused except for storage—unless the other beds in the house were filled.

Last of all, near the head of the stairs and opposite Dashwood's chambers, was the study. Double doors guarded its entrance but inside lights were ablaze. Toplady extinguished his own lamp and led the way.

"This is our sanctuary, sir—our refuge."

The study was so luxurious that it made the bedroom seem a night cellar. The walls were hung with ornamental leather, punched in patterns. Deep crimson damask covered the windows at the front of the house. Two very large tables were pushed together in the center of the room to make a work desk shared by Dashwood and Toplady. Toplady's side especially was smothered with evidence of earnest study—many books on language both opened and closed, ale bottles emptied, piles of paper for writing upon, a wallow of old newspapers, pens and blotters, an apple, a block of sandstone, a red silk garter, a toy cannon, a stale beef sandwich partially eaten and forgotten about. This is not to mention the box of pins, the set of bare quills in a red leather case, the three bottles of ink, the china cup with brown liquid at the bottom, the letter knife, or the blue paper box filled with lampwicks.

A longer and more orderly workbench flanked the entire wall across from the door. It was set carefully with several Leyden jars, an ornate globe generator and other electrical apparatus, and a rack of glass tubing. At the end of this counter, near the front windows, was a small cluster of blue chemical bottles, a large porcelain dish, and other proof of an amateur apothecary. Beneath the workbench were cabinets to the floor, with doors closed. The wall to the right held five levels of glass-fronted shelves filled with books.

Franklin sank into the huge leather sofa next to the door.

"I'll sleep here, and forget about fresh air," he said, casting an admiring eye about the room. "A Hauksbee globe! There are but two in the entire colony of Pennsylvania. Do you use it yourself?"

"I'm good for turning it," Toplady answered, sitting at the desk in the center of the room and pushing back some of his mess with a forearm. "A mule makes a good millhand."

"Ah! Then it's Dashwood who dabbles at electric fluid."

"At everything, sir—black magic! He's more of a scholar than I am, I'll grant as much."

"And Dieter Schiff, your electrician," Franklin went on, "*he* is familiar with the Hauksbee globe."

"A *fraud*," Toplady interrupted sharply. "He ingratiates

himself—a mountebank—you saw the way in which he tried to kiss your hand, as though. . . ."

His thought trailed off. There was a long silence, which explained itself.

"Then it's something of a miracle," Franklin said, "that Mr. Dashwood can hold together such contraries as are found in this Brotherhood of yours. Mr. Selwyn twits everyone without prejudice; Mr. Churchill restricts his anger, but does not control it; Mr. Dodington's a bore—what are his allegiances?—I'm thinking aloud; Mr. Schiff and Mr. Toplady don't care kindly for one another—"

"Sir! He called me a dilberry—"

"That was Mr. Churchill who called you that," Franklin said gently. "It leads me to think—which of John Raleigh's Brothers liked him the least?"

"Samuel Pennant!" Toplady said without thinking. "It was mutual. Raleigh worked for Pennant and was rewarded with hunger. And Pennant, I'm sure—he said so in many ways—was jealous of the fact that St. Francis embraced his scribbler—"

He laughed vacantly, suddenly catching himself.

"My tongue's too loose. Shall we go? There is no harmony here—and you're wrong to envy any of it. We've been like fighting cocks since this affair began."

Franklin reached for his walking stick.

"I once belonged to a Hellfire Club myself," he said, as though he were not thinking.

Toplady looked quickly across at him, surprised.

"Of course," Franklin mused, his eyes sweeping the room, "we had no such advantage as this. Dirt floor and printer's ink were more like it. We had no advantage at all, save our press and our wit. Cotton Mather named us in his all-embracing wisdom—my brother and the others of us who wrote for the *Courant* at Boston. That's a town in America, on the Charles. The Hellfire Club! He feared enlightenment!"

Franklin chuckled softly to himself and rolled forward on the leather couch.

"We'd have done well to have had a Valetta LaNeve among *us!*" he said suddenly, looking Toplady directly in the eye. "I should like very much for her to come into Pall Mall to visit *me!* Ah! If only I could stay clear of her husband—there's the rub! I'm not as old as I look, but then—not as fast as I once was!"

Toplady's mouth opened. The color had drained from his face.

"Come along, sir!" Franklin snapped cheerfully. He struggled slowly to his feet, proving his last claim. "I'm in the mood to be squeezed, that's for certain! And hope I can expect to be! I didn't come all the way from America to creep beneath the empty covers at this hour!"

He waved his walking stick bravely toward the door.

Toplady moved as though he were in a dream. A bad dream. "I will—need a moment," the lad said weakly. Then he turned and bolted from the room, leaving Franklin standing alone with his faint, fading, enigmatic smile.

Ten

It was well past midnight when Benjamin Franklin and Eugene Toplady exited the rear door of Francis Dashwood's house in Pall Mall, came round by a narrow walkway next to the mounts, crossed through the darkened cul-de-sac known as Pall Mall Court, and entered into the street itself.

They made an unlikely couple. One was short, the other tall. One was portly, the other lean. One took a great many short steps in an effort to keep abreast, the other stayed ahead by virtue of long, nervous strides.

One wore a sagathy coat and patched trousers. The other was dressed as the Devil himself.

Franklin was hardly surprised.

He'd waited patiently in the study after Toplady bolted, improving his time by inspecting Dashwood's electrical and chemical apparatus. This proved inadequate to the amount of time that had to be improved. So he browsed down the rows of books which filled the cabinets on the near wall— volumes in such variety that they offered no clue to the personality of the man who had collected them there, or rather too many clues.

He found volumes of travel, of essays, of art history, of poetry, but none on political economy. Three entire shelves were given over to venereal pleasures, and Franklin greeted the titles of the familiars—*Gentlewoman of Verona, The Merry-Mount, Roger's Folly, The Whore's Master.* With a shock of recognition he spied his own slim volume, Cave's edition of *Experiments and Observations on Electricity Made at Philadelphia in America.* It was fit snugly between *Henry's List of Covent Garden Ladies* and *Angerona,* both of which described experiments and observations quite unlike his own. In addition to these, he found a collection of volumes that touched upon demons, Satanism, black magic, the Black Mass, and other dark arts of less consequence.

Thus he was kept from surprise when Toplady, after several minutes away, bounded back through the doorway of the study clad entire in the red silk costume of a devil.

The young scholar's lips made a thin red line beneath the black mask which covered his eyes.

Franklin looked at the pointed silk ears. Then he looked at the long silk tail. He did not comment.

"This *is* a masquerade, sir," Toplady said lamely. "The first of the season. We're encouraged to dress, although God knows few will have the courage to do so. I am *known* by this costume!"

He spread his long arms out widely, turned abruptly, and led Franklin down the stairs, through the dark morning room and the sitting room, and out of the house.

Pall Mall was as changed as the hour, or Toplady's aspect. The street seemed even more noisy and crowded than it had earlier, if that were possible. The argumentative air seemed even more earnest. As they pushed their way along the walk— Toplady delicately holding his tail round in one hand—it was Franklin's turn to feel insignificant and unnoticed.

They passed the house of Mr. Harris and then the house of Lord Cobham and then the house of Lady Coleraine. The street was being fully used, so that the traffic of late carriages crept through at a walk. Franklin scanned the coaches, but saw none familiar.

A mob of a dozen young dandies, hands clasped and voices pitched high, clotted the walkway in front of the Cocoa Tree Chocolate House. But it was not so large a crowd as the one Franklin could see several doors down the street—where half the Mall was blocked by a mass of people. The two men angled out into the street so as to avoid the Cocoa Tree. They finally made their way back to the walk in front of the house of Mrs. Missenden, and found themselves at the edge of the mob. They were also at the entrance to the Schomberg House, residence of Lord Sandwich.

It was an incredibly gay and good-humored crowd that blocked their way, lit with liquor and not adverse to giving the Devil his due with whistles and loud cries. Franklin's eyes rolled upward. He pulled his coat around him and drew a deep breath.

"Let them through!" someone cried. "Back off there! The Devil's footman!"

Franklin peered out from above his spectacles, and wished he had removed them. He followed Toplady up the crowded steps.

"You want a Squeezer!" Toplady cried over his shoulder while he was being jostled about. One of his silken ears was erect, the other not.

From the outside, the house looked three times as large as Dashwood's. From the inside, six times as lavish. It fitted the magnificent degeneracy of its tenant, and was laid open to everyone who had the courage to dare the crowd. Franklin followed a bobbing scarlet head down the narrow entrance hall, which opened into a grand room of great size. Wax lights sizzled on the walls by the hundreds. Three great ceiling chandeliers cast a tremulous light on the mob inside—which seemed to gasp for breath like a dying beast.

People, perfume, and the slightly malignant odor of sweat. Goblets of cut glass were held high in the air. Heads twisted this way and that. Servants inched through the crowd with pained expressions—some elbowing their way backward—and all carrying polished ebony trays of small food.

There were many handsome women of style about, faces powdered and gowns cut so low they might never have finished dressing. Franklin blinked.

"The Breasts of Venus!" Toplady called out, twisting halfway around. He pushed a short-wigged gentleman from his path, reached back for Franklin's arm, and leaned into the crowd.

Franklin smiled at either side, nodding his head vigorously. He was met by blank, bemused faces and mouths working in constant conversation. Toplady dropped his arm, someone poked him from behind, and Franklin seemed to edge forward under his own momentum.

"Where are we going?"

"*Nice* to see you!"

Near to the magnificent staircase that dominated the far side of the room, Toplady cried out as though he had seen a familiar face—and turned sharply to the left, out of the stream. Franklin saw no familiar face. Even if he had, he could not have followed. He was a helpless, rolling stone—pushed and swept to the foot of the stairs and then carried upward by the force of the crowd, past the colorful frescoes of Berchet.

He turned his head and saw Toplady below, a flash of red surrounded by white wigs and bare shoulders. The gentle arch of the staircase intervened. Toplady was lost.

Franklin found himself locked into an odd assemblage of bodies, all moving steadfastly up the stairs. The man ahead of him wore a green coat. Step up or be trod down. He stepped up. Alongside him, another column of people made its way down the staircase.

A smile was fixed to his face.

"Hello. Hello hello! Hallo!"

He reached the landing of the second floor and was immediately swept up against a wall, nearly upsetting a small table. The crowd coursed around him as though he were a boulder left unprotected in a chalk stream, fit only to be worn down.

He inched backward into a corner.

"God damn!" he said, involuntarily.

The crowd divided at the landing, most of them turning to the left or right down dimly lighted hallways. The others pushed round and coursed up the stairway toward the floor above. From somewhere came the sound of music—flutes and hautboys. The babble from the room below had swept up the stairs with the mob and buzzed in his ears.

Franklin's back was to a papered wall. He reached discreetly around to feel the patch on his pantaloons. It was still secure. Then he set his face firmly and plunged into the crowd of people, picking his way as well as he could across the crowded landing until he had worked into the eddy that was ascending to the third floor.

He was a stranger in a house of strangers.

But halfway up the staircase he spied a familiar figure—

two familiar figures—on their way down opposite him. Charles Churchill towered above the elderly dowager who preceded him, and nearly blocked the sour visage of Samuel Pennant, who followed him.

The Bruiser spotted Franklin.

"One more floor!" he shouted across. "Dashwood's one floor more! Women up there!" He waved encouragingly and then was swept down with the crowd, Pennant trailing behind.

Franklin plunged upward.

At the second landing the crowd again divided, some going upward but most streaming off to left or right. Franklin followed a rivulet to the right, found a small backwater at the entrance to a hallway, and stopped.

Three young men—each in high red heels—passed him without a glance. They were dressed modishly as women, but Franklin's eye was neither so naïve nor so indifferent as to miss the distinction.

Toplady was right. It was a halfhearted masquerade. Not many of the guests had bothered to disguise their identities. Franklin picked out a fool, a press-gang sailor, a sad representation of a Biblical prophet complete with staff and false beard. He had his suspicions about a little man who looked curiously like Dean Swift, but whether that was an attempt at masquerade or merely a little man who looked curiously like Dean Swift, he could not really tell. Some few ladies wore silver masks, hiding their eyes if not their charms. Most of the guests were disguised only as themselves. But as Franklin recognized none of them, that was disguise enough.

It was necessary to discover members of the Hellfire Club. He thought of pursuing Charles Churchill, but gave it up. He backed through an archway in the direction the three hobbledehoys had taken and turned to enter a long hallway, leaving the landing and the staircase behind.

The view stretched down to a brilliantly lighted room at the far end of the hall. Even from a distance Franklin could see that it too was squeezed full of people. He had little enough taste for it, but he was obliged.

He had made his way only halfway down, however, when he passed a drawing room door on his right and stopped short.

"—dismiss it as magic. Some would say sorcery—the superstitious, the ignorant. Certainly it is wonderful. Isn't it wonderful?"

The door was partially open. The voice was perfectly familiar.

"—deny the marvel of golden fishes floating in the air! But is it not wonderful?"

There was a murmur of many voices from within the room.

"—first proposed a proof by which lightning could be drawn down—how much more wonderful is the natural world—met by laughter—by laughter! And yet the very proofs I proposed, when done in France with rods, showed the very sameness— opened the door—please close that door! We need it dry in here to succeed—opened the door to a new age—I beg of you, to hold in mind—the wonders of the—Electrical Kiss!"

There was a hum of anticipation.

Franklin nudged the door open gently with his stick, slipped inside the room, and sat quickly in the back row of chairs. He gave a small smile to the young lady who sat seriously erect beside him.

"This is *wonderful*!" she whispered to him.

"I see."

The room was of medium size, heavily curtained. Perhaps eighteen or twenty spectators sat in rows facing the back of the room, where a table had been set up with Leyden jars and other paraphernalia. Off to one side was a Winkler generator, which immediately caught Franklin's eye for its foot treadle, leather cushion pad, and globe capable of rotating 680 turns in a minute.

"Marvelous!" whispered the lady next to Franklin.

"Indeed," he whispered politely.

"I don't understand a word he's saying!" she confided.

"Indeed."

"Did you see the Golden Fishes?"

Franklin shook his head sympathetically.

"It's *wonderful*!" she whispered. "Do you have any sweetmeats?"

Franklin considered changing seats. But it was too late. The speaker, his back to the small audience as he adjusted a piece of equipment, spun grandly around on his heel to begin the next demonstration. Franklin did not need to see the showman's face to know that it was Dieter Schiff of Leipzig.

He reached off to the side and from a stirring of velvet curtains withdrew a stately young woman.

The crowd shifted, the better to see.

"I'll need a gentleman of some ardor," Schiff announced grandly. "One whose heart is not dulled by long marriage— who still appreciates the glories—"

Three men leaped up from their seats near the front.

"Here, sir!"

"Ho!"

"I'm your man for sure!"

Schiff beamed and selected out the first man, directing him toward the front. He was a thin, dark-eyed lad who went eagerly. The young lady flashed him a smile of equal eagerness. Schiff fluttered about with a constant patter of conversation as he positioned the young man just so.

"The ways of love are mysterious, never doubt it," he announced to his audience. "Poets have written of it. Men have died for it. The strange fires of the human heart! Yet I must declare, ladies and gentlemen, I have *never* seen such natural ardor as this gentleman displays in his face! Are you a poet, sir?"

The young man shook his head.

"Isn't this *wonderful!*" the lady next to Franklin whispered.

"Such a handsome gentleman!" Schiff said enthusiastically. "Such a handsome young lady!"

He tugged at the lad, pulling him closer to the young woman.

"Here!—here is a lady who pines away for love! Poor thing! She lives for a kiss, sir! Be so good as to satisfy her!"

Schiff stepped back.

The young man moved up, smiled nervously, and reached out to kiss the woman's lips.

A sharp crack resounded in the air. A vivid white spark issued from the woman's lips when the lad was but an inch away. It struck him on the mouth—nearly breaking his teeth—and sent him reeling backward like a rag doll.

The crowd gasped in amazement.

The young woman remained smiling, as though all her suitors were treated the same. But the young man had staggered halfway across the room. His knees were rubber. He counted his teeth with a quaking finger.

Dieter Schiff stepped briskly up to his confederate, threw a mock grimace back over his shoulder toward the audience, and planted a kiss full upon her lips—without harmful effect. Then he turned triumphantly to the crowd.

"If the electric fluid has no other use, at least it has the power to make a vain man humble!"

He bowed to the stunned young man in the corner of the room while the spectators burst into applause and elbowed each other with laughter. The woman sitting next to Franklin leaned over toward him.

"Isn't it *wonderful?*" she whispered.

He eyed her coldly.

"I can't abide the canapés downstairs," she confided, "but I have a *terrible* craving for sweetmeats."

Franklin sighed, and turned his head away to study the performance of the Garrick of electricians. If Schiff was able to view Franklin's interested face, he gave no hint of it. Instead he carried blithely on with his patter and curiosities. During the course of the next half hour he drew gasps of amazement from every member of the audience save one. He performed the trick of Mahomet's Tomb. He rang a set of eight musical bells with a vial of electrified water. He produced a shower of sand raising itself up again as fast as it fell. With the force of a long spark he made a hole through a quire of paper. He made a large golden star to twirl without touching it. He called upon the audience for a volunteer again, and drew a guinea from between a bravo's clenched teeth without coming near him. He spoke once and then again of his gala performances at the Palace in Gooch Street—where he promised the audience it could see a tit killed, or a battery of monks in energetic prayer, or a cannon fired from an island in an artificial lake.

Then he began his last exhibit of the evening—one suited for the drawing room, he said. He called it "The Conspirators."

Franklin moved at just the right moment. When Schiff turned his back on the audience to arrange a large magical picture of the King, Franklin slipped up from his seat, smiled to the lady next to him, and stepped silently from the room without standing straight up. In the empty hall outside he stood and listened through the door.

"Conspirators! Are your hands all clasped!" Schiff was saying momentarily. "If *you*, sir—yes—if you, sir, would be *brave* enough to remove the crown from the King's head— yes, that's it!—just take the crown—"

There was a loud cry. Franklin heard the crowd swoon.

"God saved the King!" Schiff shouted with a laugh. "And gentlemen—you may thank God the consequences of *your* conspiracy are not the same as those for high treason!"

Franklin suddenly had a taste for sweetmeats.

He padded down the hall, reached the stairway, and turned quickly onto it. Behind him he heard the buzzing crowd burst from the drawing room. Below him he heard the uninterrupted babble of the mob from the ground floor.

The stairs carried him to the second floor.

He did not know where he was going, but acted as though he did. At the landing he turned sharply to the left. He made his way swiftly down the hall and turned in at the first open door.

He found himself in another drawing room—this one filled not with magic but with gentlemen and smoke, both hanging low over three baize tables set to backgammon. There was a heavy smell of burning oil.

The Bruiser looked up from his game to see Franklin standing quietly in the doorway. His bony face broke into a grin, and he waved Franklin into the noisy room. He really was a democrat.

"Have you found Dashwood and the others?"

Franklin shrugged. "I found a woman who can't abide the canapés."

Churchill threw back his head.

"And I know the one!" he announced loudly. "Mary Christmas! Mary Christmas—eh? She's a remount, sir! Did you have any *sweetmeats* for the *lady*?"

Franklin's chuckle was drowned to silence by the Bruiser's horrendous, booming laugh.

The Bruiser kicked over a chair, and the man who was in it rolled off. He had Franklin sit.

"Keep your eye on me, Franklin!" he roared.

Franklin did. He watched Churchill play his game and win. There was a round of drinks, and another game. Franklin sighed, reached out, and touched the Bruiser's giant arm.

"Do you play all night?"

"At gammon?" Churchill asked without looking.

"Yes."

"It has me by the *throat*, sir! *And* the *purse*!"

Franklin sighed. "I imagine I lost Toplady within five minutes after my arrival, sir. I've not seen Mr. Dashwood, although he was to arrive before me—"

"Upstairs with Old Paul, last I saw him," the Bruiser said, still intent on his game.

"—and I believe I saw Lord Bute downstairs, but I'm not sure. I saw someone who looked like Dean Swift, who's been dead ten years. But can't be sure. I can't be sure I saw anyone, for some are dressed as women, some as sailors, some as the Devil himself! I've missed the honor of Lord Sandwich—this is his house, is it not?—unless he dresses as a lady in red-heeled shoes."

He leaned over close to Churchill.

"I've no taste for the mob, sir. Yet I'm quite lost! Wasn't it agreed that everyone was to meet here at the Squeezer."

The Bruiser turned suddenly to face Franklin. His blue eyes swam with warmth.

"Hah! Game's up!" he announced to his mates. "I seem to be the winner!"

The others nodded, as though they agreed with him. He pushed his chair back and stood up—towering over the diminutive Dr. Franklin.

"This gentleman and me's going for a stroll," he announced. "He's an *American*, boys, and never seen a Squeezer! More used to dusky maidens than batty remounts!"

The others nodded, as though they agreed with him.

Churchill and Franklin visited every room on the second floor. They barged in on some dice players, and backed politely out. They opened a door on three women changing their faces. They found a hautboy player and a flutist alone in a room with three bottles of gin, all empty except for the hautboy player and the flutist. They found a bedroom in use. In a sitting room at the end of one of the halls they found a large crowd gathered around a small man who was eating stones. But they did not find Francis Dashwood or Eugene Toplady or any other member of the Hellfire Club.

"Bloody boys are hard to find," the Bruiser said brusquely to himself.

"Toplady, sir, is dressed as the Devil. Red suit. Silk ears. He's got a tail."

"Well he ought to—"

Churchill headed for the stairs.

"Perhaps it's the hour," Franklin said encouragingly, when he caught up. "They may have gone—it must be near to—"

The Bruiser grunted. "Early to bed and early to rise— that's it, eh?" He was not an illiterate. "Not *these* bloody boys!"

The boxer's nose shifted from left to right and then to the left again, sniffing the edges of an idea.

He turned up the stairs, taking two at a time to the third story. Franklin followed. The Bruiser led the way down the hall to where Franklin had seen the Electrical Kiss, threw open the door rudely, and discovered the hautboy player and the flutist.

"Bloody hard!" he said abruptly. He slammed the door shut.

"I swear," Franklin said. "I'm lost. I thought those two particular gentlemen were on the—"

The Bruiser was nearly in a frenzy. He hurried on down the hall opening and shutting doors. There was still a sizable crowd in the drawing room Franklin had avoided at the end of the hallway, but the Bruiser elbowed his way in. He stood for a moment—a head above everyone else—and elbowed his way out.

"Half the town of London's here, and not a monk among them!"

Just then he spotted a manservant of the house walking discreetly toward them. He rushed to intercept him. "Button! Mr. Button!" he bellowed.

It was enough to capture Mr. Button's attention.

"Where in the Hell's Lord Sandwich? Lost in the stews?" the Bruiser demanded with a roar.

"Never made it home yet, sir."

Mr. Button seemed a very agreeable man. He nodded politely to Franklin and then turned his calm, enigmatic smile on Charles Churchill.

"Not come to his own Squeezer?" the Bruiser roared. "They must have some very agile Irish girls at Mother Sulphur's tonight, sir! What of Dashwood? Where's *he*? The dog was around—I saw him! And Dieter Schiff? The blockhead. He gave an entertainment, did he not? And where's Old Paul Whitehead—"

The smile didn't leave Mr. Button's face.

"Mr. Schiff was here, sir. That's true. I haven't seen the other gentlemen you mention, but you must understand—I've been very busy. Surely you're enjoying yourself, and this gentleman—"

"Oh, I'm enjoying myself, no doubt!" the Bruiser bellowed sarcastically. "As though I'm a bloody bishop! Keeping tabs on a dozen wayward monks!"

"It's *friars* you're after, sir," Mr. Button said knowingly. He pursed his lips. "That lad was here with his Devil's costume—"

"Toplady," Franklin interposed, trying to be useful.

Mr. Button smiled politely. "Mr. Pennant was here," he said. "I believe Mr. Bubb Dodington is still here, down the—"

"I'm sure!" the Bruiser said. "Unable to move."

"But there's the whole of it, sir, as I recall. There's *yourself*!" he said lightly. "I've not seen the others—"

The Bruiser shook with a sound that came closer to a horse's whinny. Mr. Button began to follow his smile on down the hall.

"—and being very busy, sir, I'm afraid I must—"

"There you are, Franklin!" Churchill said apologetically. "There's the whole of the Hellfire Club! You'll want nothing to do with Boob Dodington. Sam Pennant can hardly brighten your evening, even if you could find him. We're an irregular company, that's true enough, not like the Jesuits!"

He looked down at Franklin with his rough smile, which was warm but not necessarily polite.

"I'm afraid your evening's been laid back without reward—and the Holy Ghost Pye was the worst I've ever tasted, if you want the truth—"

"Yes," Franklin said quietly. "Lost for my purposes."

"Well, sir, damn me! It's a bloody bad way to treat a visitor—and a guest, to boot! God damn! Would you be interested in a game of dice or gammon, perhaps, to recover your lost fortunes?"

Franklin seemed to consider.

"No, sir," he said at last. "Believe me, but I've reached the age at which most of my hopes are satisfied only in sleep. If you'll permit me, I'll make my way homeward and so to bed."

"To Mr. Dashwood's, is it?"

"Indeed."

"You *may* find him there, sir, but it's bloody hard to say. He's a dog and runs the streets."

"Yes, yes. Thank you for your cordiality, sir."

The Bruiser boomed out a mighty laugh.

"Cordiality? Think nothing of it, sir! My instincts are all republican! I'd hoped to take you clean at gammon!"

They descended together to the second floor and parted at the landing—Churchill going off to his game while Franklin moved slowly into the heat and light of the great ballroom below.

The crowd was decimated by the hour. Off in one corner of the great room, surrounded by tittering ladies, fat Bubb Dodington had spread himself out on a settee. He too was snorting, probably at his own jokes. His stockings had fallen down around his ankles. Elsewhere in the room, hives of buzzing gentlemen surrounded the few homely ladies who'd been left upright and undone, with little chance of changing it. Franklin looked for a familiar face and found none.

He considered disturbing Dodington with an example of American wit, but decided against it. There was too much an air of conceit in the room to add to it. These poor souls with no place to go were the dregs of fashion, butterflies without beds.

Franklin pinched himself on the fleshy part of his arm, as he often did when he felt himself becoming too gloomy a moralist.

He came down off the bottom stair and crossed the room without drawing any notice. Why should he? He was a tired, nondescript philosopher in a sagathy coat, only the man who dared the lightning, and surely too old to struggle for the affections of a few pounds of paint, powder, and flesh—

He pinched himself again.

The servant at the front door of the Schomberg House snapped to attention when Franklin approached, and dismissed him into the night.

Except for a few scattered carriages, Pall Mall was empty

at last. The streetlamps had been extinguished in anticipation of morning, still two or three hours away. But the air already had morning's cool freshness to it. The moon hung low over Franklin's shoulder as he walked back the same way he had come with Toplady. His path led through the dark shadows of dark houses.

His brain had barely cleared of the confusing fumes of the Squeezer by the time he reached Dashwood's residence.

He blinked, and tapped on the cobbles with his stick. It was like being in the country. No one was about. He looked upward. The lamps in Dashwood's study were still ablaze—a welcoming beacon—but the remainder of the house was pitched into blackness.

He drew a deep breath and walked round through the darkness of Pall Mall Court, to let himself in by the rear door of the house. In the little areaway, where the stairs went downward to the kitchen and the quarters of Mr. Brackett, he paused for a moment. There was a faint reminder of incense.

Brimstone, he thought.

"Hellfire," he answered.

He made his way through the darkened sitting room into the morning room, and turned up the stairs.

There he stopped—as though a spider's web had touched his face.

The house was very still. Light fell out of the study doorway onto the landing above. He heard only one sound—the low hissing of the study lamps, like a ball of snakes.

His hand tightened around the walking stick.

He moved slowly upward again, reached the landing, and followed his stick into the study. He sighed. The room was empty. The lamps had been left burning so he would not lose his way on the stairs. He nodded at the kindness of Francis Dashwood.

He turned about, stepped out of the room, and went to make his way down the long hallway of the second floor.

Suddenly he stopped, drawing a short involuntary breath. His eyes widened. At the far end of the hall, between Toplady's room and his own, the shape of a man lay sprawled upon the carpet.

It did not move.

It did not speak.

And it was not quite a man.

It had silk ears and a long silk tail.

Eleven

Franklin placed a lamp down on the mauve carpet, close by Toplady's face. The lad's eyes were still half open. They stared brightly at the hissing lantern only inches away. They showed no emotion—neither hatred, nor care, nor surprise. His mouth hung unnaturally open and slightly dislocated by the pressure of his body against the flooring. In the false illumination his skin seemed bleached white, as though he were in paint and about to assume a mute role in Goldoni's *Il Servitore di Due Patroni.*

But in that anguished entertainment there are no roles for the dead.

Franklin lifted the lad's arm. It fell limply back. The dry dead hand knuckled beneath it. Franklin edged closer, noticing one awkward finger split and blackened. He reached his own arm beneath Toplady's body and lifted gently upward. The lad fell effortlessly over on his back without a sound.

Beads of perspiration suddenly showed out on Franklin's forehead, the product not only of exertion but of anger.

He threw back half of the small round rug from which he had rolled Toplady's body. The rug was damp, and when he brought his fingers to his lips they tasted faintly of salt. He ran his fingers delicately along the carpeting beneath the rug. Even blind he would have seen it: a depressed area more than a foot square, where the nap of the carpet had been pressed down.

Franklin's fingers traced an aimless pattern on Toplady's chest.

The silk costume was taut and cool to his touch. He leaned down and placed his cheek next to Toplady's lips. No matter what theorem he employed, the proof was the same.

Franklin sat abruptly upright onto his knees for a moment and then struggled to his feet. He had forgotten about his gouty leg. His head nodded imperceptibly, as though he were calculating something at a great distance—a conversation, a word dropped by mistake or intention, the hour, the absence or presence of something he could not quite name. Except for the small circle of light cast by his lamp and the glow from the study, the hallway was dark. Except for the hiss of burning whale oil and his own cetacean breathing, it was silent.

He tottered down the hall, and was about to thunder his fist against the door to Dashwood's room when he heard a commotion below. A shout, the snatch of a song, a door banging closed.

A woman laughed.

From the noise of their voices there were three or four or five of them—halfway to Bedlam.

Franklin waited.

After a moment or two they turned the corner out of the darkness and began pushing and shoving their way up the staircase—Francis Dashwood, Thomas Potter, John Wilkes, sour Samuel Pennant, a thin and ugly stranger (whose leathery face was without expression), and a round, laughing woman.

Franklin recognized her.

Her hair was drawn up onto her head, showing her ears. Her frothy pink gown matched the color of her considerable skin. The décolletage disclosed breasts like melons swaying to and fro as she marched gaily up the stairs to the urgings of John Wilkes, who marched pointedly behind her.

"There's a ladybird, she's a ladybird," the leering Wilkes said over and over.

"She's game! She's a biter!"

"Watch your arse!"

"Watch your mouth, dog!"

"Dumplins for sale!" Dashwood sang merrily, coming up sideways. He looked upward into Franklin's lamp and, like Toplady, did not blink.

"Ho! Charon at the gate!"

"Professor is it?"

"Fetch mettle, ol' Podge! That's no—"

"Dr. Franklin, sir!"

"Mary Christmas!"

The gang arrived on top with a babble of bad language. The woman, whose laughter had lighted the way up, pushed herself past Samuel Pennant.

"Mary Christmas, I say!" she said happily to Franklin, dropping into a curtsy.

Franklin blinked, holding tight to his lantern.

"Diogenes it is, then!"

Franklin lifted his arm toward the door of the study, directing them into the room and out of the hall. The stranger walked more uncertainly than the others. He cracked his shoulder roughly on the jamb, wobbled a moment once he got inside the room, and collapsed gratefully onto the long leather couch—a puppet with its strings cut.

"He's let a brewer's fart!" someone cried.

"You're dished up, Dominie—"

"It's a cheeser!" Potter gasped loudly, his little fish-eyes bulging. "God damn! It *is* a cheeser!"

Franklin heard the creaking of the stairs behind him and snapped around to see Mr. Brackett mince to the top step. In the old servant's arms were nestled three large bottles of champagne, very cold. His face carried an expression of about the same temperature. He was dressed in a pink nightshirt.

It made a crowd.

Mary Christmas—for that indeed was the name the wench went by—fell into a heap atop the angular stranger, proving it's what's in the purse that counts and not otherwise. Dashwood dropped down on the couch next to her, hoping for priority. Thomas Potter, who looked quite white and blank, akin to a puff-fish, sank next to them, and Wilkes tugged democratically on Franklin's arm in an effort to draw him onto the pile as well.

"Three to one, Professor! She's wicked!"

He laughed, she laughed, they laughed.

Samuel Pennant scowled. Drink had made his dark face even darker. He preferred his pornography on the page and not in the flesh. His nostrils flared as he breathed, and he worked his way around next to the glass-fronted bookcases.

Mr. Brackett did what was expected of him. He placed the champagne gingerly upon the work counter across the room and waited resolutely at attention, eyes straight ahead.

Between the loud cries of laughter, the squeals of Miss Christmas (whose bodice was by now quite exposed), and the fervid "Three to one! Three to one!" of John Wilkes, Franklin appeared quite helpless.

But he hammered the head of his walking stick sharply on

the edge of the huge desk with such strong effect that it made him blink.

"Sir! Sir!" he said strongly to Dashwood. "I beg to tell you that Mr. Toplady—"

But Dashwood was occupied.

"Squeeze that cat, you goat!" someone cried.

The noise grew.

"—beg—beg—Sir!"

"—and kiss my cooler, jackanapes!"

"—beg to tell you, sir—this is serious business—Mr. Toplady is—"

Franklin's voice was swallowed up by a squeal from Mary Christmas. Someone had squeezed the cat.

"Ho! Whoa!" Dashwood cried out, master of a runaway team. He waved his arms so violently that Miss Christmas, whom he'd already wrestled onto his own lap, toppled off onto the next—a bundle of pink gown, brown-eyed breasts, and merry laughter.

"Very *serious*! Very *serious*!" Dashwood cried in mock seriousness. "There's Dr. Franklin, isn't it!"

"Straighten your leg!"

"Grab that cat!"

"—Mr. Toplady has been murdered—"

"Murdered?"

Franklin winced slightly.

The room was instantly silent.

"Mr. Toplady is dead, sir. He has been murdered, I should think within the half an hour. He is—"

Mary Christmas screamed. Dashwood's arms thrashed. He was apoplectic. He struggled to get up from the sofa but could not.

"You'll find him in the hallway at the end, sir. Outside of his own room."

Dashwood lurched to his feet with a sudden effort, overcoming both drink and gravity. He bolted for the door with the others at his heels—even the grave manservant with his nightgown flying.

Only the ugly stranger, relieved at last of the weight of Miss Christmas, remained where he'd been planted—compressed into the leather sofa in his brown clothes, black hose, and plain shirt. He was a scarecrow who seemed not to have heard a word.

"Launched into eternity without benefit of an audience," Franklin said absently to him.

The stranger said nothing.

Franklin's head swirled. He could hear the others down at the end of the hallway—a hum of interrogatories punctuated by the chilling screams of Mary Christmas. She released them regularly every few seconds.

"Particularities," Franklin reminded himself. He looked about the room.

Toplady's side of the desk seemed the same in every particular as when he had left it several hours previous. It remained unordered. Franklin's eye swept over the curling mound of newspapers, the opened books, the set of quills, the plain blue box filled with wicks. He matched each against his memory, and stepped closer. Beneath the lamp, where he had placed it amidst the clutter, was a single sheet of paper. He pulled it out.

Scribblings. Toplady, the eternal scholar, had filled it with idle designs and a list of words:

Rational	Busy	Rough
Cautious	Women	Cough
Celebration	Abyss	Laughter

Beneath this was written a single line:

Emotional Women Laugh!

Franklin's eyes closed in thought. The sheet was stained in one corner with wine. Was it new or old? He could not remember. He opened his eyes and read the words to himself. Did they mean something, or were they merely the scratchings of a mind that could not rest? He couldn't tell.

"It's of no account," he said absently to the stranger, looking back over his shoulder. But the stranger was looking nowhere. He had fallen into a drunken sleep. Franklin folded the paper twice, and then once more, and slipped it into the watch pocket of his breeches.

His eyes wandered over the remainder of the desk. Particularities. The red silk garter was untouched. The beef sandwich remained only partially eaten. He lifted the pale cup with its residue of brown liquid, peered into it, and set it down again next to the wineglass. He fingered the red leather case of bare quills. An unordered life, an unordered death.

Dashwood's side of the desk was no better. Franklin closed one of the open books, noticing a thin puff of dust rise into the air.

And then he laughed—a small, satisfied laugh.

The wineglass. It was about a third filled with canary. It had not been there before. On Dashwood's side of the mountain there was another glass. Empty.

Franklin's fingers drummed on the table. His face tilted upward toward the top shelf of the bookcases. He mused.

He was still staring vacantly at the glass, noticing the reflections, when Dashwood and the others returned. The hysterical Mary Christmas had ceased her screaming. She had pulled up the bodice of her gown so that she was only immodest, and no longer half naked.

"He doesn't *look* murdered," Pennant said at once.

"But dead enough," Potter added.

"A fact? Murdered?" Dashwood said, looking directly at

Dr. Franklin. "Or merely a—speculation?" He was suddenly sobered.

"Sir, I will tell you when I speculate. What's it that Dictionary Johnson says? 'Housebreaking is a strong fact, and robbery is a strong fact, but murder is a *mighty* strong fact.' We are confronted with a *mighty* strong fact." Franklin's pleasure at discovering the wineglasses had been improved to a look of sternness.

He surveyed the circle of faces for some confirmation that his point had been understood. It had.

"I remain your guest," Franklin said. "But if you'll permit me the liberty—"

"Anything," Dashwood said abruptly. "Dr. Franklin may do *anything*." He too looked around the circle of faces to see that his point had been understood.

"Very well. Release Miss Christmas to the safety of the streets. She's an emotional woman, and I fear this is no place for an emotional woman."

Franklin smiled, and turned to Mr. Brackett. "You may wish to get dressed, sir. Your sleep has been interrupted. Morning clothes—morning draws near. On your way down you can show Miss Christmas to the door."

The servant nodded obediently. Mary Christmas looked wildly about the room—she feared to leave it—but gave no great complaint. She left meekly on Brackett's heels.

During the interval Franklin directed his attention to the remainder of the room—an enterprise in which *he* had been interrupted. The other gentlemen watched him in silence from the couch and side chairs. He searched behind the window drapery. He peered behind the long sofa. One would have thought he was going to buy the house. Finding nothing, he crossed the room to the workbench against the far wall. He carefully examined the apparatus on the bench, both electrical and chemical. So far as he could see, nothing appeared to have been touched.

He walked round to consider the mare's nest of the desk again. It told him nothing.

By the time Mr. Brackett reappeared, having exchanged his pink nightshirt for more suitable dress, Franklin had seated himself carelessly in Toplady's vacant chair. He looked into five faces set tensely to silence, and one that was quite relaxed.

"This gentleman is Lord Sandwich?"

"Lord Sandwich. Yes!" someone said.

"I suspected as much. As he's already gone, let him remain."

The innocence of sleep made Sandwich seem even more ugly than he was. His skin was cracked and bruised by hard use. His mouth hung sweetly open.

Franklin turned to Dashwood.

"You must recognize, sir, that death permits no literary criticism. It's not—let us say—like a bad verse to be dissected at our leisure. Murder cannot be parsed. It becomes necessary to make some inquiries that you might prefer unmade—"

"Very well," Dashwood said resolutely.

"Some time since," Franklin said, addressing the others, "I engaged to examine the death of one of your members— John Raleigh. The details of my engagement are unimportant. The circumstances engaged me—those and my curiosity. I boast to say it did not take me long to discover the means by which John Raleigh died. He died of the electrical fluid. I've had little enough time to interest myself in the details of Mr. Toplady's death. Beyond noticing that the evidence points all in the same direction. And—of course—seeing that he entertained his killer in this very room—sitting at this very table."

There was a low murmur. The gentlemen looked at one another.

"Many men have been struck down by lightning," Franklin went on. "Of course. In the Russias—you may know this—a foolish Swede took too great a charge from a rod set up to show the sameness of lightning and the electrical fluid. Martyrs to science, or to chance! Mr. Raleigh and Mr. Toplady are martyrs only to folly. You have here the first usage of electricity for criminal intent."

"Nonsense!" It was Thomas Potter, eyes bulging in his pouty face. "There's no danger to it. Dieter Schiff told me so himself, at one of his demonstrations."

There was immediate silence in the room. Franklin looked around from face to face.

"I make no accusations."

"It's all the rage," Samuel Pennant agreed. "Half of London has its Leyden jars and goldleaf. Look at Lord Bute! Why do you say Dieter Schiff? Consider Mr. Dashwood! Mr. Potter was—"

"*You,* sir, are a—" Potter growled.

Franklin banged his walking stick on the edge of the desk.

"What seems too obvious to one man may be intended so. Remember that!" he said. "But this is not the hour for philosophy. I make no accusations. But I require some civil answers. If that's impossible, I can retire to Craven Street and—"

"Sir!" Dashwood exclaimed.

"Very well," Franklin said quickly. "By my calculations Mr. Toplady died within the half an hour of the time I arrived upon him. Close on to three o'clock."

He glanced at the corner clock and sighed, suddenly realizing the seriousness of the hour.

"That was close on to three o'clock this morning," he continued. "Let him be dead at half past two. I saw him last after midnight, when we left this house together. We entered the Schomberg House together. But I soon lost sight of him in that—that mob. Which of you gentlemen saw him there?"

No one answered.

Franklin shook his head.

"It becomes important to calculate the hour at which he departed from the Schomberg House. He could have departed immediately—is that not so? But in that case it would hardly profit such a struggle with the devil's suit—"

"He was called away, perhaps," Wilkes offered.

"Yes. By whom? You see the difficulty, sir. I should like to know the actions of each of you." Franklin smiled. "I give you my example. I was at the Schomberg House. I met with Mr. Churchill there and saw you—Mr. Pennant—momentarily. I saw Mr. Schiff for a time. I saw Bubb Dodington at my departure, and assume him to have been there for the whole time. I was informed that Mr. Dashwood was present with Mr. Whitehead, but with my own eyes—sorry to say—"

"Easily put, sir," Dashwood spoke up. "I went down with Old Paul, not expecting you to come on. I underestimated your powers! Dodington walked with us—we left him in the clutches of the first hag we came to. We searched out Sandwich and couldn't find him—look at him! Lord Sandwich! Thus we left the house almost immediately—although we *did* spend some time in the upstairs, where there was a woman of my acquaintance. There! You have my sins as well as my schedule, sir! We crossed the Mall to the Star and Garter, and there found Sandwich too drunk to walk. Look at him!" Dashwood appeared very earnest. "I can tell you who I saw, if you wish."

"Yes."

"I did not see Mr. Pennant or Mr. Churchill. Nor did I see Dieter Schiff, although he was to present an—"

"You're telling me whom you did *not* see," Franklin said sharply.

"That's all I saw, sir."

"But did you see Toplady, is the question we're after."

Dashwood said he had not.

"I can speak for Sandwich," Pennant said helpfully.

"Do so. He cannot speak for himself."

"He got *nearly* home!" Pennant said. "He was at Mother Sulphur's—that I know. It's his habit. And was late in leaving off. It's his habit to check every familiar door on the way to home, sir. If behind the door's a woman, so be it. Dinner can wait. If behind the door's a drink, so be it as well. When he reached the Garter he most surely was drunk on diddle, for when I came into the place he was very drunk on diddle indeed."

"At which hour did you leave the Schomberg House?" Franklin asked.

"Shortly after midnight. I was with Churchill, as you saw," Pennant said. "Truth is, I tired of him—and sought to find St. Francis. I know his haunts, sir, and went straight across to the Garter—"

"He goes where the meat smells sweetest," Potter interrupted.

Samuel Pennant's scowl deepened.

"I arrived at the Garter, sir, and found them as I've told it. Dashwood, Lord Sandwich, Old Paul, William Reeve—"

"That's right!" Dashwood exclaimed. "Reeve was there as well—I nearly forgot!—although beside himself with bad dreams and no company at all."

Franklin looked irritated.

"When Wilkes came in—" Pennant began.

"Permit him his own testimony."

"Hah! Easy enough!" Wilkes spit out cheerfully. His jaw worked its way back and forth sideways. "I went *first* to the King's Head, and *then* to the Twelve Bells, and from *there* to Sadd's—I favor no man—and from *Sadd's* I went on—"

"You didn't attend the Squeezer?" Franklin asked.

"Obviously, sir, if I went *first* to the King's Head, and *then* to—"

"Very well," Franklin said.

"When I left Sadd's, finding it not so fine as it once was, I came across the upper end of the Mall, did I not, and saw the old remount—a familiar sight, sir!—Mary Christmas! I took her into the Garter—"

"And there conveniently found Mr. Dashwood, Mr. Sandwich drunk on diddle, Mr. Reeve, Mr. Whitehead, Mr. Pennant—" Franklin said.

"No!" Wilkes answered quickly. "Old Paul was not there, nor was Penny—"

"You mean to say I *was not there*?" Pennant challenged.

"Pennant *was* there, sir," Dashwood interposed. "John Roger here has taken himself a humor—"

"But where was Whitehead?"

"—a malicious humor, and he's turned it—"

"Gone to care for his wife," someone said.

"He's *domestic*, no doubt!" Potter said loudly.

"More likely lost the use of it!" Wilkes corrected him.

Franklin blinked. He was losing control.

"We have yet to hear from Mr. Potter," he said glumly. "Being the son of the Archbishop, sir, you no doubt went *first* to church, and *then*—"

The room erupted in laughter.

Potter's round face worked its way into an angry oval. He spoke with rather too much bravado for a man of his size.

"I left with the others, that's plain enough! I stopped in the mounts to relieve myself, sir, and should you wish to pursue it—check the size of the acacia! I came out of Pall Mall Court and crossed round at the Cocoa Tree—am I particular enough, sir?—and from there came round to the Schomberg

House—where I came to wonder at your presence, and by what right you sat with us tonight—"

"Potter!" Dashwood snapped.

"—as I *now* wonder," the speaker continued with sarcasm, "by what right you cast accusations and seek to examine the good gentlemen of this society."

"Spit into the wind, sir, and you spit into your own face," Franklin said.

Potter's eyes narrowed, which made him look more than ever like a puff-fish.

"Mr. Potter's memory does not serve him, that's plain enough," Franklin added.

"He came into the Garter after Wilkes and the lady, sir— I'm clear on *that*," Dashwood said, casting a sharp glance at Thomas Potter. "He was with us at the Garter—"

"For a time," Franklin said.

Potter said nothing. He had decided that silence was more insolent than words, and in that he was right.

"We've avoided Mr. Selwyn," Franklin said.

"I didn't see him!"

"Nor I!"

"Went to a hanging!"

Franklin sighed.

"And we've failed to remember Mr. Brackett," he said.

The manservant stiffened.

"Below with my lady, sir."

"The whole time?"

"Indeed, sir. I sent the two maidservants home when the last pot was washed, and then my lady—"

"But didn't you serve canary to Mr. Toplady and his killer?" Franklin inquired.

It was his trump. The question caught Brackett by surprise, and brought a gasp from Thomas Potter, who was not used to abiding by his decisions. Brackett stood with his mouth hung open.

"Did you not serve canary to Mr. Toplady and the person who murdered him, sir?" Franklin said. He rose from his seat, drawing everyone's attention with him. Franklin reached across the cluttered desk, lifted up the partially filled glass of canary in his hand, and then walked round to take the empty glass.

"Canary," he said.

"Canary," Brackett answered.

"For how else in this house would two glasses of canary find their way into this room, unless it be—"

"Canary!" Brackett suddenly cried.

He broke his posture and dashed to the worktable. Throwing back the door to one of the cabinets he reached down and fumbled about. Dr. Franklin still stood triumphant with a glass in each hand. But when Mr. Brackett turned round, he was equally triumphant. He held a bottle of canary in each hand, one bottle not even half filled.

"It's kept here, sir—some of it—for the easier use of the gentlemen—so as not to disturb—"

Franklin winced.

"You were below, in other words?" he asked.

"In other words, sir."

"Did you not hear Mr. Toplady return home, or any other awkward noise?"

"No, sir. I was below. And he—he was like a cat, sir, in his entrances and exits."

There was a look of relief on Brackett's face. But Franklin's shoulders heaved once, and then again. His spectacles had slid down to the tip of his nose.

He sighed.

"Dismiss them. Send them home."

He turned his back on the assemblage and stood silently facing the bookshelves, noticing his own wan reflection in the glass.

"Let him lie!" Wilkes said smartly, and headed for the door. But the others pulled Lord Sandwich reluctantly to his feet. He wobbled about, eyes fluttering open and shut. Samuel Pennant grabbed his arm and led him toward the stairs. The others shuffled after.

Only Dashwood remained. His eyes were upon Franklin's back, and then upon the obvious patch in Franklin's breeches—the tail of Franklin's coat standing halfway erect for his having sat badly upon it.

"It's true I'm unused to such inquiries as this . . ." Franklin said philosophically to his reflection.

Dashwood stepped forward. "It would be best to discontinue the revels. They cannot serve—there are two men dead already—the finest—"

". . . but that does not mean I cannot *think*!" Franklin said with emphasis, turning about suddenly.

Dashwood was startled.

"No, sir!" Franklin said. "Let the experiment be made!"

Twelve

The storm broke the next morning—a gray, thunderous day. Now and again the low sky was laced with a filigree of lightning. Rain fell. Yellow water ran in the streets, babbling down toward the Thames and carrying to every corner the gossip of autumn and death.

With their eyes half opened, their noses hooked to news of success and ruin, the gentlemen of London gathered around the morning fires of coffeehouses and clubs. They shivered over the night's intelligence.

"—swept away at Conduit Street, sir, and carried off—"

"—who's that, you say? Murdered?—"

"—lost a wheel before my very eyes, going round to—"

"—Eugene Toplady, I believe. So I think, although I can't swear—"

"—Yes, sir! Over on her side, throwing the driver—"

"—had her on the bridge close by the laceman's when she said her mother was expecting her—"

"—who's that, you say?—"

"—so much as that? I can't believe—"

"—Lost it all! Lost it all!—"

"—Yes—Dashwood's friend—Hellfire, indeed!—Although I can't on my honor say it was—"

"—not her mother, sir! Has she no more ingenuity than that?—"

"—dangler! Indeed! He told me—"

"—was very good—she knows her tricks, I'll say!—"

"—who's that?—Toplady, you say?—that silly scholar?—"

"—so I *think*—but on my honor I can't—"

Franklin was far removed from it. He'd arrived home close on to seven o'clock in the morning and fallen asleep almost immediately between the feathered covers of his own bed. Not quite immediately, for his mind still whirred and Peter was already bothering with the fire. Franklin had tried to silence the one while instructing the other. His orders were attended to by the black manservant while Franklin napped.

Within three short hours, however, young Polly Stevenson was bending over Dr. Franklin with buttered toast and a mess of hot chicken broth, the blouse of her gown fairly open. He was instantly awake.

He sat now at ease, in a lacquered chair near the window of his room.

The coals in the corner fireplace glowed red. He watched the rain slant down into the back courtyard below. The air was gray and gauzy. Beyond the yard loomed the dull shadow of a house standing in Northumberland Street. Behind it, in Somerset Court, Franklin could make out the faint lines of the house that once had domiciled Mr. Chippendale and the harpsichordist Thomas Barrow.

Philosophy of a sort was on Franklin's tongue.

"It's produced a wonderful clarity in my mind," he was saying aloud. "I've come to understand it's a kind of chess in which we must attend to several aspects all at once. The parallels are plain. We must look a little into futurity—in murder as well as chess—and consider the consequences of each of our actions. Even our silences! Only a fool acts without foresight, and sir!—I confess—I've acted the fool!"

Franklin wrinkled his small nose.

"In chess the player must survey the scene of action in its entirety—consider the relations of the pieces severally and in concert, the dangers to which they're exposed or which they represent, the possibilities of combination. So it is in an enterprise such as this! Each of our actions—in life and chess—carries a consequence by which we must abide. I lecture myself! I've been too cautious, sir! I've forgotten full half of what I know! Surrounded by fools!—"

Franklin shook with a sigh. He gazed deeply at the rain which streamed carelessly down the thin glass.

"But, sir," came a timid voice from across the room. "Surely you cannot rebuke yourself merely because of Mr. Toplady—"

"Beyond these likenesses," Franklin suddenly began again, "chess gives us a most important lesson for life. The habit of hope! No matter how discouraging the bad appearances of the moment, contemplation can discover the means by which we might lift ourselves over it. I believe it! I *have* that habit, sir!—was *born* with it! And I *will* have more of that fine tea. My brain is warmed, my stomach not!"

He spoke not only to the wavering reflection in the glass of the window, but to the more substantial figure of his friend William Strahan.

The latter had been rousted away from his shop early by Peter, and on this particular morning combined a new waistcoat of gold brocade with the more familiar expression of a faithful hound. Having placed yet another cup of scalding tea next to Franklin's hand—his fourth—Strahan sank back into the warming-chair.

"You compare life to a chessboard," Strahan said. "A point well taken and even better made, I credit. But *I* confess—it's my *curiosity* that's warmed, not my brain. My *brain's* cold as pudding on the matter! You were saying that the body was . . ."

Franklin turned his face back to the streaming window. Behind him, a log suddenly dropped down into the coals.

"Where did I leave off?" he sighed.

"The body had just been carried away, sir, and—"

"Very well. There are very few particularities. Very few, indeed. But they're sufficient. They're sufficient to bring us no less distant from the dark heart of a murderer! There's a most curious—there's more to this than we see, Strahan.

"I instructed Mr. Dashwood to retire so I could examine the rooms of the house in my own privacy. This he did, going down with Brackett. Dashwood's own chambers, which stand across from the study, discovered him to be in need of a house-keeper. Crucifixes and books and odd-shaped lamps! Pillows and dust and small oils of—the usual kind! That's a man's private business, and I convey it in confidence. His chambers were as disordered as the fraternity over which he presides—as disordered as his mind. I could make nothing particular of it, having nothing to measure it against.

"The adjoining room was Toplady's own—as neat as the pins in Polly's hair," Franklin continued. "A small writing table, his collection of private books, a chest, a neat bed made up. A scholar's necessaries. Here again I was at a disadvantage, not having seen the room previous. I could not tell whether anything was altered—who had been there, why they were there. But it required no familiarity to notice the window open. The wind had already come up, sir, and the curtains blew straight in. When I later put the question to Mr. Brackett, he disavowed any knowledge of it."

"The window, then!"

"I read your mind and you read mine," Franklin agreed. "The window led to the back court and down to the mounts. Even *I* could have let myself down by it, given a wager of sufficient stakes! The stones made a safe ladder by which—"

"By which the murderer could make his escape from the house," Strahan said.

Franklin looked sharply at his friend.

"A possibility, sir. He could have gone up the chimney. My own chambers—those designated to my use—were undisturbed. They lay directly across the hall. The lad himself, as I found him, lay between the two doors as though he could not determine which to enter, and instead knocked on the door to death. So far as I could see, nothing had been disturbed. The door was unlocked but closed tight—as I'd left it— everything in order, the window shut, the carpetbag undisturbed. But one doesn't look for a snake in a snowbank. Between my own chambers and the study is another room— unused—in which various objects had been stored to keep them out of the way. *That* room, sir, was very much disturbed. It had given refuge to—"

"The murderer!" Strahan exclaimed happily. "And how did you determine it?"

A faint web of irritation spread slowly across Franklin's face. He looked sharply across at Strahan.

"A flea makes itself known."

Strahan was uncertain whether that was intended to describe the murderer or himself. He sat silently.

"The murderer was so concerned to erase all evidence of his presence," Franklin continued, having made his point, "that he left a track where none existed. The bed, sir, was made up neat! The coverings were smooth! When I saw that room some hours earlier, the same coverings were wrinkled, as though someone had lain upon them. So much the evidence of my eyes tells me! Having sat upon the bed himself or taken advantage of it in some way, the murderer smoothed the coverings before he departed so as to leave no trace. He's a man of some order in his mind, for nothing else in the room gave the appearance of being disturbed, not even the table of—"

"But what of Mr. Brackett, the servant?" Strahan interrupted.

"I questioned him closely on the point. He denies being in the room for several days past—says no one goes into it—and most particularly on last evening. When the house emptied he undertook to entertain his own lady in their chambers below. He's an old man, sir, and likely to occupy himself for an hour in what takes you five minutes to accomplish—"

Franklin snorted, and finished the last of his tea.

"But you lead me astray. This same room contained a large table set with what I took to be boxes or household goods not in use, and covered with a white cloth against the dust. This was a false assumption entirely. Beneath the linen—so I discovered when I lifted it—were set one hundred twenty-one small Leyden jars neatly arranged into rows, and each with a capacity of—"

"One hundred twenty-one!" Strahan exclaimed.

"So it appeared to me, having counted them," Franklin answered dryly. "They filled the table. By my calculations they make more than enough to supply a fatal stroke if properly connected together. It was necessary only for the murderer to charge them—or to have them already charged, as I suppose—the generator was in the study, sir, and easily moved—and then to convey the stroke by wire to a conducting material of some sort. Let us say, the brass handle of one of the doors."

Strahan clapped his hands. "You've found the *wire* then, and proved it!"

Franklin shook his head with a low, whistling sigh.

"Indeed, I did *not*," he said. "I remarked that few particulars are at hand. It falls upon us to supply the remainder by conjecture. In a murder so neat and novel—the first criminal use of the electrical fluid coming to my attention, and I daresay yours—we cannot hope to have the thing laid out before us entire like an argument in the *Spectator*. And having learned the method does not smoke out the man who used it. Nor his reasons."

Strahan was seized by a curious look of enlightenment.

"There's but one man with such a knowledge of the electric fluid—I confess, I'm an ignoramus—and the practice in its use—"

"So a fool would think," Franklin said quickly. "But half of London plays with its Leyden jars. Within the Hellfire Club alone I count Francis Dashwood himself, Thomas Potter, Mr. Toplady, who said as much to me, Mr. Pennant, who raised the point of its commonality, and Dieter Schiff, who makes his livelihood from the popular interest in it. These names I have from Mr. Dashwood. Perhaps there are more. It confounds things, sir, most especially when one considers that men often act in concert for a common end."

"But my question is, do you *know* the murderer?" Strahan insisted.

"He knows *me*," Franklin sighed. "There's proof of it." He motioned toward the small chest near the foot of his bed.

Strahan rose from his chair and crossed over to find a small package atop the chest. He looked at it a moment without touching it, and then carefully pulled back the brown wrapper. Inside were the remains of a thin book that had been torn savagely into pieces and badly scorched by fire. That was not so curious to Strahan, however, as the fact that several of the pieces had been reassembled as though they were parts of a puzzle. They formed the title page: *Experiments and Observations on Electricity Made at Philadelphia in America.*

"It came to the house this morning, while I slept," Franklin said. "A warning. Mrs. Stevenson didn't keep the boy long enough to discover who sent him."

Strahan whistled to himself.

"You come too close—he only means to frighten you from—"

"Not close enough to hang him," Franklin answered. He stared out the window. "Will this rain continue?"

"I think not."

"It came up very suddenly."

"By the evidence of *this*—it's the season for surprise. The season for *murder*!"

Franklin sighed again. "You have the soul of a poet. A minor poet. Murder calls for a philosopher, and it's quite out of season in such wetness as this, I assure you. I wonder whether Fothergill has found it too much—"

"He was downstairs, sir, when I came up. I believe Mrs. Stevenson had him cornered in the parlor with some complaint or other—"

Franklin was out of his chair, had picked up his walking stick from the floor, and had left the room before Strahan could say another word.

Strahan returned to the warming-chair, his nose atwitch. There were many things he did not understand, but Franklin was the largest of them. When the American returned a few minutes later, Strahan was busily admiring the fashionable pattern of his own waistcoat. The fire had nearly burned out.

"That much is settled!" Franklin exclaimed with an air of satisfaction. He crossed to his own chair at the window, was about to seat himself, but changed his mind. "There's small chance that he'll find anything the least useful, but my mind carries me in that direction. Life's made up of small chances, and we must take them when they show themselves!"

Franklin seemed suddenly infused with energy.

"If *you* should be successful," he said to Strahan, "then perhaps some of the particularities of this affair will settle themselves into a generality."

"Anything to assist, sir!" Strahan said, standing erect. "My talents are—"

"Two good legs are the talents I'm most in need of," Franklin said. "Those you have, and add the ready talent of knowing the gossip of this town. As though you invented it. Tomorrow the Hellfire Club meets at Medmenham for a special revels. Dashwood obliges me. You'll come. I've planned on it, sir. But tomorrow is tomorrow. We have today. I want the habits of Eugene Toplady—where he might be found if he were alive, and in whose company. My mind moves in circles. There's more than one direction! Begin at Sadd's. Try the Twelve Bells—although surely there are more reasonable houses favored by students and those who fancy themselves such. Overlook none of them. Begin here—Pall Mall, Charing Cross, the Strand—but you're a familiar! Work upwards into the City. I suspect you'll not need to go as far as the Vulture Tavern."

Strahan moved eagerly for the door. Franklin stopped him.

"His companions. His acquaintances. Those in whose company he was most likely to be found," Franklin emphasized. "Most especially his women."

Strahan looked surprised (and interested).

"His women, you say?"

"Emotional women. Women who laugh."

Strahan was silent. He screwed his face into an approximation of certitude, nodded slightly, and backed from the room as though he knew where he was going and needed no eyes to tell him.

When he was gone, Franklin turned again to the window. Rain continued to fall on all of London, although more gently than before. The gray light was stronger. Beyond the yard and over across Northumberland Street he could see the black roof of a carriage moving slowly up toward the Strand, and then vanish behind a building. Franklin put his hand into his coat pocket and withdrew a small sheet of foolscap, folded several times over.

He looked at it for a long time.

He spent the remainder of the forenoon as though he were a country squire. Polly brought him a second breakfast of oysters and chocolate, and then stayed on to warm his lap. She chided him for his roguish habits. He squeezed her tiny waist. "Where's your mother?" he asked. In a pout, she demanded details of the enterprise which so occupied his mind. He offered to open his business to her, if she would do the same for him. Her laugh had sunshine in it. But in truth his heart was not much in such foolery. He was oppressed by thoughts that did not fit full together. Not all puzzles were so easy to solve. He began to talk of the contraction of various metals under cold, and their expansion under heat. But Polly had no mind for metaphor. She ran off to attend to the housekeeping.

Alone in his room, Franklin paced back and forth, counting his steps. When he reached a thousand he quitted it and descended into the parlor. There he took up a newspaper and fell asleep. It was past midafternoon when he awoke.

The rain had stopped.

He tested the air in the little garden behind the house, and found it dry and healthy—although tiny beads of water still glistened on the cress. He returned into the house, went up to the parlor, and stood for several minutes looking at the musical boxes. But he did nothing with them. For a time, he looked out the window into Craven Street. He called for the post, but Mrs. Stevenson and her daughter had gone from the house to shop while he was asleep. He was left king in the castle.

He made his way to the corner desk in the parlor and sat down at it. But he didn't last there a minute. Something stirred in his heart—something like hope. But he couldn't name it. He went downstairs to the back of the house and the kitchen. He fetched a bottle of wine up from the cellar and was sitting there at table—keeping it good company—when Mrs. Stevenson and Polly returned to discover him.

Supper was rabbits smothered in onions. Franklin ate in silence. He had consumed his store of conversation, and all of a sudden named what was in his heart. Despair.

He ordered his tea brought upstairs to his room, where he took it from Mrs. Stevenson without a word. Her skirts rustled, but she knew enough to hold her tongue.

Franklin sat at the window, watching daylight bleed from the sky until he lost all track of time. He contemplated the chessboard of Eugene Toplady's death. All he could see was stalemate. Darkness rose up from the courtyard below. He heard the hour being called, but couldn't make it out—a faraway, lonely voice drifting through the air.

"All's well," Strahan answered. "All's well—but Hell's bells—I'll be in jail—with pretty Nell!"

The portly printer stood uncertainly against the doorjamb in Franklin's room. His overcoat was in his arms, discovering his new brocade waistcoat more than a little soiled. His face was flushed ruddy, yet not enough so to disguise the rouge that smeared his left cheek. His eyes sparkled like wine.

William Strahan was full of blackstrap. He had examined every petty tavern in Westminster.

He tilted out toward the center of the room as Franklin twisted round in his chair. He threw his arms back slowly. The overcoat dropped to the carpet. One by one, Strahan carefully pulled out the pockets of his waistcoat—and then the pockets of his pants.

They were empty.

He stood absolutely still, like a small autumn bush set with strange, off-white flowers—his inside-out pockets.

"This is not triumph," he said thickly. "This is *defeat*. This is not talent. This is—"

Franklin bounced out of the chair with a happy snort. He drew Strahan over to the bed and perched him safely on the edge. Then he backed off.

"You found *nothing*?"

"*Nothing* is the *word*, sir! You've got a way with it—with *words*, sir! The *word* is *nothing*! In all this *great* town—sent out to find—sent out to find—"

Strahan wobbled his head from side to side. He began to lean precariously backward.

"—if I *remember*," he said earnestly, "sent out to find—the usual business." His eyes lit up. "Corn is going to be *very* dear—very *dear*, dear!" He laughed. "Oh, dear! Pennant is bankrupt—Samuel Montmorency Pennant—or *nearly* so, which is *all* the difference—"

"A pornographer bankrupt in *this* age?" Franklin asked.

"Indeed! A very active woman at the King's Head!" Strahan added suddenly. A smile trickled about his lips. He touched his smudged cheek. "It's not easy to—Chevenix displays a human centaur—a *human centaur*!—you must see it!—from the—and very warm in here, the way you keep it!" Strahan began to nod his head vigorously up and down, confirming everything. "He had red hair—that was plain enough!—no doubt about it!—the whole town talks about the—they think—they *think* Topbloody was poisoned by a—"

Strahan began to cough, but it was only a laugh. He jerked himself forward to prevent himself from falling backward. His sides shook.

"—a *dangler*, sir!—no doubt of it at all!—with his limp, you could hardly fail to—"

"His limp what?"

Strahan laughed gleefully to himself. He wobbled on the edge of the bed—looking now and then at Franklin, who stood over him, but then laughing all the more. He had passed far beyond the world of predicates and verbs.

"The centaur—what *is* a human centaur?—the *centaur* had red *hair?*" Franklin asked helpfully.

"The centaur?"

"Yes."

"The *centaur* was at Chevenix!—I make—don't I make it clear enough—"

"Very well. The centaur was at Chevenix. Corn is dear. Samuel Pennant is bankrupt—"

"Or nearly so!"

"Who had the red hair? Oh!" Franklin said suddenly. "The active *woman*—"

"The man with the *limp!*" Strahan cried.

Franklin straightened up, reached back for his chair, and seated himself. He scooted forward chair and all, placing his face close by Strahan's and receiving full proof of the blackstrap. He spoke somewhat more loudly than normal.

"You were to find some intelligence of Eugene Toplady. You found nothing? That's evidence as well, and often overlooked! Indeed! He had no companions. There was no emotional woman! He was never seen—"

"*Nothing?*" Strahan suddenly bellowed. He was indignant, and his face colored an even deeper red. "You say—*nothing?* The man in the disguise is *nothing?*" His voice, too, was louder than normal. He seemed almost sober.

"The man in the disguise," Franklin repeated softly. "What disguise?"

"The King's Head!" Strahan said angrily. His arms tried to flail the air. "The Three Pennies! The Red Lion! The Half Corner! Sadd's! The Black Turk! Golden Cross! You say *nothing?* A man whose *wig* comes off—a man whose *nose* is so obvious—*nothing?* You would think—you would call it *nothing* to find a man who's so loose—who's so loosely disguised that he's found out at every turn?—"

Strahan glowered at Franklin.

"He took his *hair* off at *Sadd's!* He dropped his *nose* at the *Turk's!* His—his—"

He looked incredulous.

"Very well," Franklin said calmly. "You saw a man with a—bad disguise. You saw—"

"Not *see* him!" Strahan sputtered. "He was with *Toplady!*"

Franklin's brows suddenly arched.

"Do I hear you? Toplady was in the company of a man disguised so loosely that he would surely be discovered— as though he were meant to be discovered—"

"The King's Head!" Strahan said. "The Three Pennies! The Red Lion!—" He was counting his fingers.

"A man with red hair," Franklin interrupted. "And a limp—"

"Yes," Strahan said, shaking his head energetically. "The *Frenchman*—"

Franklin sat back. He bounced to his feet. He looked lovingly down on William Strahan.

"—but I cannot tell—cannot find his *name*—"

"Very good, Strahan!" Franklin exclaimed. "Very good, indeed!"

He clapped his hands smartly together.

Strahan looked up at him through closing eyes. He tilted several ways in succession. Then he fell silently backward onto the bed.

He looked pleased.

Thirteen

"I am *not* an emotional woman!" she laughed.

"Indeed, I believe you *are*," he said.

The woman's dark eyes flashed. Dr. Franklin smiled warmly—because of the woman or because of the claret, one could not have told. Certainly it was not because of the currant pudding.

Valetta LaNeve's dark hair was drawn back from her forehead. Her neck was white and smooth as ivory. Her face was thin and finely shaped, giving her an air of delicacy. Her eyes denied it. They were misty, blue-gray pools of soft light with some deep strength and assurance in them. Half an hour after his arrival Franklin was still trying to determine their exact color—a task made more difficult by the tiny flicker of fear that danced like a candle flame in each iris. Or perhaps it was merely the reflection of the small crystal luster hanging down over the table where they sat. Franklin was not sure. He was unsettled. She handled a cold leg of mutton like a man.

It was already very late when he left the house in Craven Street, made his way across the Strand, and entered into St. Martin's Lane—coming up this time past St. Martin's Church, the Westminster Fire Office, and the Golden Bowl Tavern before he was driven across the street by the malodorous presence of the waterworks. He passed the house where twenty years earlier Dr. Misaubin had dispensed his anti-venereal pills—a scene he knew from Hogarth—and nearly turned by mistake into the narrow walk of Peter's Court. But he caught his error and pushed on in the darkness, coming at last to the tenement near to Cecil Court. There he found the LaNeve lodgings as the old Frenchman had described them.

The woman who answered his querulous knocking answered none of his notions. In all of London there could have been only a handful of women like her. None would have been so much of a handful. She was eager of company. She swept him into her apartments with tumbling laughter. She had a certain insouciance, and a kind of natural gaiety that burst from her on bolts of energy. In a phrase, she unsettled him.

"I *have* no hesitancies!" she declared cheerfully after Franklin had explained his purpose. "I'm as free as any man could be and hope to stay so. I have it from my father! The Devil be damned! If I should want a pint with the wits at Slaughter's, or should like to sing Handel with John Beard, or write for Mist's—why, I'll have it!"

"Hmmm," Franklin said.

"Ashamed? Repentent? Not so!" Valetta said, laughing. "Strange that he should think so—but he's an old French-man! The way *I* see it, sir, it's an *education*—life is *all* bad usage! I'll set my course and sail to it—Devil be damned!" She took another vicious bite of the mutton. "Didn't realize I was hungry. How's the pudding?"

"Hmmm," Franklin said. He had put off his spectacles.

"The facts of the affair are very direct, and easy enough to answer," she said, chewing mightily. "And I suppose known over half the town. John Beard won't talk to me, but the wits at Slaughter's think I'm grand!" She laughed again, and Franklin tilted his head slightly to better catch the music of it.

Valetta tasted the claret again and licked her lips.

"I came into an acquaintance with Eugene Toplady—as you mention. He was a scholar, not a soldier. *There* was the attraction—"

"That he was a scholar?"

"No—that he was *not* a soldier. I'm done with war!" she said lightly. "I knew a little of his company—of Francis Dashwood's company, I should say. And *will*! Francis Dashwood's company! The Hellfire Club! Who *hasn't* heard of them? They're fools—I'm not afraid to tell you—but very wealthy fools, sir, and said to have some wit. My curiosity was aroused, and once aroused required satisfaction. It's my nature! I went to some meetings of the Club. We smoked something—what's its name?—and we drank, of course, and gamed a bit and had high times, if you'll want to know. I needed loosening and got it. I trust you're no moralist—"

"Not I," Franklin said.

"Morality's for mice, sir, and don't bother me with it! Hadn't we better work our own salvation?"

When she laughed her chin came up, and the light from the crystal luster caught her more fully on the face. Franklin noticed a band of faint freckles across the bridge of her exquisite nose and on her cheekbones.

"You don't like your pudding," she said.

Franklin looked at it. He was nearly done.

He smiled. "I've never had any quite so good."

Valetta bent forward, the better to discover her loose gown. She liked playing to court.

"It came about that I was invited to the revels at Medmenham, and went in full knowledge of its customs—but you know of *that* if you're a friend of *St. Francis*, as he fashions himself—"

"Refresh me, madam."

Valetta looked at Franklin with a smile of surprise.

"Why! They're so funny as to be amusing—all of their rites and incantations. They have an excess of liberty, sir! But is liberty ever an excess? Ha! The mutton is good, at least, and you'll be sorry you didn't choose it when you had the chance! They assemble at the monastery, where they hold a ball of sorts—a balum rancum—do they have such hops in America?" She took another mouthful, quickly.

"I fear not, although—"

"The women are without clothes, to show their charms. It's Turkish! But very gay—there's music and food and wicked dancing for those who choose to dance!"

"Hmmm," Franklin said again. He blinked.

"It surprises me that a man of the world doesn't know of these things—but, of course, in America—"

"I didn't say I had no knowledge of them, madam. Only that I fear we have no such entertainments in America, and that no opportunity has yet shown itself here."

He leaned confidentially toward her, nearly touching her cheek, and spoke in such a soft voice that it certified a revelation.

"In America, my dear, we are more used to erecting what we call a maypole. We select a dozen or so Indian maidens of the most restless tribes and dance about the maypole—chanting to the corn plants—urging them to grow and be fruitful—shedding our clothes as we go—"

Valetta burst out with a laugh so buoyant that it blew Franklin back into his chair.

"Trumpets for you, sir!" she cried bravely, raising her

glass of claret into the air. "Take your fun where you find it!"

"Indeed," Franklin said. "But it brings me no closer to the object of my inquiries—which is to learn something of your usage at the hands of the Hellfire Club and its effect upon that fraternity. Fools or not, madam, what is plain to see—you've had a definite and deadly effect—"

Franklin saw fear in her eyes, but she hid it with a smile.

"There comes a point," she said, "when the ladies retire to their cells. You're old enough to know it. They're called nuns—after the nunneries of Mother Sulphur and Mother Douglass, you may be sure. My misfortune was to attract the attention of a monk they call the Bruiser. That was the *least* of my misfortunes. He's a gentleman of the fancy and a bit of a poet—and a bit bosky. But otherwise mannered enough, I should say. He spent some time—some *long* time, sir— and wandered away. In his place came a brute I do not know— a German—for he swore in German, he sighed in German, and he went away quite unhappy. Just as well. It was very late when the third man came to my cell. Masked. Unlike the others, he drew the curtains closed—"

"Madam! I do not require—"

"He began to beat me," Valetta said softly. "Gently at first, as though it were his expected practice. Yes—he began by slapping me. But he lost himself. He grew wild—seemed to take some pleasure in it—and I wouldn't have it. When he struck me so hard as to take my breath, I grasped at his mask— the mask of a devil, to be sure!—and tore it off. When I screamed out, he struck me with more force—was in a rage— and frankly, sir, I was no match for it. I couldn't run—I—I next remember nothing, until being wrapped in a coach for London—"

"I didn't mean for you to—"

A thin smile formed itself on Valetta's face. "You saw that I registered no surprise when you told me he is dead."

"*Murdered* is more precise. He is murdered."

The woman shook her head gently.

"I knew him very little, and if we can credit appearances—he seemed harmless enough. But life is a masquerade, sir, and we see what we wish to see—a student of languages!—a scholar! On that night he was the Devil himself. His face was—as I've never seen it. A nightmare. Mine was marked by proof that he was not harmless enough—"

"I see no trace of it, happily enough."

"Bones mend stronger than broken hearts, sir."

Franklin sighed, and settled more deeply into his chair. The woman across the table no longer looked at him. She no longer smiled.

"Hearts are the hardest of all to see into," Franklin said quietly. "Let me tell you a secret—"

"Go ahead, sir."

"On his desk, he left a message that led me to you—long before I knocked on your door."

"Yes?"

"Three words."

Valetta looked up.

"Emotional women laugh."

"I am *not* an emotional woman!" she laughed.

"Indeed, I believe you *are*," he said. "And credit you for it. I am not immune to life. Nor was Mr. Toplady. From the moment that I saw you in Pall Mall—"

"In Pall Mall, sir?" Valetta said in surprise.

"Yesterday evening, coming out of Pall Mall, you turned out atop a coach."

Valetta's face suddenly blushed. Her breath seemed to leave her.

"Yes," she said at last. "There was a Squeezer in Pall Mall, and I thought to find my husband—"

"Did you?"

"Hector? No. I came round the street several times, thinking to find him, and could not. I feared—I thought he would be there—and so tied up at Sadd's. But he was not there."

"At Sadd's?"

"No—not at Sadd's and not at the Squeezer. I pushed myself into the house and saw no one I knew—save Bubb Dodington and—Eugene—"

"You saw Toplady in the Schomberg House?"

"Yes," Valetta said. "And he saw me, I'm sure of it. He was in his famous devil's suit—I'm sure he saw me! He looked straight at me. He turned about and fled—"

"Straight to death," Franklin said. "Your husband, too, has fled. So I have it from his father—the old Frenchman. You hoped to have him back—"

"No," she said quickly. "I do not hope that. Hector's promised—I wanted to—"

"You know his habits, his disposition. Knowing the father, I'm anxious of the son."

"He's all graciousness and manner," the woman said. "Like the age—empty within."

"Then harmless enough," Franklin answered.

Valetta's eyes flashed again, but not with humor.

"Are there no hurricanes in the Indies? Where is Philadelphia in America? These storms have nothing at their center, sir, by what I read, and yet they cause great mischief."

"Then your husband is—"

"Given to frenzy, sir. In private, not public. He's a soldier, and mustered all his bravery for me. I have bruises for medals—more than those awarded by the Monks of Medmenham. Yet I feel—some responsibility for him."

She picked up the bottle of claret and poured her own glass half full. Then she held the bottle over Franklin's glass. He nodded.

"He was as unprepared for me as I for him," Valetta said. "He wears his honor like a shield, and has threatened one by one to—to kill the Friars of St. Francis. He's like a child playing war—I swear. It's true—I was in Pall Mall last night—looking for Hector and hoping to save him from some rash action—"

"Although not soon enough."

"No. Not soon enough."

"What is this plan—has he told you?"

"He's a soldier," Valetta said softly. "Or thinks he is. He came here to see me a week since—tired—dirty—would not touch me. It was the first I saw him since the revels. He talked in riddles. 'I have an army of vengeance'—or 'I'm in the army of vengeance.' I'm not sure of it. 'The pathway must be paved with thirteen hearts of souls unsaved.' I remember *that*—but don't know what it means. He said his task was hardest—not to kill, but to brave the enemy lines. He worked his way into the confidence of one of the Brotherhood—so he said—and knows their every move. A hobbledehoy—I don't know who. He could barely look at me. For a moment I was afraid, and yet—"

"Have you seen him since?"

"No—and hope not to. I've no affection for him. That's finished—I've sued before the Court." Valetta reached back and loosened the clasp from her hair, shaking it free about her face. "This wine should be more cheerful," she said.

"Yes. How large is Hector's army?"

"It's a figure of speech, perhaps. He's an excellent swordsman. I don't know—"

"It is no figure of speech," Franklin said, almost to himself. He pushed his chair back from the table.

"Do you know a painter named William Reeve?"

"Indeed," Valetta answered. "He's a member of the Club.

He lives in this street, in fact, down near to where Louis Roubillac used to have his shop in Peter's Court. The street is full of business—"

"Did William Reeve attend the revels?"

Valetta thought for a moment.

"Not that I saw," she said.

"Do you know George Selwyn?"

"The wit?"

Franklin shrugged.

"I've seen him in Slaughter's, always half asleep—"

"Yes," Franklin said.

He got up slowly from his chair and walked across to the corner window. "I have a small, hopeless task," he said. "To find the man who murdered Eugene Toplady and John Raleigh. I did not trust him from the first—" He opened his palms, and moved them up and down as though they were scales—and he was measuring the weight of conflicting ideas. Down below, St. Martin's Lane was deep in darkness.

"Those words mean nothing to you—*Emotional women laugh?*"

"No, sir. Nothing."

Franklin gazed down into the dark street. It was empty. The lamp across the way had long been extinguished.

"It becomes very late," he said. "Are there any cabs in this street?"

Valetta LaNeve did not answer.

"Devil be damned," Franklin said softly. His hands came slowly down from the lapels of his coat and fastened themselves behind his back. The room was so silent he could hear the flicker of the burning luster and the breathing of the dark-haired woman beneath it.

"Perhaps you're right," she said. "I *am* an emotional woman."

Franklin nodded his head at the reflection in the glass. His eyes were on the street below, but his mind drifted in a less desolate direction.

"Madam," he said at last, turning about with great gravity. "There's a strange man in my bed, snoring and tossing about. I will have some more of your pudding."

The bright laughter of Valetta LaNeve filled the room.

Fourteen

The small gondola, painted in bright yellow and Chinese red, was waiting for them as they pushed through the market gate and clattered down the Hungerford Stairs. The waterman looked up at them and grinned through yellowed teeth.

They made a picture.

Franklin, who reached home shortly after the morning sun first came over the roofs of London, had hurried into his old blue frock coat. One white stocking was loose from his pantaloons, and his shoes were undone. William Strahan was more carefully tailored—entirely in red, except for his gold brocade waistcoat. His face was so brightly scrubbed and beaming that he could have passed for the morning sun itself. John Fothergill was reedy and dressed in black. He walked as stiffly as a grenadier's rod, although his head wobbled loosely above his tightly buttoned collar. He carried a small valise of leather.

The black manservant Peter tottered down the stairs behind

the three cronies, balancing a large basket of yellow wicker on each shoulder.

"Ho for a fine morning!" Strahan cried carelessly, looking at the blue sky as he stepped into the swaying boat.

"Then it's morning, is it?" Franklin asked. He reached out his arm for the waterman to grasp.

"Sure as a cow's got teats and Madge smells bad."

Fothergill said nothing, but creaked into the boat unassisted to share a seat with Strahan. Peter handed the two baskets in and begged everyone a good trip. But before they could answer, the waterman had poled off from the stairs. The gondola swung out into the current of the River Thames, slid backward a bit, and then began its long slow progress upstream.

"Christ Almighty! What a load!" the boatman complained.

Hungerford Stairs glided away. The end of Craven Street passed by. Soon the small boat was inching its way past the small coppice of trees that marked the garden of Northumberland House. Franklin settled himself, having a seat of his own. He adjusted his stocking, buckled both his shoes, and gingerly ran his fingers over the small sacs that had formed beneath his eyes, hoping to flatten them out.

Then he blinked four times in succession.

He took his spectacles from the black case in his frock pocket and carefully wiped them with a white kerchief.

"Pardon me?" he said.

"I say—again I say—the river's crowded," Fothergill said, again.

"So's my mind," Franklin answered. "Congestion of the brain." He turned about in his seat to better face John Fothergill and William Strahan—riding backward. "And to think that I once swam this sewer!"

The boat slid toward the shadows of Westminster Bridge—still called New Bridge by some people, by the thin reason that it was new—and ran beneath it. The buildings of Whitehall disappeared behind the solid posts. On the other side of the river, boatmen in great numbers swarmed over a fringe of wharves and timber yards, having come down from the market gardens near to Tothill Fields.

The gondola broke into sunlight just as Franklin pressed his spectacles onto his nose and lifted his fingers to see that they would stay. At Millbank, the three travelers left the City behind.

"Is he buried?"

"Who?" Franklin asked.

"Toplady."

"No. I think not."

"Then how can they celebrate a revels—when one of their own members lies murdered and unburied?"

"Murdered?" the boatman said.

Franklin thought a moment.

"They're strangers to each other, Strahan. Very dear strangers. Whatever glue has held them together has now dissolved."

The gondola glided on in silence, through the blue smoke of the glass kilns and on past the gardens of Vauxhall, which were already filling. Beyond Vauxhall was another world—small villages that made themselves known by solitary church spires rising above the bank of the Thames, neat houses with small gardens running down to the river, birds rising above the marshes and vegetable patches. Now and then they passed a solitary cottage.

The party had just come up between Mortlake and Kew when Franklin readjusted himself upon the hard seat and reached down to once again unbuckle his shoes.

"I should like to hear of your successes, Doctor," he said pleasantly enough to Fothergill.

"It could have been done in a moment on shore," Fothergill

said sourly, "rather than come out upon this vile river to Marlow and waste the better part of a—"

"You need the fresh air, John! Your color's bad!" Strahan said happily, patting Fothergill's bony knee.

Fothergill sniffed the air, snorting out the various odors of the river and the fetid marshes that lay near by. His eyes followed the progress of a large bobbing turnip as it drifted downstream past the gondola, all split and yellowed. Strahan saw it, too, and thought of cabbages and Annie Martin.

When Fothergill lifted the valise to his lap and withdrew a small sheaf of papers, the corners of his mouth were turned far down.

"I did as you requested," he said dryly, "and inquired into the records of the Royal Society in Crane Court. They are without especial order, and the task took much longer than you suggested—"

"Thank you, sir."

"Francis Dashwood," Fothergill said, drawing his own glasses from their case and perching them on his thin nose. "An inquiry on certain Turkish vases. Published in the *Proceedings*, June 1749. He's described what he takes to be ruins of great antiquity in Buckinghamshire—a very small piece with nothing to it, sir—I don't credit it. Same year—'49. He submitted a comparison of ancient and modern modes of worship, but the Society could not see fit to publish it."

Fothergill looked up from the papers on his lap, peering at Franklin over the top of his spectacles.

"Can you blame them?" he said. "He's nothing but a merry dilettante."

"So are we all, sir."

Fothergill cleared his throat in disagreement and turned his attention back to his lap. Strahan saw a fish leap, but said nothing.

"Very well. Here we have Dr. Schiff with an inquiry upon

bell ropes and an observation on the petals of the gardenia—
which I believe comes from Carolina? You sent me some,
I believe."

"What is his observation?"

"Foolishness. On which petal does a bee land?"

Strahan burst out laughing.

"Christ Almighty!" the waterman said, hissing through
his gappy teeth and rolling his eyes. Franklin twisted round
to shoot a glare of rebuke at the eavesdropper.

"A short article concerning the roads of Sussex," Fothergill
continued. "It shows as geological science, but don't wager on
it. The man's a fraud. That's all he's had the good fortune
to publish, sir, and it's too much. In the summer of 1750—
fifteen August by the register—he sent in a paper supposing
to give proofs for drawing down lightning from clouds with
rods—doesn't he astound London with his 'Electrical Kiss'?—
he pretends to be serious—"

"To whom was this submitted?" Franklin asked.

"The committee on publications."

"Ahhh. When was it accepted?"

"Well!" Fothergill exclaimed contemptuously.

"Rejected," Franklin said.

"Of course, sir! The man's well known as a fool—a showman—he might as well sell bitters and bones on the street
corner. They call him the Garrick of—"

"I agree. A fool."

"Here's Eugene Toplady," Fothergill went on, glancing
down at his papers. "One mention—a small inquiry upon
philology. It was answered by a gentleman in Sussex. I could
find no record of him before the committee—"

"No record of the gentleman from Sussex?"

"No record of Eugene Toplady. I make myself very clear,"
Fothergill said. "Is this the lad that was—"

"Yes," Franklin sighed. "His whole reputation rests upon an inquiry answered by a gentleman in Sussex."

Fothergill nodded.

"We have Thomas Potter published here—September 1753—on shells collected from Dover. Of no consequence. Samuel Pennant—here's your pornographer—shows with a new method for the binding of books supposed to represent an improvement—this has been adopted, has it not? I believe so—"

Strahan disagreed. "It's too weak, sir—intended only for books that will never be opened."

"Nothing on John Raleigh?" Franklin interrupted.

"Not that I find, sir. But the records are—"

"Nothing on William Reeve, the painter—"

"No, sir. Nor for the other names you gave me—they're too occupied with their infidelities to bother with affairs of the mind. Do you suppose I don't recognize this list?" Fothergill asked, holding aloft a sheet of paper from his lap. "They're all members of the infamous—"

"Indeed. The infamous human race."

Franklin's eyes fell shut. The boat glided onward, and Fothergill was left to sputter his discoveries to himself.

The river curved and twisted past the village of Twickenham, as if to resist their arrival at the ruined abbey of Medmenham. The gondola moved silently beneath the shadows cast by a row of willows overhanging the bank, and then once again chopped out into the sunlight. The air was dry and crisp. The waterman began to hum a ditty—he was anticipating the easier voyage downstream. Strahan dangled his hand in the cool water. Fothergill sat erect beside him, unable to relax.

Franklin had no such difficulty. His head was slumped down upon his chest. His eyes were closed. His toes moved.

"He's thinking," Strahan explained to Fothergill.

"He's sleeping," Fothergill explained to Strahan.

"He's very fat, sirs, and it makes rowin' Christ Almighty hard!" the boatman said.

It wasn't until midafternoon that the little gondola drew near to the copse of trees marking the location of Medmenham Abbey, far up on the Thames. By then the river was consumed by shadows.

What passed for conversation among the three cronies had fallen into disuse by virtue of Franklin's prolonged and unanswerable silence. But he had long since reopened his eyes. He had rebuckled his square black shoes. He was ready for the world, and had turned about in his seat to face it. As the boat came round a small bend in the river and began to cross over, he was able to spy a flash of bright scarlet straight ahead—a robed man standing alone on a small pier that tipped into the water from the far shore.

The boat glided gently across with only a push now and then from the weary boatman. It nudged against the rotted pilings of the pier with a soft, strangulated cry, as though someone's hand or heart were caught between one wood and the other. The sound loosed a mournful bird from the bank. But no one watched it dart low across the water, or saw the panic in its flight.

Instead their eyes were fixed upon the agitated presence of Francis Dashwood. Robed all in red, but without a miter or a fillet, he was a priest whose face did penance for his thoughts. They did not need speaking. Something was obviously wrong.

"God be praised!" the waterman said softly under his breath as he fixed the gondola secure to the wooden dock.

Franklin and Strahan scrambled out of the boat. The yellow wickers were handed up and the waterman quickly slid the rope from its mooring—drifting out into the brown current. John Fothergill sat stiffly in the back of the gondola, providing the ballast of his disapproval.

From up the hill behind Dashwood came the faint, haunted piping of hautboy players, and the thick scent of unchecked vegetation—an air laden with moldering dreams. Here was an Eden from which all restraint had been banished. The boatman had been there before—at night—when the river was ablaze with firelight from the hill and the dark woods echoed with piercing cries.

But on this day, save for the piping music, the woods were nearly silent. Franklin stood quiet as a pilgrim on the pier, watching the boat drift away. His ear was cocked to the snapping of twigs and the tread of urgent footsteps. Someone was forcing his way down the overgrown pathway from the abbey—but could not be seen.

"Strahan," Franklin said, pointing to Strahan. Strahan smiled pleasantly. Dashwood didn't.

"I feared you wouldn't come," he said quickly to Franklin. "Now that you have—I fear you shouldn't have. We're too close to death—"

A thin voice came from the woods: "Pasha!"

The three men turned at once and watched Old Paul Whitehead emerge onto the pier. He was dressed in a flowing white gown and lacked breath, despite having come downhill. He looked sharply at William Strahan (who smiled pleasantly), but the old tattler had no time for prudence.

"Trouble in the Roman Room, sir!" he said excitedly. "The Bruiser! He's answered a witticism of Bubb Dodington with a right hand to the chops! Knocked him clear down— and bowled over a woman at the same time! He's cooled now—but Schiff threatens him. And Selwyn tried to have at him. It's as bad as ever you said, sir! There's nothing can be done—" Whitehead's yellow eyes were lit with excitement.

"He's cooled?"

"For the moment," Old Paul answered. "But Dodington—once we stood him up—he went for Squint—something he said—tried to have his shirt, and all the ladies laughing—"

"Has it cooled—"

"For the moment. But it's as bad as ever—"

A tight smile fixed itself on Dashwood's face.

"Very well. It's nothing, is it? Nothing. I'll see Churchill in the chapel. Tell him so. This is Strahan—the printer. Take him up—find him a robe—Dodington must have a spare. Go! Go! I'll be up in a moment—"

Whitehead beckoned obediently to William Strahan and turned on his heel.

"We'll make a Friar out of you, sir! Do as you please!" Dashwood cried as they disappeared into the woods.

"They're all here?" Franklin asked quietly.

Dashwood turned around in the silence, and looked down at Franklin. His face was sullen.

"All but Raleigh and Eugene. There's an ugly air, sir. We're too close to death and have fallen upon each other. You heard Old Paul! My authority is disregarded! God damn! The Brotherhood is ruined! This is a *charade,* a mistake in judgment—as great as—"

"Follow it through, sir. Men discover themselves in extremity," Franklin said softly.

Dashwood didn't hear him. He waved his arms wildly at the wooded hills.

"—as great as thinking you could find the rogue responsible! Not a man on earth could find a murderer who leaves no trace—who strikes by night. It's my mistake—forgive me!—but the Brotherhood is ruined—"

"Of *course* I've discovered the murderer," Franklin said benignly, peering up at Dashwood with innocent brown eyes. "Why do you think I've come? More than that, the reason for his murders."

Dashwood said nothing.

"You're a passionate man, sir. I'm a mere printer, with some practical knowledge of the world. I've attended to this affair in the only way I know—as though I were engaged in a scientific experiment. There's only one satisfactory end to it, sir. Proof. One must have proof of his hypothesis. Without it—babble to the four walls of the Round House. There's the final piece, the vaccine against error."

"But you *know* the man! Let's *have* him—"

"Indeed. I'm certain of it. But we need—"

"Let's *have* him then!" Dashwood cried impatiently. His eyes were turned to hard bright stones of hatred.

Franklin sighed aloud. He shook his head sadly. With Francis Dashwood towering over him, he seemed a very small figure indeed.

"We lack the final piece," he said. "The revels will provide it—so I trust. You say the members of your Club are at—"

"They're ugly, sir! Indeed! I've never seen the like! That's true enough, and at each other's throats—"

"There!" Franklin exclaimed, almost cheerfully. "As I hoped! So much the better! We'll have our proof when it comes to us!"

Fifteen

ashwood's blue eyes softened. The architecture of his face, excited into flying buttresses of anger and despair, came loose. He clapped his arm around Franklin's shoulder with such fraternity that Franklin almost squeaked.

The pathway to the abbey was not long, but it was filled with surprises. Franklin walked slowly and Dashwood talked fast. Coming round about by a small dry run in the woods, the two men were interrupted in their progress by the smooth white rump of a marble Venus bending over indiscreetly in the pathway. Small temples stood off from the path in other places. They were grown over with flowering vines, but left no doubt about the gods and goddesses to whom they were devoted. Near the open meadow on the brow of the hill, Dashwood plunged off the path and entered a tight grove of oaks. Franklin followed and found himself standing before a life-sized statue of Hermes. On its base were cut the words PENI TENTO NON PENITENTI.

"Macaroni Latin!" Dashwood laughed easily. "Not penitence, but a tense penis!"

"Hmmm," Franklin said. He was beginning to like the sound of the sound, and had practiced it all the way home from the apartments of Valetta LaNeve.

The restored Cistercian abbey rose up from the fringe of woods along the meadowside. Its dark stone walls were covered with ivy. Its crumbling tower, newly built in an imitation of antiquity, reached up to the crowns of the elms. They entered through the eastern porch, coming up past a statue of Harpocrates—the youthful god of silence—who pressed a stone finger to his stone lips. Above the door were the words FAY CE QUE VOUDRAS. Do as you please.

The sound of the hautboy players was very loud, as were the sounds of shouts and laughter.

"Churchill needs cooling!" Dashwood said, once they had swung open the heavy wooden doors and come into a small darkened foyer. "I'll see to it. The dance proceeds—you can hear it. So all's well! The robing room's around to the other side there—chapel's in back. Find yourself a robe or not, as you please. *Do as you please!*"

With a quick nervous laugh Dashwood darted away, leaving Franklin standing alone.

The rhythm of the hautboy players washed over him. He pulled his blue frock closer about his chest. Behind him sunlight streamed through a set of stained-glass windows of obscene design. Before him were the closed doors to the common room, behind which the volume of music and laughter swelled.

Franklin drew a finger across his forehead. He adjusted

his wire spectacles. He seemed uncertain as to which way to proceed. But then he turned abruptly and followed the hallway Dashwood had taken, alongside the common room.

No sooner had he entered the hall, however, than he was brought up short by an open doorway to his left, showing into the dancing floor.

He blinked. Twice.

The large room was lighted brilliantly with red-shaded lanterns. Perhaps it had originally been a place of worship. Now it was devoted to more earthly pleasures. Extravagant paper covered the walls with designs even more obscene than those that showed in the colored glass of the foyer windows. The vaulted ceiling high above was covered with frescoes laid up by some country Michelangelo: fleshy men and untakable women. In the far corner three hautboy players, dressed Pan-like, piped with all their hearts.

But these things Dr. Franklin did not see all at once. His eyes were diverted, as it were, to the dancers who circled about the stone floor in the center of the room and agitated the air with excitement.

There were only two of them.

One was the portly William Strahan. He'd given over his fine suit of red clothes and new brocade vest for an unremarkable white robe, which flowed and rippled as he turned. It was too large even for him. His face retained the redness, however. His mouth was held stiff and half opened. He gasped for air in quick, short breaths. His eyes bulged with undisguised strain—or perhaps it was merely the spectacle of his partner. He'd thrown his hands tightly behind his back and locked them there. The knuckles of his fingers showed white. He danced madly.

A Medmenham nun—brought up from Covent Garden—danced with equal energy before him. An Irish girl, if her scarlet hair gave any clue. She wore a glittering silver mask across her eyes and left the rest to God, who had been bountiful. Her hands whipped the air in all directions. A smile played upon her handsome face. Her quick fingers snapped—*crack! crack! crack!*—urging poor Strahan to an even faster beat.

Poor Strahan tried his best. He seemed oblivious of everyone else in the room. He huffed, and puffed, and hoped to keep it up. The dancers had the entire floor to themselves, but the attention of only half the crowd.

The other half—the Friars of St. Francis—stood across the room in two angry knots, where Franklin could see them plain enough from the doorway. He saw Reeve and Wilkes and fish-faced Thomas Potter, his hair curled and his mouth agape. Samuel Pennant cringed behind Charles Churchill and seemed to be hurling insults around the Bruiser's elbow. Whitehead glided back and forth between the contrary camps, coming to rest bravely between tiny George Selwyn and the Bruiser's pumping finger. Leathery Lord Sandwich seemed to be cackling to himself.

Only Dieter Schiff stood apart. His dark face glowered above his white robe. His eyes were fixed on Franklin.

Franklin took a cautious step into the room, edged himself sideways several feet without looking, and found his nose nearly up against the broad back of Bubb Dodington.

"—very *soft,* my dear lady, and I would *love* to touch them," Dodington was saying.

Franklin peered round the gauzy white cloud of Bubb Dodington to see a dozen Medmenham nuns lounging and laughing carelessly alongside that part of the room. They sprawled on ornate couches—all of them with eye masks, only four or five of them in pale blue robes. The others were dressed as when they came into the world, only more so.

The young woman who had Dodington's attention was robed, but the robe did little to hide her natural charms.

"My good sir!" she laughed coyly when Dodington's pudgy fingers wriggled through the air toward her. "They *are* very soft and warm, and I reserve them for just such a fine gentleman as yourself. But wouldn't you wish to touch something even *softer?*"

Franklin blinked. Dodington babbled.

"Why, *yes!*—I *would*—my *dear!*—"

The woman gaily lifted Dodington's outstretched hand to the top of his head and left it there.

Franklin could see the back of the oaf's neck flush red as a tinkle of laughter danced its way down the line of ladies, and the word was passed from one to another:

"Lout!"

"Fool!"

"Pig!"

"But he has power at Court—"

Franklin turned away and nearly knocked Dashwood from his feet.

"We must do *something!*" Dashwood whispered, catching his breath. There was a look of alarm in his eyes. "They'll tear each other to pieces—they're like dogs—"

Franklin peered across the dancing floor. Churchill had just reached round Old Paul and cuffed George Selwyn happily on the ear. The Bruiser's booming voice rose above the frenetic music:

"—daresay!—two stone underweight, Jack Pudding!—Save your ugly breath—he was hateful but I loved him—and you'll not get far—"

Reeve suddenly sat down hard on the floor. No one had touched him.

Dashwood bolted to the center of the room, waving his arms wildly—trying to get the attention of the dancers and the musicians. No one could get the attention of William

Strahan. He pumped his legs and danced in circles around the lovely Irish nun even after the music had stopped.

There was a loud sputter of noise from the Friars across the way.

"—you lousy Molly, you can—"

"—murdered who?—you jackanapes!—"

"—see your pretty face in Hell—"

Francis Dashwood's screech was the cry of a vulture, filling the room.

"If you won't dance—please!—we'll retire to the cells—" Dashwood's face matched his robe. His arms were upraised. "—for an hour, gentlemen, so do your best—*do as you please!*"

Some differences are easily settled. The Hellfire Club rushed across the room to pick its women, and Franklin was tossed and turned in the melee. His spectacles slid perilously close to the tip of his nose.

"Nice to see you, Doctor!" he heard someone say, and looked up.

It was the Bruiser. He'd lifted his little nun off the floor and had her flying over his head with a mighty laugh. He danced off with the others. The nun squealed.

"Here! Not the best! Good enough!" Dashwood tugged at Franklin's arm, and pulled him after the pack. "She's no shakes, sir!—but will do!"

They reached the back of the abbey and turned down a flight of worn stone stairs into a narrow hall beneath the dance floor. Ahead of him Franklin saw white robes gliding to the left and right. His head was spinning. He looked up into the glare of an oil lamp. By the time his eyes cleared, Dashwood had him before a narrow wooden door, knocked vigorously at it, and flung it open.

He pushed Franklin inside.

"Sister Jane!" Dashwood said boldly, backing out past Franklin with a low bow. The door slammed shut.

Franklin blinked.

He found himself looking into the large brown eyes of Sister Jane. She sat perched at the edge of a small bed, legs hanging down, with her blue robe pulled up about her knees. Beef to the heels. When she smiled he noticed a faint trace of blond hair on her upper lip.

Franklin tried to collect his thoughts, but the only thoughts he could collect were of Mrs. Stevenson. From down the hall he could hear the cries of the Brothers:

"—pretty pair!—"

"—have it *your* way!—"

"—all the same to me, my lady!—"

Franklin backed round to a straight chair set near the foot of the bed. Sister Jane had removed her mask and was not Mrs. Stevenson. He sat down heavily.

"Sister Jane?"

"*I* am Sister Jane."

"Yes."

The woman reached to blow out one of the candles that gave the small stone cell its only light.

"Madam!" Franklin said.

She tugged playfully on her hem, pulling the robe up by small fractions toward her hips.

"Madam, please! Franklin exclaimed. He raised his palm to her. "Affection can't be forced! Not upon a man of my years! Not after last night!"

He winked.

She smiled.

"You're a *he*-cat, are you? In the alley at night with Sally!"

There was a gap between her front teeth, although not so large as to bother anyone.

Franklin cleared his throat.

He ran a finger round inside his collar.

The hallway had grown very quiet. They looked at each other for a long time without speaking.

"Madam," Franklin said at last—and very softly. "Have you read any good books, or were you to any interesting places of late?"

The woman had read no books, good or bad. Or indifferent. In this Franklin's hopes were badly placed. She had, however, been to Cornwall of late. While that wasn't particularly interesting, she talked of it in particulars for more than half an hour.

Franklin listened with his eyes fallen closed. His feet were cold. He sat uncomfortably in the straight-backed chair—unable to think straight, unable to concentrate on any single thing for more than a moment. The sad fact was the woman even sounded like Mrs. Stevenson. Franklin tried counting backward from one thousand.

The sound of a faint cry from down the hall stopped him at eight hundred and eleven. Sister Jane was just about to relate the story of how her young nephew had lost his leg.

Franklin heard the banging of a door and then another shout—stronger than the first. There were footsteps in the hall and a light rap at the door to his own cell.

His eyes flew open.

He couldn't believe it—that some member of the Brotherhood was giving up the attentions of any other Medmenham nun to have a try at Sister Jane surpassed his comprehension. But his graciousness overcame his credulity.

"I yield," he said quickly. "Excuse me. Pardon me," he said politely. He stood up and backed for the door.

"—right above the knee, the surgeon says, so I says to my sister, do you think there's a chance, and she says—"

He unlatched the door and stepped into the hall.

He was not to be replaced after all. The doors to all the cells stood open, and the hall was crowded with Friars rushing down to the stairs at the end. He heard a whimpering sound— like a dog that had been stepped on—and Francis Dashwood's excited, half-strangled voice.

Churchill ran past him from behind, white robe flying and his head nearly grazing the ceiling as he loped by.

"Bloody dogs!" he snarled.

"Yes. What?"

There was no answer. The Bruiser had raced on.

Only Lord Sandwich—one eye a little larger than the other—swiveled his head round to look at Franklin when he reached the assembly of Friars at the end of the hall. He pushed his head in among the ring of bodies to see what the commotion was about.

The commotion was about Samuel Pennant.

The surly pornographer sat on the bottom stair. His black expression had given way to chalky whiteness. His dark hair was plastered back from his forehead with blood, and the forehead itself bore an ugly gash of about four inches. One eye was already swollen closed. The other stared blankly at the floor. His head trembled, and down the front of his white robe was a large, ill-shaped stain of blood.

"How many were there? Did you see him? Who was it? Did you—"

Dashwood and Old Paul Whitehead bent over the stricken man. Pennant's thick lips moved, but no words came out.

"What's happened here?"

Dashwood looked up to see Franklin peering at him, near to the Bruiser's elbow.

"It's Pennant—"

"I can see plainly enough."

"He's been beaten—"

"—near to murdered!"

"—bloody dogs!—"

Everyone started to babble at once. Franklin pushed himself into the center of the circle and stood up to his full height, which was not much. He looked over at Dieter Schiff, and was met by that gentleman's dark, glowing eyes and faint smile.

He repeated: "What has happened here?"

"—trying to tell you, sir!" Dashwood sputtered in his high, nervous voice. "Paul found him—"

Whitehead stood erect, wiping one bloody hand across his chest.

"Yes, sir. Heard him cry and went to his cell. He was on the floor—gone for a moment, sir—but he's come around—said he was jumped from behind—"

"He was alone?" Franklin asked.

"No, sir. The woman was there—"

"Where is she?"

"There still—"

Franklin bent over and looked into Samuel Pennant's good eye.

"Who did this, sir? Did you see him?"

Pennant trembled but did not answer.

"Strike me blind, sir, he may have earned it."

Everyone turned to Thomas Potter. Eyes bulging, he turned to everyone at once.

"What I mean is . . . I heard him say the Bruiser had an interest in Toplady's death. Sure to excite him. And I've heard Selwyn say—Schiff agrees—that Wilkes and the Bruiser were likely to have taken care of John Raleigh for a guinea—or less!—they hated his success with St. Francis . . . and what's more—"

Once started, Potter couldn't quit. His mouth flapped helplessly against his better judgment, which was not better at all. The Bruiser stiffened but held his place. The grinding of his teeth, however, warned everyone in the neighborhood of his intentions. It was Wilkes, however, who reached round one of the others in an effort to take Potter's lip from his face, and then suddenly there was a flurry of shoving and angry accusation.

"—more likely be in Hell!—"

"Kiss my cooler!"

"—husband of that sad whore—LaNeve!—"

"—jackanapes!"

The earnestness of the emotion sent fat Bubb Dodington gliding past Dashwood halfway up the stairs. His eyes, set so very low into his face, betrayed his fear. "Must go back to London—you'll understand—I'm sure—"

Bowing and scraping, he disappeared. George Selwyn slipped up after him, giving one last look at Samuel Pennant. "Hadn't planned to stay the night—"

Thomas Potter smiled weakly. He looked about. His mouth sucked for air. "Really am obliged to leave, sir—no hope for it—having more than my share of business—"

Dashwood cuffed him smartly alongside his ear, dropping him down two steps. Potter cringed and didn't move.

"I'll have the Bruiser on you in a moment—and see if any bones are left!" Dashwood cried. "I'm no fool! Frightened to death of your own shadows! Reserve all your bravery for the bed?"

He turned angrily from face to face—Schiff's smile was gone—and was answered with silence.

"There's nothing to it! We'll go on to West Wycombe!— Now! how's that?—and tomorrow celebrate the Mass on the Iron Woman! You'll like that, boys! Penny fell out of bed, is all—he'll do all right. Get us a dressing, Paul—eh, Penny?—this place is cold—we'll take the ladies—eh?"

Franklin edged close by to the Bruiser, whose teeth thankfully had ceased to grind, and peered up over the rims of his spectacles. "The Iron Woman?"

The Bruiser bent down, cracking a rough grin. "Quite a lady. Made of iron. A statue, sir, and fine for taking Mass from. But we'll have something soft atop, I'll say—that redhead if I have my way—"

Ten minutes later Dashwood was still haranguing the Hellfire Club. "—must all hang together or we must all hang separately!" he was saying. Franklin's lips puckered. He liked the expression.

"I should like to go."

Dashwood turned this way and that.

"Eh?"

"I should like to go," Franklin said. "Do you serve Mass from the Iron Woman? *I* will do it. The company's good and the women far better—I'm for it, sir—the used key is always bright—"

"Now! how's that!" Dashwood cried.

"If Dr. Franklin is not afraid of his shadow, I am neither," Dieter Schiff answered.

"Jolly dog!" Wilkes cried.

Sandwich cackled.

There was general agreement where a moment before had been blind mistrust. Once again there was a tight half-smile on Dieter Schiff's face.

Whitehead wrapped a dressing around Pennant's head and helped the clumsy pornographer up the steps to the chapel. Dashwood directed the closing of the cells, flushing the nuns out into the hall and driving them up toward the common room as though he were a boy with a switch after the cows. In this way Strahan was discovered still in his cell and still dancing, after a fashion. "Riding hard! Halfway to Aylesbury!" Dashwood cried out in a laugh that rang off the stone walls as he slammed shut the door. "He'll be there before us! Do as you please, William Strahan!"

Franklin sighed. He found a seat in a small alcove in the

upstairs hall and contemplated the naked woman of marble who stood opposite him in another alcove. Twice Dashwood ran by, directing the departure.

" 'Do as you please'! *There's* a fine philosophy, is it not! We'll survive this nasty affair—"

And was gone before Franklin could agree. Or disagree.

It was a half hour before the bells rang announcing the carriages ready for the journey to Dashwood's estate at West Wycombe. When Franklin answered the bell and wandered outside, he found Strahan fully dressed and standing alone behind the building in the late afternoon sun, warming his back.

"They call it here—the Temple of Cloacina!" Strahan said brightly.

"How's that?"

"Cloacina—goddess of the sewers, sir!"

"Hmmm."

Franklin saw that the two yellow wicker baskets had been lashed securely atop Dashwood's shiny black carriage. He climbed inside, seated himself, and peered silently through the round window. From one nearby carriage he saw a familiar face brooding back at him, set with dark eyes and a faint smile. Strahan ran from one carriage to another, poking his head in and drawing it out, until he'd worked his way back again to Dashwood's coach. He clambered aboard and plopped on the hard seat across from Franklin.

"Meg's in with the whores."

"And deserves to be. You're in the spirit of the thing, Strahan."

At length Dashwood himself appeared at the door of the abbey. He walked halfway across the yard, turned round to look once again at the gray stone walls of the building, and came straight over to the carriage. He pushed through to sit beside Franklin, pulling the door very gently shut behind himself.

West Wycombe was only six miles distant, yet it took them near to an hour just to reach the Oxford Road—so bad was the road that carried them. Each man bumped along to his own thoughts.

Darkness was coming.

When they had finally turned onto the Oxford Road and were making more merry time, Strahan had a thought.

"Ben."

"Hmm?"

Strahan leaned forward to catch Franklin's ear, regardless of manners.

"What have you learned?" he whispered.

They traveled on so long that Strahan had nearly forgotten the question when Franklin finally gave a little shake of his head and delivered himself of an answer.

"I've learned a great deal about Cornwall."

The several carriages became unstrung in the Oxford Road as more or less urgency pushed them forward into the settling sun. The tower and golden globe of St. Lawrence Church appeared above the trees long before they reached West Wycombe village. By then, Dashwood's carriage rode alone.

They turned into High Street and clattered through the quiet village, trailing their thoughts. They passed the White Heart and the Unicorn, came by a neat row of low brick houses with sash windows and hipped roofs, crossed the foot of Church Lane and swept past three or four more sleeping taverns. The driver slowed to turn into the narrow lane leading round to Dashwood's country seat. Stately elms lined the road. The leaves danced in the changing golden light. At last they came into a view of West Wycombe House itself, sitting out across spacious lawns.

An old man—small and dark, and dressed stiffly in servants clothes—stood to meet them in the yard. No sooner did the carriage stop than Dashwood came suddenly alive. He burst past Franklin and Strahan, threw open the door, and leaped to the ground with a great laugh.

"Mr. Cotter! Home again! And glad of it! I missed you, sir!" He threw his arm around old Jeremy Cotter, master of the servants at West Wycombe House, and turned him warmly about to face the interior of the carriage. "I bounced on his knee—and a finer man you'll never find! Here's Dr. Franklin! William Strahan! A grand man, sir—more than a father! A religious man, and the god he worships is order—everything in its place, is that right, Mr. Cotter!"

Dashwood's face was illuminated with emotion. "Home again, sir!" he cried, waving his arm about.

"Yes, sir. Your people have taken the Great Hall."

"Indeed! See that they're fed—they're hungry beasts—"

"They'll be fed, sir. The rooms are being prepared now. Everything is in order."

"Proves me right!" Dashwood said gleefully. "Here! Strahan! Come down! Do as you please, Strahan—I'm stealing Dr. Franklin. There's light enough—"

Strahan looked appealingly at Franklin's face.

"Go, sir!" Dashwood commanded. "Wine's in the Great Hall and some fine tumblers—"

He snapped around like a young athlete and led Franklin toward a path that climbed the wooded hill behind the house. In a few moments they were halfway up and turned out at a small clearing through the trees.

"Home again!" Dashwood sighed, taking quick breaths. "Born here! Grown here! And to Hell with all of London, sir!"

Franklin barely attended to the happiness of Francis Dashwood behind him. He stepped close to the edge of the clearing and peered out upon the peaceful Buckinghamshire countryside.

The sun was down.

A silver, gloomy light covered the scene before him, transfixing it with a sense of tranquillity and quietude. Below him lay Dashwood's estate. A small stream ran through it, catching the last light from the sky. The plantings of trees and shrubbery that made up the gardens were laid out in the shape of women, showing both their public and their private parts. Fountains gushed from their bushy breasts. As in most things, God's view was the most scandalous.

Lights blazed in the windows of the distant house, but the color of the ground had come to nearly match the color of the fading sky—creating a neat balance between earth and heaven, an illusion of order.

Franklin knew there was none.

He would soon find himself back in West Wycombe House, in the Great Hall that roared with lamps and the laughter of loose women. Mr. Cotter might keep the house in order. But the careless heart of the Hellfire Club would continue to beat with equal disdain for affection or death.

Sixteen

The dream was the same: doors opening and closing, women laughing, muffled voices, a piercing cry, smoke and red velvet. A man in a scarlet coat sweeping into an extravagant bow, with a look of fear in his eyes. "Dr. Fatsides!"

Franklin's eyes popped open.

It was morning. Bright sunlight poured through the open window. The house seemed strangely quiet. No birds sang.

"Strahan!" Franklin hissed.

He peered over the coverlet to the other side of the small room and the lump that was William Strahan.

"Mmmmmnh," Strahan said nicely.

"Strahan—it's very late!"

The lump stirred, and sat halfway up. Strahan's red cap made him look like a fanciful character in a fairy tale, but he threw back the covers and swung out his feet. They reached the floor, proving him real enough.

He looked sleepily across at Dr. Franklin, who remained covered to his chin.

"I believe—you slept with your spectacles on—sir—"

"No. I just now put them on, Strahan. I've been thinking."

Strahan launched himself to his feet and wobbled to the window. His red cap made a fine contrast after all with his long green gown. He blinked out into the sunlight.

"Late," he said.

"So I say—dangerously late—I want you to write to my wife—"

"Yes—you think of your wife at a time like this? Write to your wife, indeed—"

"I've been thinking—"

"It's early."

"No, sir. It's very late. I want you to go down and bring Thomas Potter up to me. I've a question for him."

Strahan sighed, just loudly enough to let Franklin know he was not a manservant. But he dressed himself quickly and left the room.

Franklin immediately threw back the covers of his own bed, showing how firmly he held to the philosophy of sleeping without clothes. He'd not been able to convince Strahan of its utility. He took a brief turn about the room—it passed for his air bath—and dressed himself. His thoughts went every which way at once and would not be reined.

"Potter," he muttered to himself. "Biscuits. Breakfast. The Iron Woman—"

He'd just moved a sitting-chair to the window when Strahan burst back into the room without bothering to rap.

"You say it's *late*?—you believe it's *late*?—"

Strahan's face was red, but not from the stairs.

"—Potter's not here, sir! Nor is Churchill! Nor Sandwich! None of them is here—"

"Not here?"

"Not here! You'd better come down the stairs directly, sir—there's been—"

Franklin was on his feet.

He followed Strahan out the door into the long hallway of the second floor, turned the staircase, and once down crossed quickly through the Great Hall, which was empty and sadly silent. They entered the Blue Drawing Room.

Over against the far corner Francis Dashwood and Old Paul Whitehead were seated side by side in separate chairs. The draperies had not yet been drawn open on the high windows. The room was nearly dark and quiet as a crypt.

Dashwood sighed absently when he saw Franklin. "Good morning, sir—I'm left with Old Paul—that's true enough—"

Whitehead's hand moved.

"Dieter Schiff's dead, sir."

Franklin stopped midway into the room. He looked from Whitehead to Dashwood to Strahan and back again.

"Wait!" he said, repeating to himself: "Dieter—Schiff—is—dead. Do you mean Dieter Schiff? Dead?"

"Strangled, sir. And beaten," Whitehead responded. "Potter found him in the ravine this morning behind the Iron Woman—"

"The Iron Woman," Franklin repeated. "Not possible—you say strangled?"

Whitehead didn't answer.

"News hurried everybody off," Dashwood said. "Couldn't hold them—no help for it. Yes—left here with Old Paul. You've come down after the fact, sir—it's quite undone. I don't wish to see you—"

He turned his face away from Franklin. His hands lifted

about an inch off the arms of the chair and wavered there a moment before collapsing back.

"Not possible—"

Franklin was already on his way out the door, Strahan at his heels. By the time they reached the portico stairs at the front of the house, Whitehead was caught up with them.

"—neck was broken, I'm sure of it, sir! We answered Potter's alarm and found him at the bottom of the ravine. We suppose the man who did it—we suppose he came out of the woods. Francis himself's broken, you can see—his spirit's crushed!—"

"No time for diplomacy!" Franklin snapped. "I must have Thomas Potter—"

Whitehead huffed to keep up.

"He's gone with the others, I'm sure of it—to London—left apart but all together! The Club's undone. They accuse each other like strangers—"

"I must have Pennant. What of Samuel Pennant?"

"Gone, too, sir! They've all flown—"

"Impossible! Is Schiff there yet?"

"Removed up to St. Lawrence, I'm afraid—"

Whitehead's eyes lifted to the hill in the distance, where the steeple and golden ball of St. Lawrence Church rose into the blue morning sky.

But the three men had come far enough around so that Franklin's were on the Iron Woman.

It was the first time he'd seen it, save for the previous evening when he stood halfway up the hill and had barely been able to make out her shape below in the growing darkness. She was aptly named on two counts: she was made of iron and she was a woman. A dark reclining figure about ten feet in length, lying on her back, amply bosomed, and with arms and legs fixed in a receptive posture. It was obvious how easily a Medmenham nun would lie atop the sculpture with her head nestled between the hard metallic breasts of the Iron Woman, the nun herself stripped bare and service enough for any Mass.

The sculpture lay balanced on two long wooden planks, not yet cemented to the massive pink base of marble beneath her. Franklin ran his fingers reflectively along the Woman's dark hip: it was rough and pitted. She had the pox of her element. He ran his fingers along one of the long boards on which she lightly rested; it was smooth to the touch, and waxy. His fingers trailed the marble base: icy cold, despite the warming sun.

He moved round to the head of the statue and placed his hand beneath the Woman's rough neck. He pushed upward. She lifted easily. She was untenanted within, merely a shell, a hollow woman without a heart.

"Empty," Franklin said.

His mouth was turned down at the corners.

The Iron Woman lay close by the house, perhaps twenty feet from the end of the right wing of the building. But behind her, only two long strides away, the ground began to slope sharply downward until it gave way to a small ravine six or seven feet in depth. Beyond it lay the woods.

Franklin stood precariously on the lip of the ditch and peered down into it. He saw a scattering of dead and curling leaves, a tangle of bare tree roots, and William Strahan.

Franklin disappeared into the ditch, a fair exercise for so early in the day.

"—lay here, sir," Whitehead said, coming down, "and we thought at first he'd fallen by accident—his neck was broken, I'm sure of it—and his face—he was beaten very forcibly, sir —quite scuffed—here!—some small blood on these leaves— fallen—but I think strangled as well, for around his neck we found—"

Franklin had already seen it.

He was bent over. His forefinger and thumb worked one end of a drawn copper wire.

"—told them to leave it—that's it!—so that nothing would be disturbed," Whitehead explained. "Wrapped once about his neck—garroted—Spanish style—or French—"

Franklin sighed.

"Where does it end!" Strahan exclaimed. He'd followed the nearly invisible wire about ten feet down the trough of leaves and stood tugging gently at it where it ran up over the edge of the ravine.

"Strahan, I would like to be removed from this ditch." Franklin's eyes were fixed on the blue sky and branches above.

Momentarily, with Strahan's shoulder beneath him, he was hoisted over.

"But it's the French manner that makes me think he's strangled," Whitehead said, scrambling up by himself.

Strahan had already run over to where the wire lay carelessly on the lip of the ravine and traced it back to its other end, near to the house.

"On the other hand," Whitehead said cautiously, brushing his legs, "perhaps—but the wire is very long, isn't it, and why someone would—"

"A measure of his haste," Franklin said coldly.

His eyes were fixed on the elm branches that overspread the lawn from across the ravine, reaching nearly to the house. Three or four pale brown ribbons fluttered from the high limbs.

"And what are those, sir?"

Whitehead squinted up at them.

"There you'll have me, sir! Perhaps Mr. Cotter put them out to frighten off the birds, or—"

"A measure of his ingenuity," Franklin said.

He looked hard at the house and turned about to face Whitehead. His small mouth was tight, his dark eyes without their customary sparkle.

"What hour was this discovered?"

"Eight-thirty o'clock, I believe—"

"By Thomas Potter?"

"Yes—he was out walking—gave the alarm—"

"Was no one else about?"

"Up early? No one . . . after last night?"

"Then what was Potter doing out?"

Whitehead looked away.

"Well, sir—I believe it's his habit. . . . Selwyn said Potty was out early to murder. I don't credit it. He gave the alarm—it caused a general disturbance, sir, that's true. They were at each other and off like crows for London—"

"I see," Franklin said. "The alarm was answered quickly, or was there—"

"*I* heard it at once—there were several others came running—" Whitehead drew a sharp breath. "The truth is—one can't say who was up or down—in or out—the nuns were here, and some were two on one, or three on one—"

"Indeed," Franklin said, gazing up at the building. "I'm anxious to know who of the Brotherhood occupied the corner room—there—on the upper floor near to the end of the hall. I passed it last night but heard no one in it."

Whitehead thought for a moment. "No one occupied that room, sir . . . to my recollection . . . that's right!—they were all in the far wing, some downstairs."

Franklin's eyes fell closed, and he seemed to shrink within himself. When he finally opened them, they seemed worn down with weariness.

"No doubt Mr. Dashwood keeps electric apparatus here as he does in London," he said softly.

"Yes, sir! In his study. Shall we see it?"

Franklin nodded. Whitehead led them round the colonnade and up the front steps of West Wycombe House. They went direct to the second story and the two rooms Franklin desired to view. The small sleeping room at the end of the hall was without a single furnishing worthy of remark. The room was drafty and little used. The door and window were closed. Everything was in its place. Dashwood's study lay down at the other end of the hall. It was larger and less disordered than the study in Pall Mall, but as mute as the sleeping room. A Kleist generator of great expense sat in one corner, covered with a dustcloth. A long bench of ash wood held a few chemical bottles and a great many smoking-pipes. Dashwood's desk was piled with papers. A collection of Leyden jars sat neatly on a rolling table in eighteen trim rows of ten, and two rows of six. Franklin asked to be taken back to the sleeping room. There he stood looking at the floor. It was neat as a pin.

He shook his head.

"Impossible."

Half an hour later Whitehead had conveyed Franklin and Strahan into the village and up the hill to St. Lawrence Church. There they found the body of Dieter Schiff sprawled on a walnut bier at the head of the nave, as though he'd been dropped from Heaven. Dashwood had sent for two surgeons, but from London, and they had not yet come.

Franklin gave the body every attention. The right side of the dead man's face was dirty and abraded—he had indeed been scuffed about. His neck indeed was broken. It held his head at an awkward angle. But death had already tugged his pale lips into a malicious smile.

Strahan looked helplessly at Franklin.

"You'll never find the man who did it—"

"No, sir," Franklin said vacantly. "The problem is not to find him. It's to find him out."

Seventeen

S trahan and Franklin were returned to London late that
morning by one of the West Wycombe carriages, without having seen Francis Dashwood. Whitehead offered
to take them back to the house, but Franklin refused. There
was nothing to say. It was a Tuesday. Franklin went directly
to his rooms in Craven Street and stayed there the remainder
of the day.

He emerged from his room the next morning to eat one
biscuit and sip half a cup of tea. For a time he prowled about
the house from one end to the other, hands thrown behind his
back, chin resting on his chest, deep in thought. He spoke to
no one, despite the most pleasant inquiries about his health
and the weather. He refused dinner.

Later in the day he went upstairs and appropriated the
parlor, playing away several hours with his musical boxes.
They made the same odd, disharmonious noises as they had
when William Strahan sat there listening to Dr. Franklin
expound on the simplicities of murder. Mrs. Stevenson came
into the room once or twice, hoping for conversation. In this

she was disappointed. Franklin said nothing. He stared at her coldly, as though she were not there. On the third time, she stood in the doorway with her hands on her hips and stared back. "It *is* my house, sir," she said as she departed.

She returned at suppertime with a plate of breaded fish and a mess of beans. Franklin was seated before the parlor window, gazing absently out into the empty street. His lips moved, but he did not speak. The musical boxes were scattered about the floor behind him. They were silent as his thoughts.

When Mrs. Stevenson returned an hour later to collect the dishes, Franklin was gone. His supper had not been touched.

He remained entirely in his room on Thursday morning, with the door closed tightly against intrusion. He would not eat. He would not speak, even when Mrs. Stevenson burned the lamb and the odor filled the house. Peter was banished to the kitchen. The circle of Franklin's acquaintance was steadily growing smaller.

Mrs. Stevenson wiped her hands over and over on her apron, and began to worry for him.

That forenoon, however, he was brought out of exile by the occasion of a visitor who appeared unexpectedly at the front door of the house in Craven Street. Valetta LaNeve was dressed in a pink-colored capuchin edged with ermine and earned an irritated welcome from Mrs. Stevenson—whose suspicions sometimes outran her good sense. Nevertheless, the landlady showed the visitor to the second-floor parlor, seated her, and went up to tell Dr. Franklin.

He closed the parlor doors forcefully behind him when he went into the room, leaving Mrs. Stevenson with one ear pressed tightly against them. But she heard nothing to reward her suspicions.

"—paid me another flying visit, good sir. He declared that the wrongs which were done him were now righted—did not say how—and said he was going off to America. You may find him there. Good riddance. He had nothing else to declare, in one manner or the other. He began to speak of his father, but could not—his voice was full of tears. Let him go! I thought you would wish to know of this, and so I came—"

Franklin himself escorted the woman down the stairs and showed her from the house. Mrs. Stevenson had slipped down to the kitchen to fix tea, thinking it her obligation. But Franklin returned straightaway to his room without tea or sympathy. The intelligence carried to him by Valetta LaNeve was not calculated to elevate his spirits.

Franklin left the sanctuary of his room only once more on that day. Mrs. Stevenson found him alone in the parlor near to evening. The lamps had not been lighted. The room was nearly dark. Franklin sat in his chair at the window. On his right knee he had spread out a sheet of paper which had been folded three times, and often unfolded. It contained a list of nine words, and at the bottom:

Emotional Women Laugh!

But he did not look at it. His attention was fixed on the gathering night. He seemed the model of repose.

Yet so fierce were the wars that raged within him, a small red boil had appeared on his chin.

The next morning Franklin appeared in the downstairs hallway dressed for the street. He wore a narrow-brimmed hat that Mrs. Stevenson hadn't seen before. He tottered weakly on his walking stick, and had forgotten his spectacles.

"I'm going to be bled," he announced sourly.

"You are *not*, sir!" Mrs. Stevenson corrected him abruptly, happy at last to have been spoken to. "If you'd only consent to eat, this black humor would pass off of itself, sir. Such low spirits are unlike you. If you'll allow me to bring—"

"I am *not*, sir," Franklin replied with resignation. He was hot. He turned abruptly about and disappeared up the stairs to his room.

Not long thereafter, Mrs. Stevenson sent her daughter up the stairs with a breakfast of chicken soup and chocolate. The landlady's good sense sometimes outran her suspicions. Polly found Franklin seated in his chair at the back window, looking out over the courtyard below. He would not speak, nor even turn to see her. When she returned for the bowl, the soup remained in it. Cold. The chocolate was untouched.

Polly tried to be gay. She chirped of the weather. She told him of the man who had been killed for his purse at the end of Craven Street. She confessed how very much she missed him, and asked whether he'd return. She kissed him lightly on the cheek, as in earlier days.

But he remained in his chair, and neither moved nor spoke.

That settled things for Polly's mother. She sent for William Strahan.

"Had no *idea*!" Strahan said cheerfully as he entered the house, less than an hour after being called away from his shop. He pattted the landlady on her hip on the way upstairs. "Nothing to worry!" he said. He returned a few minutes later with Dr. Franklin shuffling along behind in his blue hat.

At the door, Franklin turned to Mrs. Stevenson.

"I am going to be *bled*."

In the taverns and coffeehouses of London, one could find many things. Lords and ladies, to be sure, wastrels and scriveners and mountebanks; gamblers and authors, which are the same after all, both riding the stallions of chance until they're thrown; students and smiths and merchants, all complaining of bad business. There was more. At Adam's, a fly-cap monkey in a cage and a piece of the True Cross. At the sign of the Blue Gate, teeth that grew in a fish's belly. Behind the glass boxes at Garaway's, Job's ears, Wat Tyler's spurs, the original keys to the Garden of Eden, the white skeleton of a guinea pig. At the Round Wife, a bullfinch that flew free and sang a pretty tune.

But these were mild curiosities compared to the attractions of the haunts to which Strahan led Dr. Franklin. His notion was to relieve the latter's mind of its dark and strenuous thoughts. What better way than to see the poor Porcupine Man and His Son, all covered with ugly quills? Or the Man without Hands carrying his tea between his great and second toes?

Strahan led Franklin on a tour of the freaks of London.

"We'll not talk of Francis Dashwood or his Brotherhood—not even of pretty Meg, sure enough!" he exclaimed heartily. "Why dwell on failure? We're only human, sir, so leave it off. Think instead on this—"

They were at the George Inn, in Fenchurch Street, and Strahan pointed up to the Slav who sat on a wooden box and dangled his monstrous knobbly legs over the side. He was the Man with the World's Largest Feet.

Franklin said nothing.

At Clifford's Inn, even Strahan stood mute before the fine collection of Nature's Mistakes: Elephant-Nose Boy, Frog Boy, Cyclops, the Worm. At Burhop's, where drapers usually gathered, they each paid a penny to view a three-legged girl and a gigantic man so nearly smothered by rolls of fat that he was said to weigh a thousand pounds. At the Cupper, the Corsican Fairy balanced delicately on his master's knee.

Franklin blinked.

He sighed.

In a small tavern near to Newgate, he ate two biscuits and drank half a cup of ale. A dark-skinned man across the room from him ate melted pitch from a spoon, and suffered burning coals and water to be placed within his mouth.

"That's it! Drink it up!" Strahan said. "We'll catch Cholmondeley next—the Human Centaur—he's very wonderful!" He wolfed his mutton and wiped a greasy hand on the side of his coat.

But their path did not lay direct to Mr. Cholmondeley.

It took them to the Heath Cock, where they watched the Crab Man—an unfortunate legless sailor—scurry about the floor on his hands. And to the Buffalo Head, where the Lizard Lady sat safely behind gauze curtains with her scaly limbs exposed. And to Tudway's, where the Ethiopian Savage and the Wonderful Giant wrestled at opposite ends of a long bar of iron, which they twisted in their hands.

Franklin finished his halibut and asked for another plate—his third.

"A wonderful amount of credulity in the world, Strahan—haven't I said?" He wiped his mouth carefully with the side of the tablecloth and reached for his ale.

"Drink your ale—that's it!" Strahan said.

They'd worked their way round to near Charing Cross once again—past two plates of beef each, with a mess of carrots and onions, three chops, a bacon slab, cherry tarts well iced, and a pinhead who had no need of hair, in the shop of John Simes, perukier—when Franklin suddenly stopped in the street.

"We're all of us dwarfs or giants, are we not?"

He waved to Strahan's great bulk, and his own.

"In this form—stuffed with philosophy—we're but illusions. The mistakes of nature lie within us—"

He spun his walking stick erect into the air.

"I agree! More ale will do it!" Strahan exclaimed happily. "The Salt Box lies round the corner, and—"

"No," Franklin answered. "*There* is Chevenix."

He pointed his stick across the street to the toyshop of

Chevenix. Several gentlemen stood idly on the walk out front, gazing at the color posters by which Chevenix advertised the oddity of Mr. Cholmondeley, the Human Centaur.

Strahan hopped to keep up with Franklin as he crossed the street. They paid a shilling each at the door, were directed down a long center aisle to the rear of the shop (where a dozen or more marionettes hung by their strings from hooks, startled faces watching all who passed), and exited into an open, high-walled courtyard. There a number of spectators—most of them women—had already gathered.

A golden rope kept the small crowd back from Mr. Cholmondeley.

He was thin and raw-boned, and wore a black peruke that accentuated the dark pits on his face. His dingy frock came down over his forelocks, which gave way beneath the fringe of his coat to a semblance of horse's legs. The entire remainder of his body—back to his flowing black tail—was indisputably that of a bay horse.

As Franklin and Strahan entered the yard, Mr. Cholmondeley looked over at them and carelessly dunged. This drew a slight reaction from the ladies, who were not used to it, but Mr. Cholmondeley noticed it not at all. With one hand he stuffed fresh grass into his mouth, and from a golden cup held in the other he washed it down with French wine.

For about ten minutes a dark young man gave Cholmondeley's history, one hand resting lightly on the creature's flank and being careful all the while of his feet. He looked enough like the Centaur to be his brother—if that were possible. The story was even more wonderful than the newspaper made it out to be. Cholmondeley had been foaled in the Alps, where he was captured, and brought out in the possession of a Dutch nobleman who tried unsuccessfully to enter him in army service as a cavalry. The nobleman sold him to an itinerant Frenchman and he was taken all over

Europe, being unfairly taxed now as a horse and again as a human. In France a match had been made for him with a lady of high spirits and low character. The issue, nine months later, was of a blue-eyed baby boy, proving—so the exhibitor declared—the superiority and preponderance of humankind over the animal creation. And on and on.

Halfway through this curious account, which grew more and more curious, Strahan turned to Franklin in befuddlement.

"A stuffed horse, no doubt," Strahan whispered.

"No doubt, sir."

"But—then how does he dung?" Strahan's eyes were round and wide.

"Indeed."

The exhibitor closed his history with an invitation to the ladies present to register for a ride upon Mr. Cholmondeley's back in the city streets or for a private audience with the Centaur, notwithstanding the newspapers had reported his conversation to be generally lewd and indecent. Several ladies stepped forward to do so.

But Strahan and Franklin turned about and proceeded back into the toyshop. They exited to the street, shaking their heads with worldly wisdom.

"We'll have to eat—" Strahan said as he crossed over toward the Mews Wall. "You've not had enough to keep a centaur alive, much less an American—not of your stature, sir! We can go down to the Golden Cross, I'm sure, or cut through to St. Martin's Lane and go up to Slaughter's if you wish, where the beef is very fine, or we can—are you tired yet? I hope not!—we can go to a place onto King Street where the lamb is said to be better—"

Strahan babbled on. Hunger had narrowed his vision. He was nearly to the Mews Gate when he suddenly realized that Dr. Franklin was no longer at his side.

Nor behind him.

Strahan looked back across the street. Between the shoulders of the gentlemen who stood so avidly reading the posters that advertised the Human Centaur, and debating whether to go in, he spotted the blue hat and coat of Dr. Franklin.

He hurried across, pushed past a silken gentleman, and peered round at Franklin's face. It was lighted with something like joy.

"What does it *say*, Strahan? What does it *say!*" Franklin asked excitedly.

Strahan looked at the poster. He nodded knowingly, and answered with equal excitement: "The Human Centaur!"

Franklin sighed.

"Above that."

"Oh! *Above* that?" Strahan looked at the poster again. "Cholmondeley, sir! John Cholmondeley!" he answered, even more excited than before. He pronounced the word "Chumley," as it was meant to be said.

"Precisely!"

Strahan looked curiously at Franklin.

"Precisely *what*? If I may ask—"

"That's precisely what it *says!* And not at all what it seems to say!"

Franklin pursed his lips. A small whistle escaped him. He rocked back on his heels.

"Willie," he said with a satisfied air. "This affair has been like a string confounded with false knots. One tug at either end—and the string is straight! There'll be no more murders in the Hellfire Club!"

One of the gentlemen turned to him.

"The Hellfire Club, you say?—"

But Franklin's hand was already in his pocket. His face was a mask of benign contentment.

Eighteen

William Strahan was always flattered when Franklin called him Willie. It meant that Franklin was pleased with him. It recollected times past, when both men moved in more modest circumstances unencumbered by the baggage of reputation. In this instance it made him answer all the more easily when Franklin laid two final tasks upon him. One was to find Francis Dashwood, trying Pall Mall, and arrange for a meeting of the Hellfire Club at the earliest chance. The other was reserved for whispers.

Strahan sniffed the air like a hound at the hunt, although without the finer instincts such as are only bred through generations. He had to be instructed, after all. But having been so, he broke from the gate with eagerness and enthusiasm. He yelped inside—and left Franklin to make his way home from Chevenix alone.

Franklin dallied down to Charing Cross and its crowds. After so much close thought, he felt the need for close company. At the Strand, where the sign of a golden cross stood high above the street, he entered for an ale. He was buffeted about by sailors and travelers, but didn't mind. When he reached into his pocket for his purse, his short fingers moved delicately along the edges of the paper Eugene Toplady had left in Dashwood's study. He turned about with a faint smile—and half his ale was knocked onto the front of his shirt by someone else's elbow. Even this he didn't mind. When the deep voices of the sailors sent the words of a sea chant rolling over the heads of the crowd, Franklin hummed happily along. He ordered another ale. He minded nothing.

A warm feeling overcame him, not like contentment at all. There was something tremulous within him—something large and deep. He was glad of life.

He wandered up the Strand. He examined the new map of Pennsylvania in the window of Thomas Jeffery's printshop. He saw that Deard's toyshop was still closed against him. By the time he entered down into Craven Street, darkness was falling. He walked slowly, past the house at No. 7, and on down to the timberyard at the foot of the street. The steps led down to the Thames.

For a long time he stood on the bottom step with his back to the street, near to the water. A few gondolas and barges drifted by, already lighted against the night with small twinkling lanterns. Franklin's thoughts followed the river—down to the sea, out across the rolling ocean, home to America.

"There's a dangerous place, sir, where you stand—"

It startled him, notwithstanding it was a soft, sweet, feminine voice. He turned quickly about to the shining face of Polly Stevenson, who stood close behind him. Her sparkling eyes gave way proof of her gaiety. She stretched herself up to give Franklin a soft, perfumed peck on the cheek.

"You're not going to throw yourself in—"

Franklin threw back his head and laughed. It startled her.

He spent the evening at backgammon, losing two games and winning one. He ate heartily of the supper that had been saved for him. His stomach growled. Everyone was glad of his being broken out of his black humor, and for the occasion Mrs. Stevenson lighted every lamp in the house. They were not extinguished until very late, and even then one particular lamp on the third story burned brighter and much longer than the rest. It was Polly's.

The following day Strahan's manservant came by at an early hour to announce that the gentlemen in question would assemble together one last time—at the Vulture Tavern that evening for supper. Mr. Strahan himself was attending to the remainder of Franklin's instructions and hoped to return by the hour that had been set.

This news Dr. Franklin received from Mrs. Stevenson when he descended the stairs for breakfast at noon. Polly was still in her room, earning the complaints of her mother—her tardiness at chores, her lassitude in the mornings, her endless infatuations. "Madam! Don't burn my house to roast your eggs!" Franklin declared, reaching for the newspaper. But the meaning escaped her.

The day could not pass quickly enough. As the supper hour approached, it passed too quickly. He stood alone in the parlor, looking down upon a street that was both empty and silent. He paced in small circles and rehearsed his thoughts. He stationed himself at the window once again. He was dressed. He was ready. But the hound had not come home from the hunt.

At last he went downstairs and pulled Peter away from his supper. In a few moments Franklin's carriage stood out front. He entered impatiently, and Peter was not slow to catch his mood. He turned the coach about in the narrow street so abruptly that it struck a curb and Franklin was thrown from the right side of the seat to the left, as though he were a full sack of coffee beans.

"Faster," he said.

The Strand flew by at miraculous speed. Temple Bar swept over the coach like the shadow of a hawk diving down for the kill. When Peter eventually drew into King Street and jarred to a halt in front of the Vulture Tavern, Franklin's heart was beating hard. Not from the ride, but from the thought that Strahan had failed.

He stepped gingerly from the carriage, waved Peter on his way, and entered the Vulture. There he was immediately embraced by Mr. Henley, keeper of the place.

"Frinkman!—Frankman!—is that it?—thank God!—you've brought 'em back, sir!—and to think I'd never see 'em again—" He tugged at Franklin's sleeve and pulled him over toward the closed door of the gaming room, past a sea of astonished faces. "God! Thank God!" Henley sputtered in gratitude, having put two and two together and knowing it made good business. He opened the door and urged Franklin inside.

Ten faces turned toward him as the door clicked shut.

The room was silent. It had an uneasy, awkward air. Wilkes and Churchill sat together off in one corner drinking sullen wine. The others were scattered about the edges of the room—well off from a large dining table and well away from one another. Even Bubb Dodington sat alone from George Selwyn, who looked hurt by the distance between them. Paul Whitehead stood alone. Dashwood balanced back in his chair against the far wall and fixed Franklin with thin eyes. Sandwich sat with his legs folded and arms crossed; one foot swung to music he alone could hear. William Reeve was nearly hidden beneath an outlandish pink hat whose brim extended near to his shoulders. Scowling Samuel Pennant sat in an opposite corner, his eyes darting about from one untrusting face to another. Thomas Potter looked at no one.

The table was littered with the scraps of supper, which had already been eaten. Franklin surveyed it.

"You could not wait?"

"Damned busy!—"

"—jackanapes!"

"—soon to go!—"

"What have you got—"

Franklin sighed.

"Not even Holy Ghost Pye, I see."

He moved round to the head of the table, pulled out a chair, and sat in it. He sighed again, and folded his hands carefully before him.

"My pleasure also is to be elsewhere," he said quietly. "I find it hard to suffer fools—"

"Who's he to say—"

"Shut up!"

Franklin lifted his head and seemed to address the red eyes of the vulture that swung silently from the ceiling above him.

"—but I am here to announce the solution to the crime of murder in the Hellfire Club. You may listen or not, as you wish."

He addressed his folded hands.

"Some time since, Mr. Dashwood invited me to examine a piece of poor poetry received at his door. It threatened death to the members of the Hellfire Club—to each of you in turn, and to Mr. Dashwood himself in his appropriate turn. It exercised him. By itself it signified nothing. In combination with the death of John Raleigh it signified a great deal more than nothing. It exercised *me*. From what Mr. Dashwood told me—"

Franklin stopped to watch the Bruiser separate himself from the wall and come over to the table near the opposite end, taking a seat.

He addressed the Bruiser.

"—from what Mr. Dashwood told me of Raleigh's affairs, half of London had cause to see him dead. Yet half of London did not kill him. John Raleigh was murdered by the electrical fluid—the easiest of all deaths. The method was both deceptively simple and inherently—"

Franklin stopped again. Thomas Potter and Francis Dashwood had left their seats at the wall and come up to the table, joining Churchill. Franklin fixed his eyes on Dashwood.

"—and inherently dangerous, yet obvious to me at once. You, sir, know something of the electrical fluid. Its effects are immediate. They're not to be revoked."

Franklin turned his gaze toward Thomas Potter.

"When Mr. Dashwood brought me to this place with my friend William Strahan, the day John Raleigh was murdered, I found all the necessaries required—"

"I didn't bring William Strahan—he was already here—"

Franklin brushed Dashwood away.

"You are right, sir—pay attention to particularities. I found all the necessaries required to account not only for Raleigh's death but the manner of it. I reiterate my thoughts. The room in which Raleigh died was locked from the inside—a fact that is only curious. It mattered as little as your manners, which are poor enough, or your allegiance. Raleigh himself threw the bolt after he entered the room. A reasonable man can't think otherwise. As for his business in the room—I'm not prepared to answer, and require none. In his employment as porter it was his business to look after the rooms of this tavern. That will be sufficient. He was found on the—"

"Do you mean that a threat was made against *all* of us?" Potter interrupted. His cheeks pulsed in and out like the gills of a fish.

Franklin looked sharply at him.

"I've said that, sir—"

"That's right!" Dashwood agreed, glaring with impatience. But Franklin was already continuing.

"Raleigh was found on the floor at the side of a bed, near to a small table which served as a stand for the water basin. The rug next to the bed was soaked well in saltwater—I tasted it with my fingers. The basin was not in place, but lay across the room under a table as though it had been thrown there—near to the base of the wall in which a small hole had been cut to approximate a mousehole—"

"A mousehole!"

Bubb Dodington had come up to the table, listening closely. Selwyn quickly joined him. The fat man looked increduously across at Dr. Franklin with heavily lidded eyes.

Franklin addressed them.

"Indeed, sir—a mousehole. It led through the wall into the vacant building next to this, where the murderer placed himself with his apparatus. By my own calculations—consider a Leyden jar three inches in diameter, coated inside and out and up the sides for three inches with tinfoil. Provide a table perhaps three feet square, covering it with bottles. Eleven in a row, eleven rows. Charge them fully with a generator—Mr. Dashwood, your own machine can throw a charge some seventeen or eighteen feet, as you may know. Connect the jars together. Now! From the outer coating run a bare wire of copper through the mousehole and into the room, laying it beneath the rug. Likewise, take a wire coated with beeswax—to protect against the loss of fluid—and bring it from the inner coating of the Leyden jars through the same hole. Scrape its end bare, and bring it up to connect with the basin—through the nailhole in its lip. Darkness hides it well enough. I'm giving you a receipt for murder—"

Franklin's eyes brightened as he once again realized the ingeniousness of the scheme. There was silence in the room.

"It's sufficient for the victim to reach for the basin—he can't avoid the rug, even so, and thus need not touch the basin at all. When his hand's close enough, death will leap to meet him. As for the murderer, he need only disconnect the wires at his end of the experiment and draw them through the wall. A tug loosens the wires from the basin—which spills and comes across the room. We must expect great things, gentlemen, and I account for them. The murderer is freed from any connection with his victim, without entering the room again. He throws into confusion any person who examines the evidence without knowing the power of the electrical fluid, or the means to transmit it—"

Dashwood held his forehead in his cupped hand. His eyes had grown small and hard.

"You merely speculate, of course, and have no means to prove—"

"Indeed," Franklin answered. "Without speculation we're brutes, are we not? I find everything as I've described it. The table on which the basin sits is itself fixed with a coat of beeswax—hardly to be noticed from the natural color of the wood, yet saving the electrified object from any loss of fluid. Some evidence is very plain, sir! And on Raleigh's hand is the certain stigmata of having taken a charge of great proportions—described to me by the man who examined him— burnt flesh, like so—"

Franklin raised his own hand, showing a brown scar at the base of his thumb.

"I too have taken the force of the electric fluid, although thankfully not in so great a proportion—"

A low murmur of agreement swept around the table.

"And nearly killed you, did you say?" Churchill asked.

"So I *did* say, sir, on the evening of the Squeezer. Your memory's very sharp! Such an infant science claims its victims. Well! I could use some wine. I expected—"

Lord Sandwich, who had his hand on the bottle, passed it down.

"—I expected William Strahan here, but don't see him," Franklin said. "Let me proceed—"

He filled his own glass and tasted it.

"In science," he continued, "one must look beyond an effect to discover its cause—and often find a nest of causes. So it is in murder. It's not enough to discover the mode of murder. One must also seek to learn what moves the heart of the murderer, and urges him to his actions. It became clear to me—having learned of it—that I must pay my attention to the affair of Valetta LaNeve. The dead man—Raleigh—had connection with it. He boasted of having the woman, did he not? Toplady had connection with it. He introduced the woman into this Club, did he not? Dieter Schiff also had connection with it—as his own reaction told me, and as the woman herself inadvertently confided—"

"Valetta?—"

"You found LaNeve?"

"Sad whore—"

Franklin stopped them.

"The murderer was most certainly aware of it—and here's the key to it—he seized upon this unnatural abuse of Valetta LaNeve as a diversion from his true intent! From the very beginning this affair was a Trojan horse, ridden by a doddering French officer—a dullard, a natural cuckold, a coward. A lack-a-brain!"

Franklin leaned forward.

"Consider it," he said, letting his glance drift from one

earnest face to another. "The verse received by Mr. Dashwood came hard upon your summer revels. It claimed a grievance— a grievance which all of you knew to be true, although it was not stated. What thought leapt up in Mr. Dashwood's mind? That the members of the Hellfire Club were placed in great danger. Just so. For what reason? For the abuse of Valetta LaNeve. Indeed. There's my catechism! Did not members of the Hellfire Club die? Indeed! Even the beating suffered by Mr. Pennant at the Abbey—even that, sir!—was in the cause of making you believe vengeance was being done. And behind it all lay—Hector LaNeve! Not as the murderer, mind you, but as a stalking horse. He was, after all, the most aggrieved. He was drawn—"

"If you disregard the feelings of the lady," Whitehead said.

Franklin looked at him sharply. "Bless you. Hector LaNeve was drawn into a plot that didn't exist—to kill members of the Hellfire Club as vengeance for the sins committed upon his wife. What the murderer promised him, who can know? A fool's vengeance. Hector was encouraged to think he was a spy, told to disguise himself and work his way into the confidence of—let me say this, Hector LaNeve was often seen in the company of Eugene Toplady, in a disguise so transparent that he was easily remembered in taverns throughout Westminster."

A chorus of hums greeted this announcement. Dashwood's complexion took on a deeper cast of red, but whether from embarassment or anger was not apparent.

"Irregular," Bubb Dodington announced.

Franklin glanced up at the vulture overhead. "As though they were intended to be remembered together, for indeed they were. Intended and remembered. The murderer took an additional precaution. He shared with LaNeve the verse which Mr. Dashwood received—encouraged him to learn it—hoped *that* would strike so close to the nerve that he could not keep it to himself. And in that calculation was proved correct."

"Toplady, you say?" Dashwood asked, having recovered his voice. "LaNeve seen with Toplady?"

"Indeed," Franklin said quickly. "For good reason. Whether there was irony in it, I cannot say. Certainly there was malice. For the murderer, I well suspect, realized the truth of what was told me by Valetta LaNeve herself. That it was Toplady who entered her cell lastly at the revels, and who so roughly—"

The room erupted again.

"*That* fiddle without a stick?—"

"Never—"

"—can't believe what you say—"

Franklin blinked.

"The murderer himself believed it well enough," he said. "Should all else fail and discovery be close at hand, *there* would be Hector LaNeve to point his finger at. Parading about town in paltry disguises. With the very man who's had his wife, although Hector would have no idea of *that*. Vowing vengeance all the same. Prattling deadly verse. A stalking horse! And all to hide the true intent of the murderer. But let it be—"

"What *was* his true intent?" Charles Churchill said thickly.

"Let it be. Comes the murder of Eugene Toplady. The mode was the same as with John Raleigh, the circumstances somewhat different, and the error more condemning for the murderer. For he hangs himself."

Franklin sighed. "I found the lad myself at the end of the hall on the upper story of Mr. Dashwood's house, near to his own room. The rug on which he lay was both salted and moistened—the better for conduction of the fluid, and especially so if a metal sheet is placed beneath it and a bare wire be run out to ground itself. Of course I found no sheet beneath the rug—who would be so careless as to leave it? Who would think that it would leave its own impression on the carpet underneath? The murderer removed it, as he removed the wires. He had no need to remove the Leyden jars or the generator that Mr. Dashwood so kindly provided for his amusement! In an unused room near to the study I found more than one hundred twenty Leyden jars, most of them more than three inches in width. In the study was the generator—a wonderful machine—where the murderer had so nicely returned it. Sufficient! By running a coated wire to the brass knob on the door Mr. Toplady touched—and by charging the bottles to their capacity nearly to the point at which Mr. Toplady touched it—some of you saw the results, did you not?" Franklin shook his head. "Death by the electric fluid."

He made a church steeple with his fingers. Everyone was deathly quiet.

"So much I observed with my own eyes," he continued. "But let us speculate on the event. Mr. Toplady returns home from the Squeezer, enters the house, and climbs to the second floor. The murderer has preceded him to prepare his deadly web—and is surprised in his presence by Mr. Toplady. But not *so* surprised that Mr. Toplady has the least guess as to why he's there. He's been there before. He *belongs* there! He's in place. I boasted to Mr. Toplady that I could name him but he disbelieved me—I didn't pursue it. If I had, he would surely not be dead—"

Franklin's voice grew suddenly quiet.

"—nor would we find two glasses of wine on the table in the study. One does not willingly sit to drink with death. I create the circumstances for you. I believe the murderer hoped to get Toplady drunk, and so to sleep. He was already upset. Wine was spilled over his papers. The bottle was better than half empty. There could not have been much time—particularities! The spider and the fly! As they talk, Toplady picks out his pen and takes paper and attempts to create order where he feels only disorder—innocent enough! His mind turns to his dearest thoughts—those of language and words and the rules of their relation. The murderer merely listens—and calculates how best the spider can escape the fly. It's easy enough! The lad's in his cups. His mind's elsewhere. Rise and pretend to leave—a merry good-night! But instead of descending the stairs, go instead to the unused room—where the jars are stored and the generator waits."

Franklin's hand made a circular motion, over and over. Thomas Potter's eyes followed it hypnotically.

"He charges the bottles little by little, so as to have the charge as full as possible. It's a dangerous gamble—a gamble of trust and habit. He waits—a minute?—half an hour?—an hour? He waits silently for the fly to reach the web—until—"

Franklin brought the palm of his hand down forcibly on the tabletop, rattling the dishes.

"—Toplady is dead!" he concluded.

"B'God! The world's gone to Hell!" Sandwich cried, startled out of his wits.

Potter's face was white.

"Holy Mother!" Selwyn squeaked.

Franklin smiled ruefully and shook his head. "Forgive me," he said.

The door to the gaming room suddenly flew open.

"Yes, sir!" Henley asked, poking his head in and addressing Francis Dashwood. He was used to answering grunts and thuds, and was brought to the door by Franklin's dramatic fist.

Dashwood's jaw trembled. "We'll have more wine—"

Franklin shuddered at his own powers, and calmed himself with a glass of canary from a fresh bottle.

"As it is," he said apologetically, "the murderer cleared his traces, leaving behind only one thing. The noose to hang himself by. *Emotional women laugh!* He neglected the thoughts of a man about to die—there it is—*Emotional Women Laugh!*—I leave you to puzzle over it! God knows I did! And bear the scar!"

Franklin fingered the boil which still bothered his chin.

He shrugged, and as he did so the door burst open once again. This time it was not Henley's head that so hesitantly appeared, but William Strahan's.

"Willie!" Franklin said, rising abruptly to his feet. No one else moved.

Strahan beamed mightily. He looked about from face to face, and then his eyes fell unhappily on the table with its soiled dishes and greasy napkins.

"You could not wait?" he asked.

"We're having Holy Ghost Pye—right now!" Franklin said, drawing Strahan into the room.

"We're having fairy tales," Dashwood corrected him sullenly.

"Emotional women laugh!" the Bruiser said. He boomed out a mighty laugh.

Franklin turned quickly about to confront the Hellfire Club. His face betrayed his anger, and brought them to silence. He seated Strahan. Then he took his seat himself. Franklin's eyes were cool and impassive, but the color was full into his cheeks.

"I'm not of a mind to bear assertion without proof," he said icily. "Nor to live with doubt. I have my proof—that satisfies the niceties of the thing, but it doesn't satisfy me. I had one surmise left, and asked of Mr. Strahan to prove it for me." He looked at Strahan. "I have no hint—no more than you—as to whether he's met with success. You gentlemen are familiar with Mr. Cotter?—"

"Cotter?"

"But of course—"

"My servant, sir," Dashwood answered at last.

"And he is what kind of man?" Franklin asked.

"You won't find a better!" Dashwood said with a little sound of surprise. "Bounced me on his knee—a very orderly and efficient gentleman—I *call* him a gentleman!—he is only a servant—everything in its place—but what he has to do with this business—"

"Precisely," Franklin interrupted. "Everything in its place—"

He turned to Strahan.

"Be good enough to tell these gentlemen—I *call* them gentlemen—of my instructions to you last evening, sir—"

"Yes," Strahan nodded. "To go to West Wycombe and to there see Mr. Cotter alone—"

"And you did go?"

"Just returned, missing supper . . ." Strahan's eyes roamed hungrily down the length of the table until they came to rest on the three chins of Bubb Dodington.

"Did you have any questions of Mr. Cotter?"

"Why! Yes, sir!" Strahan sputtered, incredulous. "The question you *instructed* me to ask of him—"

"Which was—"

"Which was, how many Leyden jars did Mr. Cotter find to be broken in the corner bedroom on the morning Dieter Schiff was murdered, before he—"

A low growl rumbled in the throat of Francis Dashwood.

"Proceed," Franklin said. "There was more?"

Strahan swallowed, and spoke very quickly. "Yes. Before he removed all the apparatus back to Mr. Dashwood's study in West Wycombe House, sir—"

Dashwood was on his feet, red-faced. There was a loud clanking of dirty silver against the goblets on the table. "Are you accusing me?—you say Mr. Cotter did what?—" Franklin lifted his hands and turned again to Strahan.

"I presume Mr. Cotter had an answer for you—"

"*Eight*," Strahan gulped.

"Eight Leyden jars?—"

"So he estimates," Strahan answered rapidly. He looked straight at Franklin, not being able to look at the others. "They were smashed, of course. He told me he went into the room very early on the morning—never connected the two things, as you so obviously saw. But! well, he found the electrical machine and the jars—as you said—quite out of place, belonging in the study down the hall; and he noticed those that were dashed upon the floor—he removed them—so he said—swept off the mess and disposed—Christ!—I didn't ask where he disposed of them—is it important?—"

For a moment Strahan feared he'd failed in the entire inquiry. But the gentle smile that was fixed on Franklin's face told him he hadn't.

Franklin had tilted back in his chair and was gazing severely down the table at Francis Dashwood. "You say that Mr. Cotter had not heard of Mr. Schiff's death then, to connect the two?" he asked Strahan, without turning to him.

"He heard of it *eventually*, as we all did, sir. The body was not found until some time later. And as all the gentlemen said he'd been dusted in a scuffle—neck was broken, he was beaten—you can see, Mr. Cotter didn't imagine—"

Franklin sighed.

He placed his spectacles back upon his nose.

"Comes the death of Dieter Schiff," he said dryly, peering over the rims of his glasses at the Hellfire Club. "For a time it confounded me—I freely confess. It overthrew all my speculations—"

The room had fallen silent. Franklin stared up at the vulture once again.

"Run a charging line down from the window of the bedroom on the second floor of West Wycombe House," he said absently. "Fix it into the trees with silk ribbon. Attach one end stripped bare to the Iron Woman. Attend to your grounding line. Very much the better if your Woman's hollow—as she is—for she may then be lifted and two boards be placed beneath her—impregnanted with beeswax—to prevent the electrical fluid from running into the ground. Charge your bottles to their fullest. You have a receipt for death. Should anyone touch the Iron Woman—"

Franklin sighed, and looked down at Francis Dashwood.

"Let us take it as speculation, sir," Franklin said softly. "The Leyden jars have been moved during the night into the corner bedroom. The generator along with them. The jars are charged to their capacity, and need to be. Morning has come. Dieter Schiff is up to greet it. He descends the stairs while the house sleeps and enters the yard. The grass is wet with morning dew. He nears the Iron Woman—"

"Please!" George Selwyn squealed. "Don't *do* it that way! Can't you speculate *straight*?—"

"—he's an electrician after all, and conscious of its power. But all the same—forgetful of his own jeopardy. It's a peril of the single-minded, gentlemen—in any endeavor, doubly so in murder. Do I need repeat my own experience—nearly killed in my own house by carelessness? No! It's an infant science! And here was Dieter Schiff, his connection with the earth made more certain by the wetness of the grass. Through insufficiency of mind he comes too close to the devilish trap he himself created: the spark leaps out! He's dead— in an instant!—and his body's thrown back by the force of the charge. The wire snares around his neck and pulls out its connection with the Leyden jars, crashing some of them to the floor. He's a dead man dancing!—headlong into the ravine, where his face is scrubbed, his neck snapped—so!" Franklin snapped his fingers with a crack.

Thomas Potter was ghostly white.

"As I found him!" he shuddered.

Voices began to babble all around the table. Strahan leaned over to whisper in Franklin's ear: "You *exceed* yourself, sir!" But Dashwood's cry came louder than the others.

"Too easy! Too easy!" he shouted at Franklin. "Dieter Schiff? his own *trap*? You cannot prove a word! The murderer might as well be here!" He looked frantically about from friend to friend. "Where was his cause to see us dead? He *had* none—"

The silence waited for an answer.

"You underestimate the power of the freak within us, sir," Franklin said without emotion. "For a man to take himself so seriously within as to publish on the roads of Sussex and upon bell ropes and the petals of the gardenia . . . to see the similarity between lightning and the electric fluid, and suggest a proof to show it—to have a scientific mind, sir—and yet to be taken on the *outside* for a fool, a buffoon, a mountebank and charlatan—even in his own company—most surely cries for correction."

"He *was* a fool!" someone cried.

"A fraud!"

"A good-for-nothing!"

Franklin raised his hands into the air, being proved right.

"It plunged me into a black humor," he confessed, once

the Brotherhood stopped ranting. "For if Dieter Schiff was himself murdered—then by whom? I had all of London again to choose from. Or each of *you*. It soon cleared off, for it came to me that here alone was an instance in which the murderer had not removed his apparatus—the wire remained. Why was it not removed? Because the murderer *himself* was dead! Mr. Strahan accounts for the rest. Yet this plunged me into a humor far blacker than the first. For if the murderer was dead—how could I hope to prove him the murderer?"

"You haven't proved it, sir!" Dashwood said. He glared up at Franklin. "You've taken the easiest way, is the truth— and hope to blame this affair on the man who seems most obvious—a Friar of this Brotherhood who cannot talk to tell the truth. *Too easy!*" A malicious grin spread itself crookedly across Dashwood's face.

"But then it came to me," Franklin said calmly, as though Dashwood had not spoken, "that a weather vane points in two directions, although we read it only by the point of its arrow. It shows us the way from which the wind blows, as well as the direction to which it goes. It came to me that my attention was fixed in the wrong direction—"

He seemed to sigh, but didn't.

"*Too easy!*" he thundered, his brown eyes flashing. Everyone jumped. "Have you smoked it? *Emotional women laugh!*"

The Brotherhood was dumbfounded. They hadn't heard such strength of passion from Dr. Franklin and looked down at him now with wide eyes.

"I carried that too long in my pocket, gentlemen!" he said angrily. "Indeed! But thanks to William Strahan and a— human centaur called—called—"

"Chumley," Strahan helped.

"Called *Chumley!*" Franklin cried. "Spelled *Cholmon-*

delay! Called *Chumley*! The language itself is a freak! Few things are what they seem! Our letters lie silent! Their sounds don't correspond! And which of your number cared more about such things than Eugene Toplady—"

He looked sharply about.

"—sitting there in the study with the man who would murder him—the lamps hissing, the darkness all around and drawing nearer—"

"Please!" said Selwyn.

"—and all the while his mind at work—drawing out a list of words to correspond to the man who sat across from him —*Rational—Busy—Rough—Cautious—Abyss—Laughter*—I have them here! Until at last he found the order that answered not only to the evil face across from him, but to the evil fears within: *Emotional Women Laugh!*"

Franklin's voice became suddenly very quiet.

"If you will take the sound of *ti* from the word 'emo*ti*onal,' " he said, "the first vowel in 'women'—add to it the sound of *gh* in 'lau*gh*'—"

"*Schiff!*" cried Thomas Potter, not meaning to.

"You will excuse me!" Franklin announced, standing abruptly and bowing hard in the direction of Francis Dashwood. He stalked forcefully from the room, with Strahan meekly at his heels.

Epilogue

Not even a full supper of mutton, carrots, and sauce cooled Franklin's passion. Those contrary emotions over which he seemed to exercise such strict control were at last broken loose. He took his meal with Strahan in the eating room of the Vulture, washing it liberally down with ale and complaint. "Too easy! Too easy!" Dashwood himself came out once to beg Franklin's pardon—he knew not what for—but Franklin bellowed him back into the gaming room with the others. By the time Franklin and Strahan departed the Vulture, the noise and cries from the gaming room were as loud as ever they'd been when the two cronies first came with a third to sit there.

But now Franklin sat in the corner of Strahan's gold carriage, still simmering. Strahan brimmed with solicitude.

"This isn't like you—not at all!" he said as the coach moved off into the darkness of King Street. "Who'd have guessed so much of the Garrick in you!—"

"Easy allegiance!" Franklin sputtered. "Idle minds! Great wealth to no purpose! Character so easily corrupted! Useless! To lose two men so innocently, and give not a care!—"

It sounded as though Franklin spit. Strahan hoped not.

"They wounded your pride by saying your solution was—"

"My *pride?*" Franklin snapped. "I'm *alive,* am I not? And glad enough of it!" He turned his head away to watch the lamps glide slowly by on the street. Their faint glow gave Strahan a profile.

"You bring it up, sir—I meant to ask," Strahan said in a small voice. "It was *you* who was to celebrate the Mass on the Iron Woman, was it not?"

Franklin did not answer. The carriage rocked along over the cobbled streets.

"What I mean, sir, is you gave no victim for the Iron Woman—"

Franklin's head turned back, and the lamps from the other side of the street reflected his eyes. Strahan heard him sigh and knew that he was calmed.

"Dear Strahan, of course," he said softly. "In each instance, *I* was to be the victim—"

Strahan couldn't speak—and had no need to.

"The whole affair, as you heard me say, was a diversion from the true intent of the murderer. It was a plot against myself, sir, disguised to seem a plot against the Hellfire Club. From the very first I suspected as much. Dashwood's verse was received not long after my arrival in this country. It aroused me—and more so that the difficulties of the crossing, the incompetence of the captain, the foolishness of the governor in America—these things so long delayed me and made my arrival impossible to predict. Coincidence is a bad companion, Strahan. I was led to consider I'd been noted in Falmouth on the seventeenth July, and a scheme set in motion to disrupt my mission to the Penns. One disregards such things at risk—"

Franklin reached for his walking stick and set it upright on the carriage floor.

"—considered it, I say. Well! Politics had nothing to do with it, and the Penns be damned! But then, sir, when Dashwood told me the porter at the Vulture was found dead—I *knew* the man! He set that woman on me, and tried to have me back to the very room in which he died! I've already lost her name—"

"Annie Martin—"

"Indeed. There are two coincidences within the hour. Two points. They made a line, Strahan, and it pointed straight at me. I began to suspect that something had gone terribly wrong for the murderer. It came home to me most fully as I sat and talked to you of murder—and its simplicities." Franklin loosed a little sigh. "In *that* light—the circumstances of John Raleigh's death were better read. His task and hers, unknowing why, was to get me in that room, leaving the rest to God or the Devil! That they failed signified nothing to them. Raleigh wandered in—he was porter, was he not?—and died. Annie Martin wandered all about and she died, too— so that she'd never wonder. And in that very place it was Dieter Schiff who set Dashwood upon me—Toplady said as much, while still alive to say it. There was Schiff's very plan. To draw me into the heart of the Hellfire Club. Dr. Fatsides! Do you remember it? If Annie had me, I was dead. If not, there would be another chance. As it was, he heard poor Raleigh go into that room and thought he had—I say! What's that! Two women fighting?—"

Franklin twisted quickly about to peer from the window onto the Strand, but the carriage had already passed by the struggling women. He settled back in his seat.

"Ahh, London," he sighed. "City of commanding grace." He was quiet for a moment. "The charge that Toplady took was intended for me as well—don't doubt it. It was *my* door wired, not his. So I surmise. They're straight across and close enough to touch with either hand. The lad had reason—he said he'd air the room and turn the covers back—no doubt he tried to do so—but was the wrong fly in the web nonetheless. There's why I say Schiff tried to make him sleep—and waited there in silence for *my* steps, not some other's. *I* was the fly he wanted—a humble-bee!—and once in place, he was unable to open the door to his nest and watch the hall, for fear of being discovered. Those were two *women* fighting, weren't they?—"

"I didn't see them—"

"Well, Strahan, it's a wide world, ain't it? I early set on Dieter Schiff—that's true—but couldn't smoke him out and could not smoke his reason. He fawned on me like a fox. I feared to touch him—not knowing whether we would both go to Hell together. You saw the book he sent me— my own *Observations,* torn apart as though it were *my* body! I'd be blind not to see what he intended. At the Squeezer, I happened in on his little demonstration—the Electrical Kiss, the Golden Fishes, the Conspirators. I've seen them all and thought up half of them myself! But was ill prepared by a claim he made—that he'd induced the experiments lately performed in France with rods to prove the sameness of lightning and the electric fluid. Why make such a claim—in a town that could refute him—if in fact he hadn't done as much?"

"He *was* a fraud, sir, a showmaster—"

"The world credits me—and hoots at Dieter Schiff! Understand that, Strahan! He's kept on a leash to laugh at! There's his motive force—the darkness in his heart. Envy! There's the dwarf within him—"

"You mean he had *cause?*—"

"You heard Fothergill, did you not?" Franklin said. "I had him search out the records of the Royal Society for *all* the members of the Hellfire Club, hoping to keep my purpose to myself. You heard the date on which Dieter Schiff proposed his proof—and marked rejected! Laughed at by the connoisseurs! As I myself was! My own communication on the subject, although written some two weeks sooner, came later into the hands of the same connoisseurs, for its passage across the ocean. And save for some small parts was rejected in the same manner. Not until the experiment was made and proven did Mr. Cave bring out my letters in their fullness. By then Schiff no doubt felt his thunder stolen—and *I*, sir, as you said, put myself forward for the Iron Woman to steal *his* thunder. I trusted him to strike—he grabbed the chance, did he not? Ahh!—you were halfway to Aylesbury at the time, riding hard!"

Franklin laughed out loud. The carriage was drawing near to Craven Street.

"I hoped only to expose him—couldn't think to prove him guilty unless it was to offer him the chance to try the Iron Woman before me! I thought to leap upon the Woman first and offer him my hand. He wouldn't take it—there's a wager! I'd be safe for having the coated boards beneath me, and he'd be—dead! The decipherment of Mr. Toplady's list came long after—and thanks to you, sir! It's a wide world full of mysteries—you've said it, or was it I?—but never wide enough at all for the canker of ambition. Or the worm of envy!"

Franklin laughed again, and Strahan joined him.

"I philosophize—stop me!—here's Craven! I'll have more ale, but you'll find none here—"

The coach had turned into the street and come to a stop before the house of Mrs. Stevenson.

"Let me clasp your hand, dear Strahan, to suffer me! There!"

Franklin reached for Strahan in the dark, then opened the door to the carriage and stepped carefully into the street. "Can you see?" he asked. "The house is dark, save for a single lamp—"

Strahan leaned down to look up. Indeed only one lamp burned—in a window on the third story.

"There's hope for old printers such as us," Franklin said congenially. "For someone waits through the night—"

He moved slowly up the curb toward the front door of the house, and Strahan—reaching over to draw shut the door—couldn't help but hear him muttering under his breath:

"Too easy! Too easy!"

But whether it was the Hellfire Club or Polly he referred to, was as great a mystery as ever.